Louise Miller
Mysteries
BOOK TWO

Protesting Trouble

KAREN CULLEN, DVM

Library and Archives Canada Cataloguing in Publication.
Cullen, Karen. Louise Miller Mysteries: Protesting Trouble.

ISBN paperback: 978-1-7781519-4-1
ISBN EBook: 978-1-7781519-5-8

Published by: IV Lines Publishing

Cover Design: Britt Wilson - Indie Publishing Group
Formatting: Chrissy Hobbs - Indie Publishing Group

This book is dedicated to Sandra Kane-McBride.
Forever loved by her human, four-legged, and feathered friends.
Brave, Courageous, and Tough-as-nails,
Loving, Kind, and Thoughtful.
Proud of her Scottish heritage.
Resting in God's hands.

Also By Karen Cullen

LOUISE MILLER MYSTERIES

Breeding Trouble (Book 1)
Protesting Trouble (Book 2)

SPUD ISLE MYSTERIES

Body in the Paddock

Chapter 1

LOUISE SPRANG UPRIGHT in her bed at the sound of a stranger in the house. The female voice was unknown to her. Louise whispered to herself, "Someone's in my house, and she's yelling at me in . . . Is that *French*?"

Louise grabbed the blankets she had kicked off overnight and pulled them close to her chest. Her eyes darted around the room as she looked for the baseball bat she kept handy in case of a midnight intruder, and for her phone. Her heart sank at the realization that the bat was across the room in her closet, but hope returned at the sight of the phone, easily within reach on her nightstand.

As Louise grabbed the phone with a shaky hand, her mind

whirled at the proximity of the voice: it was coming from the hallway just outside her bedroom. The intruder was close. Common sense told her to dial 911, but instead she opened the contacts app to call her friend Alex Hines, a homicide detective. Louise and Alex had been friends since their university years, and whenever she felt unsafe, she thought of him first.

About to tap on Alex's name, she caught sight of her three-legged tabby cat, Oscar, who was sleeping peacefully at the foot of the bed. The woman continued to scream, and Louise was puzzled as to why Oscar wasn't upset, or even awake. He was a friendly cat to those he knew, but not to strangers, especially loud ones.

There was a notable pattern to the home intruder's speech. Louise couldn't understand the words, but it sounded as if she were repeating a short sentence over and over again with an intensity that made Louise wonder if the woman was trying to warn her of danger. While it would be great to have such a caring neighbour, none of hers had a key to the house. *How did she get in?*

Louise lowered her legs to the floor and tucked her feet into her slippers. If the intruder was going to enter the bedroom, she'd already had plenty of time. Tiptoeing slowly toward her closet, Louise held her breath, then opened the door, hoping it wouldn't make its usual squeak. The hinges were louder than normal, forcing her to freeze in place, certain the intruder would barge in.

She held her position for what felt like minutes but was probably only seconds, then dove into the closet and retrieved her trusty baseball bat. With the bat perched on her shoulder, ready to swing at any would-be murderer, she made her way to the bedroom door. Shielding herself with the door as she opened it, she peeked out. The hallway, lit by the glow of the rising sun, was intruder-free. Her frightened state waning, she relaxed her shoulder muscles as she lowered the bat.

With the door open, the screaming was louder. Louise listened as the woman continued to scream her unintelligible message. *It definitely sounds like French.* Louise had taken French years ago in grade school but had never been skilled at learning it, or any other language. When a new acquaintance inquired if she knew a second language, Louise would answer that some days it was a wonder she could hold a conversation in her mother tongue, English.

"*Batterie? Batterie?* That sounds familiar." Sleepily, Louise scratched her head. She looked back at her furry companion, still curled up and snoring, then up at the hallway ceiling, where she spotted a flashing red light.

The screaming was coming from the carbon monoxide detector. "*La batterie est faible!*"

"*Batterie? Batterie?* Battery!" *Something about the battery.* "Is it screaming that the battery's low?" Louise slapped her forehead. "Argh!"

Dr. Louise Miller sped into the parking lot of the Black Creek Animal Hospital in Coverdale, screeched to a halt, and threw the transmission into park. Initially surprised that the spot closest to the back door was still free, she didn't give it a second thought as she grabbed her laptop bag and breakfast from the back seat and rushed into the clinic. The early-morning low battery announcement had sent her on a search for a ladder to put a halt to the warnings from the "intruder." *What's wrong with a series of beeps like in the good ol' days?* Louise's sleep had been cut short, but she was relieved that what had disturbed her peace of mind was artificial, not flesh and blood.

After finding the A-frame ladder she'd purchased shortly after closing on her dream home—a red brick two-storey historical with a creek running through the backyard—she'd climbed up and removed the battery from the carbon monoxide detector. She expected the screaming voice to cease her warnings once the battery was removed, but it didn't. Louise scratched her head, then got down from the ladder and found her phone sitting on the bed, where she'd flung it earlier. A quick internet search revealed that some of these devices were hard-wired into a home's electricity, and that the only way to stop the ear-piercing noise was to either find a new battery or turn the house's electricity off. Turning it off would have meant forgoing her morning coffee. No caffeine was not an option, leaving Louise with no choice but to search for a battery.

She started in her home office, thinking that would be a logical place to store batteries, but if they were in there, they were likely buried under the piles of papers and books she'd been meaning to organize for the past few months. Giving up on the office, she next tried the junk drawer in the kitchen, and finding nothing, she headed into the garage. A triumphant shout escaped her lips when she noticed a package of two 9V batteries on the workbench. "No idea when I bought these, but they'll do."

Louise re-entered the house through the door that connected the kitchen to the garage and found Oscar, with his characteristic scowl, sitting by his food bowl. While her tiny housemate's expression was permanent, created by a scar on his upper lip, it made Louise laugh. He looked as displeased by the early-morning disruption as she felt.

"Sorry, buddy. Let me replace the battery. Then we can both have breakfast." Louise glanced at the clock on the microwave. "Shoot. It's a lot later than I thought. I guess that explains why you're down here and not still in bed." She shrugged. "Nothing I can do about it now. I'll replace the battery, get dressed, feed you, and race to work."

Happy there hadn't been any speed checks on her way to the clinic, Louise had stopped at the local sandwich shop for a caramel latte and a muffin. Balancing her laptop bag over her shoulder and the coffee and muffin in one hand, she searched for her key to the clinic with the other. "Another marvel of technology. If I'd had to use a key to turn the car on, I'd now have the keys in my hand and not have to search for them."

Frustration with modern advances that rarely made her life easier was common for Louise when she was tired, and late. She sat the cup and muffin on her car, then put the laptop bag on the ground and opened it as wide as possible. She shook it a few times, then hearing the familiar rattle of the keys, dug them out.

Louise unlocked the door and pushed it open. She was greeted with the familiar smells of antiseptic cleaner, rubbing alcohol, and a nauseating all-too-familiar odour emanating from the far end of the hallway.

"Oh no," she said to the empty entryway. "It smells like we have a case of parvo today." At the end of the hall was a litter box serving as a footbath to disinfect shoes, and an accompanying towel to dry them. The isolation room was around the far corner. The litter box confirmed her fears that they had a patient with an infectious disease.

Compared to a couple of decades ago, parvovirus was a

rarity, but it still showed up occasionally. Usually in improperly vaccinated pups from puppy mills, backyard breeders, or unscrupulous pet stores that sourced their dogs from the mills. While the producers of the dogs made money, the losers were the pups who suffered and often died, and the clients who, after laying out thousands of dollars to purchase a puppy, were now faced with the veterinary bills.

Louise sighed. When they were presented with the medical bill, it wasn't unheard of for these clients to become upset with the veterinary team, who had either pulled the family pet from the brink of death or done their best to do so. Rarely was their anger directed at who deserved it—the party who'd sold them the puppy. Louise felt her blood pressure rise as she retrieved her laptop bag and breakfast, then went upstairs.

Cringing that her bad start to the day was turning into something worse, she pushed open the door to the doctors' office, the first room on the right at the top of the stairs, with her foot. The room consisted of a row of filing cabinets to Louise's right, a window directly across from where she now stood, and two desks to her left. Dr. Daphne Carling, Louise's best friend and business partner, was seated at her desk and typing at her computer.

The fair-skinned blonde veterinarian raised her head when Louise dropped her bag to the floor. "Oh, good, you're finally here. It's been quite the morning. I admitted a diabetic cat who hasn't been doing well for the past few days. The client brought him in because he seemed a bit flat—they were waiting in the parking lot when Rita got here."

Rita, a registered veterinary technician, or RVT, Louise had met when working at a clinic as a veterinary student, was their office manager. Like most RVTs who'd spent much of their career dealing with anxious large dogs, Rita had a bad back and could no longer handle the physical demands the job required. Fortunately for Louise and Daphne, Rita was ready to take on a managerial role just when they decided to open their own veterinary hospital.

Daphne continued her update as Louise placed her coffee in the microwave and set it for forty seconds. "I think the two cat neuters have been admitted and Heidi's working on the pre-op bloods now. Oh, and I admitted Jack, a pup that probably has parvo. We're still waiting on the test."

The microwave beeped. Louise wasted no time in raising the cup to her lips. "That hits the spot." She took another sip, then said, "I didn't have time for coffee at home. I'll tell you all about it later. Anything else?"

Daphne pursed her lips and rubbed her chin. "Other than the coyote coming from Sydney's for an ultrasound, I don't think so."

"Perfect. I'll head down and get the cat neuters done so that's out of the way when Sandra arrives with Major." Louise took a bite of her muffin and headed toward the hallway.

Sydney's Wildlife Rehabilitation Facility, also called SWaRF, had been founded by Sandra Kelly, a woman who chose to help the area's injured wildlife when she found herself with an unexpected inheritance from a distant relative. The money had been enough for the initial set-up, but as SWaRF grew to aid the growing needs of the animal kingdom, the facility became reliant on government assistance and the generosity of donors and volunteers.

Louise and Daphne had been introduced to Sandra by their part-time kennel assistant, Melanie, Sandra's niece. They both had an interest in learning to treat some of the undomesticated animals the centre cared for, and Sandra needed a new veterinarian after her previous one retired.

"Oh, wait!" Daphne called after Louise. "Alex was here this morning before anyone else arrived."

Louise laughed. That explained the empty parking spot by the door. It wouldn't be the first time he'd arrived at the clinic before anyone who actually worked there, often with a message for Louise or a treat for the staff. After finding him sitting in his car in the parking lot on multiple occasions, she gave him a key to the building and his own security code so he could let himself in. He wasn't there every day, but the clinic had been broken into by a couple of thugs a few months earlier, so Louise and Daphne agreed that having an armed homicide detective be the first one in wasn't a bad idea, even if it wasn't every day.

"Did he say what he wanted? Did he leave chocolate?" Louise grinned in hopes of a sweet treat after the cat neuters.

"Sorry, no. He did say he had a surprise for you, but then he got a call and had to run. It sounded like something was happening at the airport. He said he'd try to make it back later. Then *poof,* off he went." Daphne looked at the time display on her monitor. "He's probably there already." She looked at the time again, squinted, then turned back to Louise. "Why *are* you so late? It's been a while since he left, so he could be on his way back by now."

Louise had just opened her mouth to start the story about the intrusive carbon monoxide detector when Rita rushed into the office, winded from running up the stairs. Her pupils were dilated and her face flushed. "Have you heard the news?" She leaned on the wall, then took a few deep breaths to calm herself. "There's been a huge explosion at the airport. At least two dead and many more injured."

Chapter 2

ARLY NEWS REPORTS were vague about the number injured, but from what Louise witnessed as she rushed down the hallway toward the emergency department, the small local hospital was quickly becoming overwhelmed. Several ambulances had already delivered patients and were now racing back to the airport. In addition to the patients already admitted, Louise had counted three ambulances in the parking lot unloading victims in a frenzied rush to save lives.

The hallways were lined with people in various stages of consciousness—some in hospital beds and others still strapped onto ambulance gurneys, paramedics standing guard over them. A young EMT who couldn't have been more than twenty-five paced nervously next to his patient while glancing repeatedly at the clock on the wall.

As Louise hurried past him, he called to a colleague tending to her own patient a few yards ahead. "We have to get back out there." His voice was frantic. Was this his first serious incident? Louise didn't want to think about the carnage the first responders were dealing with at the airport.

The female EMT in uniform, apparently a good decade older than the young EMT, was alternating between filling one of her kits with bags of intravenous fluids and extension sets from a nearby cabinet and returning to her patient to ensure he was still breathing.

She tried to reassure her co-worker. "Take a deep breath, John. We can't leave these two until a nurse or doctor is available to see them. They may need respiratory support, or CPR if they code." Louise could see the fear and stress in the EMT's eyes as she hurried by.

As Louise passed IV poles and gurneys, she pulled the collar of her shirt up to shield her nose from the unmistakable smell of burnt flesh. Many of the patients she'd seen had temporary bandages on their faces and hands. She prayed for them, not knowing how deep their burns were but knowing that if they survived, they could be facing life-altering injuries and years of suffering.

Tobin Memorial Airport, the site of the explosion, served a small rural area, and the users were mainly owners of private planes. Some were business people who made use of the facilities for quick access to meetings in cities across Ontario and Quebec. Others were hobbyists who enjoyed flying and were fortunate to have the funds for membership in the airport's flying club.

Normally, only a handful of people were at the airport on a weekday morning, but according to the news Louise had listened to on her way to the hospital, today organizers of a children's charity had been preparing for a special occasion: their annual week-long fundraising event, due to start tomorrow. There was to be an air show that included vintage planes and newer, never-before-seen models.

Along with the regulars at the airport were volunteers from the charity, patrons who supported it, owners of the planes to be displayed, and vendors setting up to sell everything from model planes to hot dogs as part of the fundraising efforts.

The offices, one of the hangars, and the surrounding area were crowded with people when an explosion ripped through the office building. Police had been on site before the explosion, but the radio announcer didn't know their reason for being there. When Rita had entered the doctors' office at the veterinary clinic, she reported that two people had died. The information had since been updated—one of those killed was a member of the Bathurst Region Police Department.

Louise scanned the emergency department for any sign of Alex, but she was certain that none of the bandaged heads belonged to her . . . Her what? What *was* Alex to her? He was her friend, one of her best friends, but lately she'd been wondering if he was more than that. She shook off the distraction and flew down the hallway that would take her from the ER to the more secure areas of the hospital.

She was frantic when she reached the door that declared no entry beyond this point. She pushed on it. It was locked; a key card was needed. Louise banged on the door with her fist. She had called the police station from her car, but the receptionist couldn't tell her who'd died, or where Alex was. *Is he dead?* This couldn't be happening again. She couldn't lose him. She had to get past this door to see if he was in surgery or in intensive care.

She fell back against the wall. *Think, Louise, think.* She cupped her head in her hands, and when she looked at the floor, she saw surgical-green scrub pants. *Her* surgical-green scrub pants. In her rush to get to work this morning, she had grabbed a pair of scrubs rather than selecting a work-appropriate outfit.

She threw off her jacket and dropped it to the floor—now she'd blend in with the hospital staff. All she was missing was a stethoscope, a badge, and a key card to open the door. Should she return to the car to get the stethoscope she kept with her for family pet emergencies? No, that would take too long. The medical doctors in the ER hadn't been wearing stethoscopes, only the nurses, so she'd pretend to be a doctor. *You are a doctor, Louise—only your patients have more hair than these ones.*

While she had the outfit, she still didn't have a badge or key card. She was pondering the many ways in which she might get them when a young volunteer came through the door. Louise stuck her foot in the gap before the door swung closed. The dark-haired girl, who reminded her of their student, Melanie, viewed Louise suspiciously.

Louise smiled at her. "Thank goodness. Perfect timing. I forgot my key card in my office and I have to get to the OR stat."

The volunteer stood tall and, with a serious tone that told Louise the ploy had worked, said, "Of course, Doctor." She held the door open for Louise, giving her full access to the restricted area.

Louise scanned her surroundings for security cameras.

Not seeing any, she continued down the hall toward a central nursing desk. No waiting patients lined this hallway. Instead, it was lined with various-sized carts carrying defibrillators, ultrasound machines, bandaging materials, chest tubes in sterile packages, and assorted other items that might be needed in an emergency. Some of the carts were almost bare, and these were obviously what the orderly with a trolley, who was jogging in Louise's direction, intended to fill with more sterile packages.

The badge hanging from his left pocket reminded Louise of her badge-free scrub top. She placed her hand over the place where a badge should have been and pretended to scratch an itch. It was an unnecessary precaution, because the flustered orderly dropped his items onto the supply cart, then spun around and headed the way he'd come.

Louise sighed deeply; he had paid her no attention, and she hoped her luck would continue. She had to get to Alex, and she was certain he'd be in this unit. She knew in her heart that he had to be seriously hurt. That was the only reason he wouldn't have called her by now, and it was the only reasonable explanation for why the receptionist at the police station hadn't told her where he was. She didn't really need to tell Louise his location—only that he was okay. But she hadn't said he was okay, so obviously he wasn't.

Tears threatened to overtake Louise as she moved closer to the nurses' station. It was manned by a single nurse. He appeared to be in his forties and had a phone pressed between his ear and shoulder while he was typing on a keyboard. His hair was dishevelled and his green scrub top was decorated with a variety of colours—probably from a mixture of blood, vomit, and other human-produced liquids. She gagged but suppressed the urge to vomit. Animal wastes didn't bother Louise, but anything coming out of a human turned her stomach.

As she crept by the nurse, keeping her body turned to hide her face and her lack of an identity badge, she overheard part of his conversation.

"I'm sorry, ma'am, but we don't have any patients by that name in this department. Yes, but there was an explosion, and we're currently handling patients who require intensive care or are waiting for emergency surgery. If your husband was here today for a tonsillectomy, his surgery has been cancelled and will be rescheduled." The nurse paused.

In a mirror meant to warn people when someone was coming around the corner, Louise saw his reflection just as he rolled his eyes. She shook her head in understanding. It wasn't easy to keep your cool in the midst of an emergency when the person you were talking to was oblivious to the situation and focused only on their own issues.

The nurse continued. "Yes, I'm sure it's very inconvenient for you to have to take another day off work, but think how lucky you are that you weren't at the airport this morning." He slammed the phone down. She wanted to turn and give him a thumbs-up, but the beeping of EKG monitors reminded her that she needed to find Alex.

As she rounded the corner, she spotted a group of doctors and nurses huddled at the far end of the hall. A curly-haired blonde woman lowered her face into her hands as one of her colleagues rubbed the woman's back. Louise's heart sank. The message was unmistakable—another victim had probably died of their injuries.

The group of colleagues broke up and slowly spread out, some going into patient rooms, others heading into offices or toward the nurses' desk. Louise turned toward the wall to shield her face and found herself looking at a paper label outside a patient room. Her heart raced when she saw detective alex hines written on it. If he was in this section, his injuries could be serious, but more importantly, he was alive!

Louise looked over her shoulder to see if anyone was around. Assured she was alone, she slowly pushed the door open. The first bed was occupied by a young man with dark hair. His right leg was in an elevated cast and his right arm was bandaged. She glanced back at the label, then back into the room—Officer Norman Talbot was sleeping soundly, judging by his snoring.

She opened the door wider to bring the second bed into view. She expected to see Alex also sleeping peacefully and snoring. Louise let out a guttural sound from deep within, then froze in place as her eyes were met with the empty bed. Not a bed with messy sheets and a dented pillow, left empty by a patient who was in the bathroom or who'd gone for tests. No, this bed was stripped to the mattress, and the floor around it recently mopped. *If Alex was in that bed . . .* Louise began hyperventilating at the thought. *If Alex was in that bed, he's gone forever and I'll never see him again.*

Chapter 3

LOUISE'S KNEES WEAKENED as the room started to spin. A staticky voice that sounded miles away called, "Code blue." Another soul was at risk of being lost, and Alex had already lost his battle. Louise fell against the door frame to steady herself against the nightmare unfolding around her.

A tear ran down her cheek as a familiar grief overwhelmed her. She'd vowed not to become romantically involved with Alex because of the inherent dangers of his profession. Her fiancé, Zack, had died in a car accident shortly after they graduated from high school. The man she'd planned to spend her life with had been killed by a drunk driver. Now it was happening again; she'd allowed herself to think of Alex as more than a friend, to consider a future with him—but just like Zack, he'd been taken away from her in a flash.

Louise wiped her eyes, then fixed her gaze on Norman, the sleeping police officer who'd been wounded in the explosion. She didn't know the extent of the injuries to his leg and arm, but she was happy for his loved ones that he was alive. "God, please be with Norman and his family." She sniffled a few times, then wiped her eyes with a tissue. "Don't let another family lose someone special today."

"The doctors say he'll be good to go in a couple of weeks. He'll need a lot of physiotherapy, but they suspect he won't have any permanent injuries."

Louise's eyes widened. "God?"

"Nope. Just me, Alex."

Louise whirled around and gasped at the sight of the man standing before her. Alex's wavy brown hair was matted with blood, he had a bandage over his right eye, his arms were littered with scratches, and his clothes were torn and bloody. Louise grabbed him into a bear hug.

He winced. "Not too tight. There's a bit of bruising around my . . . well, everywhere."

Louise squeezed him tighter. "I thought you were dead!" She pulled away and slapped his shoulder.

"Ouch. What was that for?"

"You could have been killed. I thought you had been. The receptionist at the station didn't tell me if you were okay or not, so I snuck in here. The bed you were supposed to be in has been stripped. That's what they do when a patient dies!" She slapped him again, unable to control her conflicting sense of annoyance and relief.

Alex rubbed his shoulder. "It's also what they do when a

patient is discharged. The scene at the airport is pure carnage, and a lot of people need medical attention, so when a patient is discharged, they don't waste any time making room for the next one."

As though on cue, an orderly and nurse with a patient on a gurney raced toward Alex and Louise. Alex stepped out of the way, then grabbed Louise's arm to pull her out of the way. They watched as the patient was transferred to the bed Alex had occupied.

Louise sniffled and made eye contact with Alex. "So you're okay? Are you sure? Why are they releasing you so soon? What injuries do you have? What happened at the airport?" She palpated his chest and abdomen; there was no swelling or pain response.

"Did they take radiographs? If you're not injured, why are you bruised all over?" As her fingers made their way from Alex's chest to his abdomen, she noted his lean body mass accentuated by rippling musculature. Heat rushed through her body and she snapped her hands back to her side, then covered her face. "Um . . . sorry."

Alex smiled. "Not a problem." He placed his arm around Louise's shoulder and guided her down the hall toward the nurses' station.

A woman Louise guessed was in her mid-twenties, her mascara running down her cheeks, rushed toward them. "Alex, I'm so glad to see you. The desk sergeant called to let me know Norman was injured and told me what you did for him."

Alex, moving stiffly, gave the woman a brief hug. "The doctors say he's going to be okay, Jean. Several days in hospital, then a few weeks in physiotherapy, and he'll be as good as new."

"Thanks to you. If you hadn't pulled him away from the falling debris when you did, we might have lost him." Jean kissed his cheek, then hurried into Norman's room.

Louise used her tissue to wipe the lipstick from Alex's face. "You're a hero—you saved that young officer." She smiled at him.

"I did what any of us would have done in that situation. I heard the blast, and then in a flash the walls were falling in around us and glass was flying everywhere. I pulled Norman down by his shirt. Then there was a second blast. Once things settled, I was lying on top of him, and a few inches of drywall were lying on top of me. The drywall's the real hero. It kept the glass shards from reaching us."

A nurse carrying a clipboard waved at Alex, then handed him a pen. "I need you to sign this AMA before you go, Mr. Hines." She shook her head and tsked at him.

The nurse's face told Louise that something was amiss. "What do you mean, an AMA?"

Alex shrugged. "Nothing. It's nothing. Just a formality."

Louise's brow furrowed and she stared at him. "No, it's not *nothing*! It's an Against Medical Advice form." She addressed the nurse. "Isn't it?"

The woman nodded.

"What are you doing, Alex? If the doctors don't want you to leave, it's because they're worried you might have serious injuries." Louise grabbed the pen from his hand.

Alex grabbed the pen back and pointed it at Louise. "What is it you said earlier about sneaking in here?" He looked at the nurse. "She's not supposed to be in here."

The nurse rolled her eyes. "And *you're*"—she jabbed her finger at Alex—"not supposed to *leave* here. Seems neither one of you have good sense." She thrust the clipboard at Alex. After he signed the form, she snatched her pen from him, turned on her heel, and walked away.

Chapter 4

LOUISE STORMED INTO the clinic, then into the treatment room, sending its door slamming into the wall.

Heidi, the head RVT, who sported scrubs decorated playfully with cartoon dog skeletons, had her blonde hair pulled into a ponytail. She was removing a bandage from the front leg of a small dog while the other RVT, Jenny, held the canine still. Heidi snapped her head up and stared with fright at Louise. "Oh no. Alex! Is he . . . ?"

Louise glanced back at the wall and door she'd just assaulted, then mouthed *Phew*, as neither was damaged. "He's okay, Heidi. That's what he claims, anyway. The man is as stubborn as . . . well, I don't know as what. He signed himself out of the hospital against doctor's orders so he could rush back to the airport. He's determined to find out what's responsible for the explosion."

Heidi placed her hand over her heart. "That's a relief. Not that he's stubborn, but that he's not, you know . . . dead."

"That's for sure." Jenny, her dark hair newly cut short around her ears, tossed the soiled bandage into the garbage. "We'd all be bummed if something happened to Alex. He's a great guy."

"He can be so headstrong at times. Just rushes off into action, not thinking about the potential dangers." Louise sat down on a stool next to Heidi and scratched the dog's chin while admiring Jenny's newest tattoo—a heart and ribbon with the letters *RVT* in the ribbon.

"Hmm." Heidi rubbed her chin in a mocking way. "Sounds like someone else I know. It wasn't long ago that a certain someone got herself trapped on a boat with drug dealers and murderers. The two of you are like . . . What's that old expression? Corn on a cob? Rats in a row? Pigs in a pen? No, that's not it."

Louise laughed. "Peas in a pod!"

Heidi snapped her fingers. "Right. That's it."

Rita entered the treatment area, massaging her chronically irritated back muscles. "It's good to see you're laughing. Alex must be okay."

Louise raised her brows and shook her head. "Physically, yes—so far—but as Heidi and I were just saying, he's too stubborn to have good sense. One of the nurses said as much."

Heidi gave Louise the side-eye. "I'm not sure we were *both* saying that." She laughed and scooped the dog from the table and into her arms.

"What do you mean 'so far'?" Rita opened the door to a cage so Heidi could place her patient inside.

"He says he's fine, just some bruising, but they made him sign an AMA before allowing him to leave the hospital."

Rita stared at Louise. "Oh." She closed the kennel door and secured the latch.

Meeting Rita's gaze, Louise raised her eyebrows. "Exactly. He could have internal injuries that may reveal themselves later." She raised her hands in surrender. "Sadly, there's nothing I can do about it. He's a grown man. I'll check in with him later to see how he's doing, but for now, I have to get set up to ultrasound Major. Has he arrived yet? I didn't spot Sandra's van in the parking lot."

With a slight frown, Rita cocked her head. "Um, hate to be the bearer of bad news twice in one day, but something's going on at the rehab centre. Daphne's on the phone with Sandra right now. She asked me to send you up to the office if you came back."

Louise tilted her head. "*If?*"

Rita shrugged. "We didn't know . . . you know . . . if Alex—"

"Right. Sorry. I'm sure you were all worried about him too." Louise pushed open the door she'd slammed earlier. "Off to see what today's strike three is all about."

Daphne was hanging up the phone as Louise entered the office. "I'm so glad to hear that Alex isn't seriously injured."

"News travels fast around here." Louise plugged in the Keurig she kept on the cabinet behind her desk, selected a Vanilla Biscotti pod from her vast collection of coffee flavours, and hit On. She turned toward Daphne and was about to speak.

"No mug?" Daphne smirked.

"Shoot!" Louise turned around and threw a mug under the spout seconds before the hot liquid started flowing. "That would have made a nice mess, which would have been fitting given the day so far. Rita says there's a problem with Major?"

"Not Major, but Sandra can't get him here today. The entrance to Sydney's is being blocked by a group of protestors, and they won't let any vehicles in or out. Sandra called the police, but with the explosion at the airport, they told her that unless human lives were in danger, they wouldn't be able to respond for hours, if at all today."

Louise sipped her drink, sighed, then sipped again. "I guess I can take a drive over there after office hours." She sat at her desk and pulled up the schedule. "This is odd. It looks like we have an unusually light afternoon with only a handful of appointments. How did that happen?"

"The phones have been ringing steadily since you left, but not to book appointments. Understandably, the explosion has people shaken up, and from what some clients are telling us, the roads are a mess. Several who were on the books for today have called to reschedule. Mary and Shirley are stretching them out over the next few weeks so we don't get slammed next week."

"Good planning on their part." Mary and Shirley were the clinic's receptionists—the front-line staff as Louise liked to think about them. "I've been racing in and out of the side-door today, I haven't even seen either of them yet."

With a small gust of wind, a tree branch tapped on the office window, drawing Louise's attention. Buds were forming—a sign that spring and warmer temperatures were on the horizon. Soon the plants in her garden would be flowering and baby bunnies would be hopping across the backyard. As she watched the budding limbs swaying in the breeze, she was reminded that even when things seem dark, there's always hope of brighter days. No one knew yet if the explosion was deliberate or accidental, and Louise felt blessed that so far Alex was safe. She'd continue to pray for the families of those who died or were seriously injured.

"I wish there was something we could do for the victims of the explosion. So many people at the hospital had what looked like serious injuries."

Daphne turned her monitor to face Louise. "I was thinking the same thing. I've been jotting down some ideas for a fundraiser. I think we could get the staff involved. I'll chat with them over the lunch break."

"That's a great idea. In the meantime, I'd better get the two cat neuters done."

"Already done. In fact, both patients are already recovered and have discharge appointments set up for later."

Louise looked questioningly at her friend.

Daphne shrugged. "With the cancellations this morning, it wasn't hard to squeeze in a couple of cat neuters. The diabetic cat, on the other hand, is a bit of a concern."

Earlier, Louise had simply run off after Rita's announcement of the explosion, leaving Daphne to carry the weight of the clinic on her own. Louise's stomach did a flip-flop. Not long ago she'd been leaving the workload to Daphne while chasing down bad guys and a wayward locum veterinarian.

"Sorry about leaving earlier. What's going on with the cat? How's the puppy? Was parvo confirmed?"

"Parvo was confirmed, but thankfully Jack is responding to fluids and supportive care. I've spoken to the client about monoclonal antibodies, but they're concerned about costs. They're still paying off the six thousand dollars they paid for the cute little mongrel. Their credit card is maxed out, so we helped them apply for one of the veterinary emergency credit services."

Louise knew that not only would Daphne help Jack's family apply for credit, but she'd also likely discount their bill to help them out. It was something they both did occasionally and selectively, knowing that if they did it too often, they'd soon have trouble paying their own bills. To prevent a client base that expected cheap—or free—veterinary care from forming, they rarely told clients about the discount. Sadly, the populace was becoming more demanding and entitled, and while happily many pet owners were seeking better quality care for their pets, they didn't understand that such care was costly for the veterinary community to provide. If they didn't pass the costs on to the clients, there'd soon be no veterinary community left to provide the care.

"The Morrisons—they're the puppy's people—can't take him to the emergency clinic for overnight care, and I'm not comfortable leaving him alone here overnight, so we'll send him home with the IV catheter in, but bandaged. He'll come back in the morning for reassessment and continued treatment. I'll keep him here today as late as possible."

Louise glanced at the calendar on her monitor's taskbar. "Isn't there something going on at Ella's preschool tonight? Something for Easter, or is it just a springtime thing?"

After graduation from veterinary college, Louise had thrown herself into her new profession, leaving little time for a social life or new relationships. Daphne, on the other hand, married her college boyfriend, Joe Carling, soon after becoming a licensed veterinarian. Opening a new clinic with Louise while starting a new life with Joe had made for a busy time for Daphne, but after a few years the young couple found themselves happily settled with two beautiful children and a home in the country.

Their eldest child, a four-year-old girl named Ella, was enjoying her first year in kindergarten. The last time Louise saw their second child, Ben, who was a couple weeks shy of six months, she was amused by his new-found voice. His favourite word was "ba," which he repeated often, emphasizing it in various ways as though he was conveying an important message.

Daphne slapped her palm to her mouth. "Shoot. I'd completely forgotten. Joe's going to feed the kids early, and we have to be at the school by five thirty. We arranged to meet there."

"It's still early in the day. Since you've done my surgeries for me, I'll take a drive to the rehab centre now to see what's going on with Major. Maybe I can assess him from afar and we can get the ultrasound done tomorrow. I'll be back in plenty of time for you to get out of here for Ella's show."

"Great idea."

The intercom on Daphne's desk beeped. She pushed the button.

Heidi's voice came over the speaker system. "Perdy's non-responsive."

Daphne looked at Louise. "That's the diabetic cat who came in this morning."

They raced to the staircase and then the treatment area.

Chapter 5

DAPHNE FLEW THROUGH the treatment room door, Louise on her heels. Heidi and Jenny had Perdy wrapped in a warming blanket and had an oxygen mask fixed over his face. Multiple coloured wires ran from under the blanket to the ECG monitor at the end of the stainless steel treatment table.

Jenny handed a sheet of paper to Daphne. "He was so dehydrated when he came in, we were only able to get a urine sample a few minutes ago. He crashed while I was waiting for the stick results. He's got ketones in his urine."

Louise studied the readout on the ECG machine. "His QT interval is prolonged. What was his blood potassium level?"

"Mid-normal when he first presented. We added a maintenance dose of potassium chloride to his fluids to keep it from bottoming out." Daphne, who had been auscultating Perdy's thorax with a stethoscope, looked up at Heidi. "Let's get another electrolyte panel on him. We may need to increase the potassium in his fluids. What was his last blood glucose?"

Jenny held Perdy's hospital chart up for Daphne to see. "Coming down, but still higher than normal. We've been giving the insulin as prescribed."

Daphne shook her head. "If only the *client* had been giving the insulin as prescribed, we probably wouldn't be here right now."

Louise eyed her friend; it was unusual for Daphne to be openly critical of clients, especially in front of the staff.

Daphne sighed. "I've had Mary calling them for weeks to schedule an appointment for a recheck exam and a fructosamine level." Measuring fructosamine levels gave the veterinary staff an idea of the patient's glucose fluctuations over a two-to-three-week period, often negating the need for a glucose curve. A curve involved a day's hospitalization and multiple blood draws, which could be quite stressful for a cat, compromising the results, as stress alone increases glucose values.

"The client kept telling Mary that the appointment wasn't necessary because Perdy was getting his medicine and doing okay. They would have run out of insulin days ago, yet they haven't called for a refill. I suspect they weren't giving the right amount, if they were giving it at all."

Daphne lifted Perdy's lip, then pushed on his gums to check his mucosal refill time. "He's so dehydrated, my finger is sticking to his gums." She looked at Jenny. "Let's run his renal and liver values, as well as get another glucose."

Jenny rolled the skin over Perdy's right foreleg to raise a vein.

Heidi applied some isopropyl alcohol, then collected a blood sample. She glanced at one of the beeping monitors. "His blood pressure and oxygen are improving."

As if on cue, Perdy shook his head, causing the oxygen mask attached to the Bain Circuit's long blue tube to drop to the floor. Heidi massaged his head to stimulate him. "That's a boy—give it another shake." Perdy didn't respond. Heidi retrieved the oxygen mask and placed it back over his face.

Jenny prepped the blood sample for analysis in the catalyst. "They said something about herbs and the internet when they brought Perdy in this morning."

Louise rolled her eyes. "Oh, great. Good ol' Dr. Google and his magic herbs. Why bother with a professional with a university education and years of experience, scientific research, and proven treatment protocols behind them when all you have to do is ask Dr. Google?" Louise put her palm to her forehead and sighed. "I hate to rush off before Perdy's stable, but I need to get to the rehab centre now if I'm going to get back in time for you to leave early, Daphne."

Daphne gave her a playful shove toward the door. "You're still here? We have this covered. I'll call Perdy's mom to discuss transferring him to a 24/7 facility."

Louise drove north on Rural Route 24—Sydney's Wildlife Rehabilitation Facility was about thirty minutes north of the Black Creek Animal Hospital. The drive afforded her plenty of time to rehash the day's events in her mind, and to work out the worst-case scenarios. She knew she was needlessly torturing herself; she couldn't change anything by worrying. *Trust in God, He's in control.* She'd seen it on a bumper sticker a few months ago, and more importantly, it was in the Bible. Trusting others was something Louise struggled with, but why did she resist trusting God?

She turned on the radio to get an update on the explosion at the airport—she didn't have to wait long. The reporter sped through the weather report and then was back on the lead story. They had no new information on the cause of the blast, but sadly, the death toll had risen to four, with at least thirty-four people injured, many seriously.

Louise glanced at the clock on the dashboard. It was already half past one and she still hadn't heard from Alex. Was he okay? Would he take himself back to the hospital if he was feeling unwell? She was tempted to call his mobile but didn't. If he was at the airport or the police department, he'd be immersed in the chaos of trying to find clues as to what caused the explosion.

She reminded herself that he was surrounded by fellow officers, not to mention firefighters and EMTs, so if he wasn't well, they'd be there for him. Yet she couldn't ease the anxiety she felt knowing he could have died, and that he could still be in danger.

The reporter had said that scattered showers were expected in the early afternoon, and as if on cue, the clear, sunny sky was replaced by dark clouds seconds before heavy droplets pelted the windshield.

"This weather better suits the day so far." Louise turned the wipers on, then keeping her left hand on the steering wheel and her eyes on the road, she rummaged through her bag for a cereal bar. The crinkling of the wrapper lightened her mood.

She'd forgotten to grab lunch before leaving the clinic and was becoming hangry. "Whoever invented that word was a genius. And happily, the skies north of here look clear. Hopefully no rain at the rehab centre."

Louise balanced the cereal bar between her hands at the top of the steering wheel and tugged on the edge of the wrapper. Nothing happened. She used her teeth and was excited to feel the plastic rip, but her joy was short-lived, as a blaring horn assaulted her ears. She looked up, and directly in front of her were the headlights of a half-ton truck.

Louise screamed while yanking the steering wheel to return her car to its own lane. She caught a glimpse of the driver's angry face as the pickup truck sped past, the rapid short beeps of his horn expressing his opinion about her driving.

Louise slapped her forehead. "Stupid, stupid, stupid." She'd allowed her "hanger," if that was the right noun for the feeling of being both hungry and angry, to affect her driving.

Chapter 6

THE CEREAL BAR wasn't enough to soothe Louise's hunger, which became evident when she found herself instantly annoyed at the group of protestors blocking the entrance to the wildlife rehab centre.

She counted five women loitering in front of SWaRF. After parking her car, she gripped the steering wheel tighter and inhaled deeply. *God, give me patience.* She exited the vehicle and grabbed her travel kit from the trunk, then approached the band of troublemakers.

The women, all middle-aged or older and with various body shapes and hair colours, were holding signs that hung low in front of their legs. When they saw Louise approaching, they thrust their signs into the air and shouted an obviously practiced chant: "Free the animals. Free the animals. No more captivity. Animals have rights too." Their signs said the same thing, as well as Go Vegan.

Louise shook her head and surged forward. She needed to see what was going on with Major, and she had no patience for these protestors. She had a sick patient, Alex still hadn't called to update her on his condition, Daphne needed to get home early, and she—Louise—was still hungry. She threw a cold stare at the woman who appeared to be the group's leader; she was the only person not holding up a sign.

The heavy-set, short woman with shoulder-length brown hair wearing a well-rehearsed grimace met Louise's gaze and held it. She also met Louise's pace in an attempt to block her access to the centre. The main gate was the width and height of one found on a standard backyard fence, with a padlock to keep people out.

The woman straightened to her full height—still not as tall as Louise—and crossed her arms. "We're not allowing anyone access to this facility until we know that the animals aren't in harm's way."

Louise's blood pressure surged and an uncomfortable wave of heat made its way to her head. "The only animal in harm's way at the moment is *you*." Louise pointed her finger into the woman's face. This vet wasn't going to back down when a patient needed her. "I don't care what your politics are, what your views on conservation are"—she glanced back at the Go Vegan sign—"or what you eat for dinner. All I care about is the sick animal you're preventing from getting medical attention. So get your whiny big butt out of my way."

Louise and the protestor stared at each other for what

seemed like an eternity. *Why isn't she backing down? Where's Sandra?* Louise stepped closer to her opponent. "I said—"

Before she could finish her sentence, she heard honking and . . . Was that Scottish highland music? Bagpipes? She turned her head toward the west end of the privacy fence in time to see a golf cart pull into view. Sitting in the driver's seat was Sandra Kelly, a woman of Scottish descent in her mid-forties who had bobbed white hair, a square chin, and a huge toothy grin. She was bopping to the music being blasted for all to hear from a large boom box sitting on the passenger seat.

"Over here, Louise. I'll give you a ride."

Behind the golf cart was a small band of four men and women, all holding their cellphones in the air. Louise hopped in after Sandra put the boom box on the cart's floor. Then Sandra made an announcement to the protestors. "If any of you attempt to follow us, my friends here will call 911. Stay where you are, or go to jail for trespassing. We have you on video."

Louise doubted that would work. Why wouldn't they simply follow the golf cart to gain entry into the facility, then flee when the police arrived?

Sandra must have guessed Louise's thoughts. "They've already been warned by authorities to keep off the property. They were hanging out at the back parking lot today too, until I reminded them there's a court order prohibiting them from that area. That's why we couldn't get Major to the clinic earlier."

Sandra expertly manoeuvred around a large hole. "They shouldn't even be so close to this entrance, but the police are tied up with the explosion at the airport, so the dimwits know they can get away with it today. If they get farther onto the property, though, they could face jail time, and most of them aren't all that committed to the cause. They're mostly middle-aged empty nesters with nothing better to do with their time. Other than Madame Grumpy Face and a couple of others, I haven't seen any of the serious protestors in a few days."

Louise smiled at the nickname Sandra gave to the woman with the twisted, cranky face who'd tried to block Louise's access. "How long has this been going on?"

Sandra yanked the steering wheel left, then right, executing hairpin turns to avoid exposed tree trunks, rocks, and low shrubs before coming to a clear path. Fifty yards ahead, a parking lot with two vans and a few cars could be seen. "For a few days. We've had issues in the past with people misunderstanding our purpose and trying to cause trouble. That's why we chose this secluded location, but we can't be completely hidden if we want to solicit supporters. And, of course, we have volunteers who come and go over time. It's possible that a recent one was here on a mission that had nothing to do with helping us."

Louise pried her fingers from the frame of her seat. Despite Sandra's obvious expertise in driving a golf cart over rough terrain, the bumpy ride made Louise offer a silent prayer of thanks for their safe arrival. "What type of mission?"

Sandra chuckled. "Some of them see themselves as real-life spies and will"—she made air quotes—"'infiltrate' our centre to get"—she made air quotes again—"'evidence.'"

"Evidence of what?"

Sandra shrugged as she parked the golf cart in front of a mobile office trailer and removed the key from the ignition. "Beats me. Whatever they think will back up whatever stories they make up to get media attention, I suppose. That's what this is usually about. They want media attention so they can lead their followers into thinking they're fighting the good fight and saving animals. The more followers they have, the more money people send to them. Sadly, that money rarely goes to helping animals. If anything, their misguided antics hurt more animals than they help."

Louise shook her head. "Sad that so many are taken in so easily. Do people have nothing better to do with their time than sit in front of a computer and look for reasons to get angry?"

"No, I guess. This recent wave of protests started after someone, possibly a fake volunteer, posted a static-riddled voice recording on Facebook. She made some crazy claim that we were doing something unethical, but the audio is so bad, I don't know why anyone would take it seriously."

"What was she accusing you of?"

"I have no idea. I didn't listen to it myself. One of our regular staff found it and said it was mostly incoherent gibberish, and now here we are with a group of determined protestors."

"Keyboard warriors with too much time and not enough sense."

Sandra glanced at a small pond that was playing host to a family of mallard ducks. "You got that right, sister."

Louise's stomach grumbled. She couldn't stop that, but she did stop grumbling about what she'd witnessed at the front entrance. Sandra needed her support, not her negativity. "You wouldn't happen to have anything to eat around here, would you? Doughnuts? Cereal bars? Anything, really. I missed lunch."

Sandra laughed. "No problem. We keep a ready supply for the staff—it's not unusual for some of them to be here for long hours, even overnight, watching over sick animals or new arrivals. The new arrivals are often transported here because they've been seriously injured or orphaned, so we watch them closely for the first twenty-four to forty-eight hours."

Sandra led Louise into a trailer, where there was a kitchen with a table and chairs, a stove, a refrigerator, and a laminated counter sporting a coffee maker and teakettle. Louise gratefully scarfed down the sandwich Sandra made for her, and then they headed out to see Major, the sick coyote.

"I'm happy to say he's perked up as the day's gone by. With the protestors out there, I assumed he wouldn't be getting any sedation at the clinic today, so I had his caretaker go ahead and offer him food. He gobbled it right up. That was encouraging, as he hasn't been eating well for a couple of days."

After observing Major in his habitat—an indoor enclosure set up to mimic a wooded area, with the added benefit of straw and heat lamps to keep the patient warm—Louise and Sandra agreed that he was stable enough to wait until the morning to be transported to the animal hospital for further tests if needed. "If the protestors show up again tomorrow, Sandra, call me in the morning. I'll come here with a tech and we'll see what we can do on site."

"Sounds good. While you're here, let me show you our newest project. Our maintenance man and all-around handyman, Bailey, has been creating a pond for some of the waterfowl we get in here. It'll be wonderful for their rehabilitation before we release them."

"The pond we passed on the way here?"

"No, that one's natural and outside the security fence. The new one's strictly for rehabilitation." Sandra chuckled. "Not that we can keep the other birds away, but we do want to keep nosy humans away, so this pond is in a secluded area near the back periphery of the property. As well as working on the pond, Bailey's been working on improving the fencing. This past winter, some young people took advantage of a snowstorm and the resulting snowbanks to climb over the fence, damaging it in the process. One of our many unexpected expenses this year."

Louise sighed. "Argh!"

"You got that right, my vet friend. Argh!"

They trekked down a dirt path through a wooded area that led to a small clearing. "Over here." Sandra turned left and waved for Louise to follow her, but Louise stumbled on a rock.

She dropped to her knees, then rolled her body so she could sit on a log. "Ouch." She removed her shoe and massaged her foot. When she was done, she noticed Sandra about forty yards ahead of her, staring at the pond.

Her face drained of colour, Sandra had one hand over her mouth and the other pointing at the water. A bush at the water's edge blocked Louise's view, so she hurried to her client's side to see what the trouble was.

Louise let out a gasp. Floating face down in the pond was the body of a woman.

Chapter 7

AFTER FINDING THE woman floating in the new pond, Louise immediately called 911. Sandra and her crew wanted to pull the victim out of the water to try CPR or, if it was too late for that, to show her body due respect, but Louise's prior experience with a crime scene had taught her to leave everything as they found it. It was obvious the woman was beyond help, and if this was a crime and not a terrible accident, they needed to preserve any evidence.

The first officers to respond were familiar to Louise. Wayne Carter attended the same church as Louise and Alex, and it was he and his partner, Brian Tomlin, who'd responded to the break-in at the Black Creek Animal Hospital a few months prior.

Brian, who had a moustache and a goatee, and soared well over six feet in height, secured the body to its current location by slipping a loop around one leg, then tying the other end of the rope around a rock on the adjacent grassy area.

Wayne, not much taller than Louise and clean-shaven, approached Louise and Sandra with his notepad and pen ready. "Hey, Louise. So you two were just walking around and stumbled upon the victim? Did you see anyone else in the area?"

Sandra zipped up her jacket, then crossed her arms tightly against her chest. "I didn't see anyone. No one should be back here, especially not someone who doesn't work here."

Wayne spoke with a soft, reassuring voice. "The victim isn't one of your employees?"

Sandra shook her head.

"What about a volunteer?"

Sandra shook her head again. "No, I don't think so. She's not wearing one of our work shirts, and all of my people are accounted for. They were all up front filming the protestors when Louise and I came back here. Unless . . . Oh my. What if one of them came back while we were with Major and tripped?" Sandra covered her face with her hands and lowered herself onto a nearby rock. "There is something familiar about her, but I couldn't see her face . . . What if she *is* a volunteer here?" Quickly tapping her foot, Sandra flattened the dirt underneath it. "No, the shirt isn't right. All of our people would be wearing an orange-and-black SWaRF shirt."

Wayne tapped his pen on the notepad. "Okay, Ms. Kelly. We'll have to wait for the coroner's report to confirm it, but it looks like the body has been here for a couple of hours, if not longer. It's unlikely it's any of your people if they were all accounted for when Dr. Miller arrived."

Sandra sniffled, then rose to her feet. "That's good news. And the only employee who didn't show up today for work is a man." She turned her attention to Louise. "Bailey—the caretaker I told you about. The one who constructed this pond for us. He was going to work on it over the weekend but called me Saturday morning to say he wasn't feeling well and would be back Monday."

"He told you he'd be here today but then didn't show up for work? Hmm." Wayne tapped his pen again. "What's Bailey's last name?"

Sandra thrust her fists onto her hips. "Nelson. Bailey Nelson. He's been with me for a few months. He's a good man, and very trustworthy."

Wayne, expressionless, held Sandra's gaze. "I see."

Sandra's lips tightened and her nostrils flared. Louise gently pulled her away from Wayne, afraid for the officer's safety. "He's just doing his job, Sandra."

Sandra wagged a finger at Wayne. "He thinks Bailey did this. He thinks Bailey's a suspect!"

"Everyone's a suspect at this point." Louise hugged the rehab director's shoulder.

"The good doctor's right about that. If this is a crime scene, everyone's a suspect until they're cleared. That includes the two of you." The booming voice made Louise, who'd been facing the pond, turn around.

She had been longing to see Alex since parting ways with him earlier at the hospital, but this wasn't the reunion she'd hoped for. "What are you doing here? Are you okay?" She wanted to run to him and throw her arms around him, but they had an audience. Then what he'd just said hit her. "Wait! What do you mean, that includes the *two* of us?"

While Sandra was in the bathroom, Louise sat in a chair beside Alex in Sandra's office—located in the trailer the women had visited when Louise arrived at SWaRF. It contained a desk chair, a weathered desk piled high with papers, and two chairs for visitors. A computer monitor sat on top of a small filing cabinet positioned under a window. In the far corner, a photo of a green bird with red feathers next to its beak hung on the wall.

"What type of bird is that?" Alex nodded at the photo.

Louise shrugged without looking at him. "I don't know."

"You're a vet and you don't know what type of bird that is?"

"You're a cop. Do you know all the traffic laws in Australia?"

"Point taken."

What was this chit-chat about a bird photo? Was he trying to make up for his earlier behaviour? Louise crossed her arms and stared out the window, ignoring the man who refused to give her any information about the events at the airport. And as they'd made their way from the pond to the trailer, she'd asked Alex why he was at the rehab centre and he evaded that question as well. She wasn't pleased with his refusal to share his knowledge, even though she knew he wasn't allowed to reveal information about an active investigation to civilians, including her.

Blessed with excellent peripheral vision, she knew he was staring at her. What was that in his eyes? Was he silently pleading for her understanding or forgiveness? Perhaps he felt guilty for not calling after the explosion, or after parting ways at the hospital. He should feel guilty for calling her and Sandra suspects. Maybe he had a brain injury?

Louise turned her full attention to him and stared into his eyes. His pupils were the same size, and the diameter she'd expect for the amount of light in the room. He looked tired but alert. She squinted while attempting to assess his mentation, then raised her finger in the air. "Follow my finger." She moved it right, then left.

"What are you doing?" Alex grabbed her hand and pulled it down, away from his face.

"Good reflexes. When Sandra gets back, I'll ask her if she has a penlight."

"For what?"

"To check your pupillary light reflex. To make sure you don't have a brain injury."

"A what? Why would you think that?" Alex shot to his feet, causing the chair to rock backwards.

Louise caught the back of the chair and kept it from falling over. "Well, let's see. You were in an explosion earlier today, and now you're accusing me of being a murderer."

Alex sat at the edge of Sandra's desk. "Two things wrong with your theory. One, I haven't told you it was a crime, or murder. And two, Officer Carter told me that the body appeared to have been in the water for a few hours. As per the timeline of your movements that I got from Mary, you haven't been here long enough to have committed the murder—if that's indeed what it is."

"You don't *have* to tell me anything, as your presence here screams that it's a murder. You are, after all, a homicide detective. And I know I didn't do it—*you're* the one who put me on the suspect list. I don't need to be a detective to figure any of that out."

"Do you need to be a detective to figure out that I called the clinic earlier to let you know I was okay? Or that after informing me you weren't there, Mary said you were here? Or that soon after I ended my call with her, a blast came over the police radio that something was going on at the wildlife rehab centre, the very place Mary had just said you were at?"

Louise frowned. That made sense, but she didn't want to admit that it was a good reason for Alex to show up at the pond.

He returned to his chair, then continued. "I thought I'd better head over here before going home to shower clotted blood, and who knows what else, out of my hair—to make sure you were okay."

Louise softened. He was concerned about her, and he'd rushed here to make sure she wasn't in danger.

But then he said, "I wanted to make sure you weren't getting yourself into trouble." He frowned, or was that a smirk? "It looks like I might be too late."

"You can't be serious. We *found* the body in the pond— we didn't *put* it there." Louise was about to stomp out of the office when Sandra appeared in the doorway.

"Hey, guys, sorry I kept you a bit. That . . . that . . . scene at the pond. It really shook me up. I needed to splash some water on my face and take a few minutes to breathe." Sandra closed the door, then sat at her desk. "I think I'm okay to talk now, Detective."

Alex, who had stood when Sandra entered the room, sat down. "I realize this is difficult, Sandra, but I do have a few questions for you. I'd like to start by asking about the absent employee. What was his name? Bailey—?"

"Nelson." Sandra clasped her hands beneath her chin, then tapped it with her knuckle. "He's only been with us a short while, but he's a great guy and very reliable. I don't remember him ever calling in sick—he came in to work on the pond while he had the flu this winter. He thought it'd be okay since he wasn't around the other employees, or the volunteers, but I insisted he go home to protect his own health."

Alex nodded as though trying to accept what a great employee Bailey was. "And why isn't he at work today?"

"Like I told the other officer, he wasn't feeling well. He called me Saturday morning to say he was sick. He was going to work on the pond over the weekend but decided to hold off until today." Sandra paused, as if reluctant to continue. "I guess he's still not feeling well."

Alex made some notes on his notepad. "So not long ago he was willing to work through the flu, but now he's calling in sick? Did he say what was ailing him?"

Sandra, her eyes wide as though she'd just seen a ghost, shot a look at Louise.

Louise picked up on Alex's doubt and Sandra's fear. "I'm sure Bailey now knows that Sandra doesn't want him here when he's not well, so he stayed home. It's obvious."

Alex turned to address Louise. "Nothing is obvious in an investigation."

His phone dinged. He read the message, typed in a response, then returned his attention to Louise. "And sadly, it's been confirmed that we do have a murder investigation on our hands. The text was from Officer Tomlin. Our victim had marks around her neck consistent with an attack."

Sandra pursed her lips, then looked at Louise. When Sandra turned back to the detective, she thrust her shoulders back and, without wavering, held his gaze. "Bailey didn't do this. I'm certain of it. He's a kind, gentle man. What would his motive be?" She flung her arm up, as if in protest. "No, I don't believe it. You can't suspect him."

Alex spoke softly. "I'm sorry, Sandra—we have to suspect him. He's familiar with the area, and he's unusually absent from work at the same time a dead body shows up in his work area. We can't clear anyone at this point. As I said earlier, *everyone* is a suspect." He fixed his eyes on Louise and held her gaze for several seconds, then looked at Sandra. "I'll need a list of all of your employees and volunteers."

Sandra rose and unlocked the top drawer of the filing cabinet. "Of course. No one here has anything to hide." She opened the drawer and rummaged through the files, then pulled out a single sheet of paper. "This is a list of our current employees and volunteers. I put it together before Christmas in preparation for our staff's Secret Santa."

Alex took the list from her. "Thank you. What about previous employees or volunteers? Has anyone left in the past few months under negative circumstances? Fired? Not getting along with others? Stealing?"

Sandra shook her head. "No, nothing like that. As I told Louise earlier, we occasionally get the odd fake volunteer, but we haven't had to let anyone go lately. I can give you a list of the volunteers who've come and gone over the past year, but it'll take time to get their names together. I told Louise about one volunteer who released a voice recording on Facebook." She repeated the story to Alex.

"We'll look into the person who made the recording, and

I'd appreciate that list as soon as possible. One more thing. The victim had an identification badge in her pocket, but it was damaged by the water. The only text we could make out was the last three letters of her last name—*ell*. Does that mean anything to you?"

Sandra shook her head again. "No. I don't know anyone with a name that ends in *ell*."

Louise reached for the cellphone Alex had placed face down on Sandra's desk. "Where's the badge from? That should tell us who she is."

He plucked the phone from her hand before she had a chance to see the screen. "I can't reveal that at this time. It's part of another investigation."

Louise lifted her palms in frustration. "How can that be? What other investigation?"

Alex ignored her questions and swiped the screen on the phone before addressing Sandra. "I have a photo of the victim we took from the badge." He held the screen toward Sandra. "Do you recognize this person?"

Sandra slunk into her chair. "Now I'll be a suspect too. That's . . . that's. I'm sure it's her."

Alex and Louise asked in unison, "Her who?"

Sandra lowered her head into her hands. "She's one of the protestors. Well, *was* one of them. I haven't seen her for a couple of days. She and a few of the other regulars, except for Madame Grumpy Face and a couple of the others, just disappeared."

Alex swiped the screen again. "She was wearing a shirt with a logo on it. Does the acronym ARS mean anything to you?"

Sandra wiped her face. "I think it stands for Animal Rights Soldiers."

"Why are they here? What's their purpose?" Alex tucked his phone into his pocket.

Sandra shrugged. "I assumed their purpose was to make my life miserable. Recently, they've championed themselves not only as animal rights activists, but also saviours of the environment."

Louise felt compassion for her friend, but she couldn't suppress her smile as she thought about the group's purpose and name. "Animal rights soldiers and environmentalists? A. R. S. E. So a bunch of—"

Alex gave Louise a sidelong glance and pointed his index finger at her. "Don't say it!"

Chapter 8

WITH THE DISCOVERY of a dead body and the commotion that followed, Louise had lost track of time. Her plan when she headed to Sydney's Wildlife Rehabilitation Facility earlier in the day was to quickly check on Major, the sick coyote, then head back to the animal hospital to allow Daphne's early departure. Louise wanted her friend to get to Ella's school play on time, and to do so without worrying about the sick patients under their care.

After Alex had finished questioning Louise and Sandra, Louise walked him back to his car, intending to convince him that Sandra and her crew couldn't possibly be responsible for the murder. It didn't work. He continued his spiel that everyone was a suspect until the police ruled them out with concrete evidence. *No doubt something he'd learned in detective school—How to Be Persuasive when Talking to a Witness 101.*

Louise replayed the conversation in her head as she drove back to Coverdale. When she reached the clinic and pulled into the parking lot, the clock on her dash told her it was quarter after five. She had called the clinic on her drive back to inform Daphne she was on her way. Louise didn't know how long it would take to get from the vet hospital to Ella's school—she could only hope that Daphne would have plenty of time. Louise threw the car into park, turned off the engine, grabbed her bag, and rushed through the back entrance. Having cleared the doorway, she stepped to the side just in time to avoid a collision with her business partner, who was flying in the opposite direction.

Daphne pushed on the horizontal bar that released the latch and cracked the door open. She looked over her shoulder at Louise. "Thanks for the call earlier. If I hurry, I should be able to make it to the school before Ella's class goes on. Heidi will fill you in on the cases." And as quickly as Daphne had appeared, she was gone.

Louise watched as the black metal door swung closed and made its usual clicking sound. The hallway behind her was quiet as she stood staring at the exit. "Bye."

She turned around and let out a scream. Standing directly in front of her was Heidi. "Where did you come from?"

With a toss of her head, Heidi indicated the treatment area. "Over there. You must have been deep in thought just now. My shoes are squeaky today."

Louise frowned. "Not squeaky enough. I've had enough

excitement for one day, thank you. I don't need anyone sneaking up on me."

"You *are* a bit jumpy, but it's understandable after finding a dead body."

Louise dropped her bag at the base of the stairs and headed for the treatment room. "Fill me in on the cases. Who's still here? Did the diabetic cat—Perdy, was it?—go to the referral clinic?"

Heidi followed Louise into the back area, which was set up with kennels along the walls, two treatment tables in the middle of the room, and a wet station for cleaning dirty wounds and performing dentistry. "The parvo puppy, Jack, is scheduled to go home at six thirty. Perdy Theobald is still here. Daphne was hoping the owners would pick him up for transfer before she left, but they were being difficult."

Louise sighed. "Difficult how?"

Heidi retrieved Perdy's clipboard from the hook on his cage. "They started with the ol' phone switch routine. Mr. Theobald kept Daphne on the phone for about fifteen minutes, asking questions about costs and prognosis and whatever, and then he said—"

Louise rolled her eyes. "No!"

Heidi nodded. "Yes! Yes, he did! He said"—the senior tech mimicked the man's goofy voice—"'Can you tell all that to my wife? She's right here.'"

They both sighed at this ridiculous habit some pet owners had. Whether they were married couples or couples dating, siblings, or other relatives, they thought nothing of expecting the veterinarian to repeat themselves multiple times to multiple people.

"Poor Daphne, but better her than me. I have no patience

for that foolishness anymore. The last time a man assured me that I could speak to him about his pet, then once I was done asked if I'd repeat everything to his wife because she made all the decisions about said pet, I told him I wouldn't repeat the instructions and they'd just have to learn how to communicate among themselves."

Heidi smiled. "Did you really? Who was it?"

Louise laughed. "No, I didn't. But someday I will—I promise."

Heidi handed the clipboard to Louise. "As you can see, shortly after you left, we were able to stabilize Perdy. He's been more responsive, and he's even eaten a bit of the diabetic food for us."

"That's good news." Louise flipped through the chart that gave her an overview of what treatments the overweight tabby had gotten during the day, and the results of his lab tests. "Why am I thinking there's more to the story? Why haven't they picked him up yet? I'm sure Daphne stressed the need to get him to the referral centre ASAP for ongoing observation and treatment."

Heidi sat down on a stool. "Oh, she did. She reminded them we don't have anyone here overnight and that he needed 24/7 observation. They promised they'd be here by five o'clock, but as you can see, they're not."

"Let's head up front and see if Shirley has heard from them." Louise headed for the front office.

Heidi followed. "Shirley's off this evening. Mary's training Miranda, a new part-time receptionist. She's a high school student—grade twelve—but she has a lot of experience working with the public and handling cash. I think her last job was as a cashier at a grocery store. Rita hired her last week."

Louise had mixed feelings about having a new staff member she'd known nothing about until this moment. It was odd to have no input into a new hire, but at the same time it was great to have an office manager who could oversee hiring and, if needed, firing. Lucky for Louise and Daphne, after over eight years in practice, they hadn't yet needed to fire any staff. Their last locum veterinarian lost his license before they had a chance to fire him for involving the clinic in a drug-smuggling ring. They did, however, fire the client he'd been working with, and Louise had to admit that it had filled her with guilty pleasure at the time.

Louise and Heidi used one of the exam rooms as a passage to the front office, but before they made it through, Mary popped into the room and closed the door partway. "Mrs. Victoria is here to buy food for her pups."

With fascination, Louise observed the no-nonsense receptionist in her mid-fifties peek into the reception area. Mary was a fun character who could play a kindly grandmother type one minute, then pull out her tough-as-nails persona the next if she needed to defend those she cared about. Louise often wondered if the toughness was related to losing her husband in a construction accident when her kids were little. Raising three young children on her own couldn't have been easy.

Mary glanced back at Louise and Heidi, then placed her index finger over her lips. She whispered, "Miranda's helping Mrs. Victoria. I want to see how she does."

Louise felt a surge of compassion for Miranda. Mrs. Victoria had a reputation for being haughty and rude to all staff not only at their clinic, but also at neighbouring ones. She thought herself more important than any other clients, or for that matter, any other people.

The three women stood in the exam room out of sight. Louise and Heidi couldn't see what was going on beyond the cracked-open door, but they could hear voices. Louise leaned over Mary—she had to see what was happening.

Mrs. Victoria slammed a bag of dog food onto the counter and said in a booming voice, "Where's Shirley? I prefer to deal with Shirley. She knows what I need."

Miranda smiled and tapped on the keyboard. "Shirley's off this evening. I'd be happy to help you. Did you need anything other than the food?" The teenager, who wore her long curly black hair in braids, could easily be mistaken for someone in her twenties.

Mrs. Victoria leaned over the counter, bringing her face closer to Miranda's. "You look young. Are you new? How old are you? Are you old enough to be working here?"

Miranda backed up a few inches. "My name's Miranda, and I'm plenty old enough to sell a bag of dog food. We don't sell liquor here, so age isn't really a big concern."

Louise clapped her hand over her mouth in shock, and to stifle a laugh. Miranda's tone suggested she didn't have an ounce of meekness; this new hire had spunk. Mary punched the air with her fist.

Louise was expecting the client to blast Miranda, but instead the woman said, "I guess you'll do for now. But you should know, young lady, that I'm one of their best clients here. I've spent so much money here over the past couple of years, I'm sure I must own the second floor by now."

Miranda, who'd been focusing on the computer, looked Mrs. Victoria straight in the eyes and, wearing a poker face, said, "It says here in your file that you've spent a total of six hundred and eighty dollars in the past two years on three pets.

I can't be sure, but I doubt that even covers the monthly utility bills. And if I'm reading this correctly, your last invoice is a few weeks overdue."

Her mouth open wide and her hands clasped together, Mary looked back at Louise. She gave Louise her best attempt at puppy dog eyes and asked, "Can we keep her? Please?"

Louise, who'd stepped back when Mary turned around, suppressed another laugh. She rolled her eyes and shook her head at Mary, then gave her a little shove on the shoulder. "I have work to do upstairs. You can deal with the fallout."

As Louise and Heidi raced for the stairs that would take them to safety on the upper level, they heard Mrs. Victoria yelling, "There you are, Mary. Did you hear what this young woman just said to me?"

Mary's voice rang through the halls. "I'm sorry. I didn't hear a word."

Chapter 9

LOUISE AND HEIDI parted ways at the upper landing. Heidi headed for the staff room, no doubt to grab a cola from the refrigerator. Louise entered her office and turned on her computer monitor before making herself a coffee.

Cupping the mugful of the sanity-saving hot beverage in her hand, Louise sat down at her desk and opened her internet search engine. She typed in *Animal Rights Soldiers and Environmentalists* and their new acronym, *ARSE*.

There was a long list of links to articles in local newspapers about the protestors. A quick scan told her that while some seemed sympathetic to the group's cause, others were critical of its actions. Besides the articles, there was a link to the group's Facebook page. Louise clicked on it, then said, "Nuts!" The group was private, and she'd have to request to join it before she could see names and pictures of the members.

"Darn! I wanted to see if I could get the names of the people who were at Sandra's today." She noted that she was talking to herself again—something she was doing more and more as she grew older. Louise shrugged. "Oh well, at least I don't have to worry about a rude response."

Next, she clicked on the first news article and was disappointed by the lack of photos of group members, until she scrolled down a couple of screen lengths. There she was— Madame Grumpy Face, as Sandra called her, holding a take-out soda cup. What was that protruding from the top of the cup? Louise enlarged the photo. Poking out of the disposable cup was a plastic straw.

Louise chuckled. "Didn't Sandra say that the group also championed themselves as saviours of the environment?"

The article was dated 2013. "Oh well, it's a few years old." She pointed at the woman in the photo. "I guess you weren't as sanctimonious then as you are now, or maybe being against plastic straws wasn't yet media worthy."

Reading through the article, Louise hoped to learn Madame Grumpy Face's name, but sadly, no group members were identified, and their purpose wasn't discussed. The reporter focused on their use of a megaphone, and the resulting noise complaints from people living near the small zoo in Western Ontario that had been the focus of the 2013 protests.

Louise closed the site and was about to click on the next article when her phone buzzed. She sighed, relieved to see that the text was from Alex, but then tensed as she wondered if he had good news or bad. The explosion had been several hours ago, and he might now be suffering the complications of injuries he'd earlier refused to admit were possible. Or maybe he was fine but messaging to say that they'd arrested Sandra on some trumped-up charges. Dread from a mixture of exasperation and concern flooded her, and her finger hovered over the text message. *Just open the message and read it. Why are you always making up worst-case scenarios in your head?*

The intercom buzzed before Louise tapped the screen. It was Mary. "Mrs. Theobald, Perdy's mom, is here to pick him up."

Louise pressed the voice button. "Thanks, Mary. I'll be right down." Rather than reading the text message, she looked at the time display. "Six o'clock? How did so much time go by since I got back?" She grabbed a white lab coat and made her way to the treatment room.

When she entered the treatment room, Louise saw Heidi and Jenny preparing Perdy for transfer to the Bathurst Region Emergency Clinic—commonly referred to by veterinary teams as B-REC. Louise watched as Heidi removed the bandage around Perdy's right front leg and detached the intravenous tubing from the catheter that fed under his skin into his cephalic vein. Heidi then screwed a sterile injection cap over the opening and flushed the catheter with saline before replacing the bandage. Leaving the catheter in place would allow the emergency clinic to continue the intravenous fluid therapy without having to place a new catheter immediately upon arrival—as long as it was still in place and patent after the trip.

"He's looking much better than earlier today. I see he's

now holding his head up and is alert." Louise rubbed the short-haired cat's chin and was rewarded with a purr.

Jenny scooped Perdy into her arms, gave him a gentle hug, then placed him in his plastic travel carrier. "I'm happy to say he's feeling much better. He's not only more alert, but he's also eaten for us again and is using his litter box. He really is a sweet little guy."

Jenny handed the clipboard with Perdy's chart to Louise, who then scanned the information indicating his progress over the day as per blood results and vital signs, such as heart rate and body temperature. The last page was detailed instructions that Daphne had written for the clients, informing them that Perdy was still critical and thus needed ongoing hospitalization. Included was a map to the emergency clinic, as a well as the contact information for B-REC.

"We've already called B-REC to let them know we're transferring a patient, and Mary sent his records to them earlier." Heidi chugged the last of her cola, then expertly tossed the can into a garbage can across the room. She opened a new can and took a sip.

Louise shook her head, unsure if she should be impressed by her young technician's skill at can tossing or worried about the damage to her stomach lining from all the cola she drank. Of course, Louise drank more coffee than was probably wise, so she refrained from lecturing her fellow caffeine junkie. It was a side effect of working non-stop five to six days a week, some of those days lasting ten to twelve hours.

Jenny lifted the carrier and offered it to Louise. "Mrs. Theobald's in the front office. She didn't want to wait for you in an exam room."

Louise pursed her lips. To decrease distractions and afford

the client privacy should other people be in the waiting room, it was preferable to use an exam room. Was Mrs. Theobald claustrophobic or just difficult? Weary of what was awaiting her after an already long and stressful day, Louise feigned a happy face, then took the carrier from Jenny and headed for the front office.

Mary and Miranda were hovering over a computer monitor, Mary instructing the girl on various features. Louise held back a grin—she was sure Mary was simply avoiding eye contact with the huffy-looking, well-dressed woman wearing what Louise thought might be a cashmere sweater. Her arms folded, Mrs. Theobald was standing to the side of the desk. She was adorned with fake eyelashes and fake fingernails, and she had unnaturally full lips. Her thin face was punctuated with high cheekbones and lacked wrinkles, though she was obviously middle-aged. Louise choked when the chemicals from the woman's overpowering perfume hit her nostrils and entered her lungs.

Making eye contact with her client, Louise nodded toward exam room 1. "Would you like to talk in here, Mrs. Theobald? I have some instructions for you from Dr. Carling, and if you have any questions . . ."

The plasticized woman rolled her eyes and huffed. "I don't have time for this. I've been waiting here patiently—I don't know what took you so long. Guess you were just waiting for me to pay the bill before bringing my cat out." Mrs. Theobald turned for the door.

"Did you want to take the cat with you?" Louise lifted the carrier higher.

"My car's right there. You can put the carrier in the back seat. I paid enough for not even a full day of care, and now I'm supposed to take him to a different clinic? The least you can do it put it in the car for me."

Louise felt the heat rising in her chest but tried to remain professional. "The *least* we did was save your cat's life. I'd be happy to help you to the car, but I'd rather first make sure that you're familiar with the emergency clinic and how to get there. It's important that Perdy be taken there immediately for continued care. He's responded nicely today."

The client rolled her eyes again and opened the clinic door. She threw her arm in the air as if waving at an imaginary fly. "Sure, sure. Let's get going. Some of us have important things to do."

Louise glanced over at Mary, who held her palms up and shrugged.

"I'm right behind you." Louise followed the woman to a pristine, brand-new Tesla with a green licence plate. "As I was saying, Perdy has responded to treatment today, but he isn't out of the woods yet. He needs ongoing care, which he can only get in a hospital setting. Once he's released, it'll be important to continue the insulin treatment and to monitor him on a very regular basis." Remembering Daphne's earlier comments on Mrs. Theobald's habit of ignoring recheck visits for Perdy, Louise emphasized the words "very" and "regular."

As soon as she heard the doors unlock, Louise opened the back driver's-side door and placed Perdy's carrier on the seat. She then reached over and secured the seat belt around the carrier. She whispered to her patient, "I'm not terribly confident in the skill of your driver, but thankfully it's only a short trip to B-REC." She closed the door and handed the paperwork to Mrs. Theobald.

"What's all this?" Mrs. Theobald grabbed the papers, then ruffled them.

"Directions to the emergency clinic, as well as their contact information should you need it. We've already sent Perdy's records to them. They know you're on your way and will be ready for you when you get there." Louise made her best effort to smile at the woman, who rolled her eyes yet again.

Without another word, Mrs. Theobald got into her car and drove away. Louise said a prayer for Perdy's safety, and for the people on duty at B-REC.

Chapter 10

AFTER A LONG and trying day filled with an obnoxious carbon monoxide detector, an airport explosion and Alex's brush with death, protestors blocking access to a patient, and an entitled client, Louise knew she should have gone straight home and straight to bed. The trouble was that once she was certain Alex was out of danger—she'd responded to his earlier text with a phone call—she'd begun to obsess about the deceased woman she and Sandra had found at the rehab centre.

Upon leaving the clinic parking lot, Louise could have turned right and headed home, but instead she'd turned left onto Main Street, then right onto Rural Route 24. That was approximately twenty minutes ago, and the sun had since set.

As she drew closer to Sydney's Wildlife Rehabilitation Facility, she strained her eyes in the darkness to find the driveway. "Yeah!" she shouted to the air when it came into view. Louise slowed enough to safely make the turn into the main parking lot, and as she placed the car into park, she spotted Sandra waiting for her in the golf cart they'd ridden in that afternoon.

Sandra situated the cart beside Louise's car, hopped out, then opened the car door for her. "I almost missed your call. I was about to do the nightly rounds for our resident critters when my phone buzzed. I have to admit, I'm glad to have the company—I let the staff leave early today to de-stress after all the excitement. I've never felt nervous being here alone before, but after . . . well . . . you know."

Louise jumped out of the car, then wrapped her arm around Sandra's shoulder. "I know. And no worries—I'm happy to keep you company. I wouldn't mind a bit of company myself right now." What Louise really wanted was to return to the area where she'd stumbled earlier because something that seemed innocuous at the time had caught her eye. Now, in light of the dead body they found in the pond, she wanted to investigate it further, then head home to bed. However, leaving Sandra alone in the dark after someone was murdered on the property wasn't an option. "I'm surprised the police aren't still here."

Louise hopped into the cart, and Sandra kicked it into gear and headed for the path through the woods. "There's one officer stationed near the back parking lot. He said he'd be here until I'm done my checks. Once everything's locked up and secure, he's been ordered to leave and return to patrol. It sounds like they're down a few officers tonight."

"Yeah. Alex called earlier to let me know he was feeling

okay but was staying with friends overnight in case he had a concussion. He mentioned that they had to call several officers from the night shift in to cover the day shift. More than a few officers were injured in the explosion, and sadly, the death toll's up to five. Two members of the force and three civilians." Louise took a deep breath to fight back the tears that threatened. The damaged buildings could be repaired, but some victims would have their lives altered forever. And nothing could bring back those who'd lost their lives.

Sandra sniffled. "That's horrible. Do they know yet what caused it?"

Louise dug a solitary tissue from the side pocket of her scrub pants. She raised it to her face and recoiled from the smell of waxy ears, no doubt from a patient she'd seen earlier, before blowing her nose. "Got any tissues in your office?"

Sandra sniffled again. "Tons."

"That's good news." Louise wiped her nose on the sleeve of her jacket in hopes of displacing the dog ear smell. "Alex couldn't tell me much about the investigation, but he did hint that it's looking more and more like a deliberate act. Who could be that hateful?"

"A few people come to mind." Sandra swung the golf cart into a spot by the mobile trailer and slammed it into park.

After collecting a box of tissues, a couple of high-powered flashlights, a box of plastic sandwich bags, and two travel mugs filled with hot chocolate from Sandra's office, they rode the golf cart toward the pond.

Sandra stopped the cart outside the area still surrounded by yellow police tape. "What are the sandwich bags for?"

Louise frowned. "They were going to be for evidence collection—you know, in case we saw something that should be bagged. But the tape tells me the police aren't done here yet."

Sandra shone her flashlight at the pond. "No. I was told they might be here for several days and to not disturb anything."

Louise exited the cart and headed back to the spot where her foot had earlier met the tree stump. She bent down, facing the pond, then scanned the area for the fabric she'd discovered earlier. It didn't take long to see it swaying in the wind, attached to a tree branch. "Sandra, can you shine your light on this tree over here for me?"

Once her friend highlighted the object of her focus, Louise took photos on her phone of it from multiple angles. "I'd love to put this in a baggie and take it with us, but I'd better leave it here. I don't want a lecture from Alex on tampering with evidence." Instead of plucking the fabric from the twig, Louise placed a sandwich bag over it, then zipped either end to tighten it. "That should keep it in place until the forensics team returns tomorrow. It might not be important, but it could be from the killer."

"Or the victim."

Louise nodded. "True. Could be. Do you remember what she was wearing?"

Sandra shook her head. "No, not really. I know she wasn't wearing one of our shirts, but other than that, I can't really remember what I saw. It all happened so fast. Pond. Body. Police. My mind has been spinning all evening."

Louise headed back to the pond and lifted the yellow barrier.

Sandra called out to her, "Remember the part about not

letting anyone disturb anything? I think going beyond the tape counts."

Louise continued on her path. "I'm not going to disturb anything. I'm looking with my eyes, not my hands—I promise. Shine your light over here for me." Louise pointed to a cluster of stones adjacent to where the body had been lying.

Sandra sighed. "Sure. What do you see?"

"A cigarette butt. Does Bailey smoke?"

"No."

"Anyone else who works here smoke?"

"I'm not sure, but even if they did, no one's allowed to smoke on SWaRF grounds. We had a fright a while back when a fire in the surrounding woods threatened to overtake our property. I doubt anyone would sneak back here to smoke, because if they got caught, they'd be fired immediately."

Louise placed a plastic sandwich bag over the cigarette and held it in place with a stone at each corner. She then searched the edge of the pond with her flashlight. "Other than the blood-soaked grass, I don't see anything else out of the ordinary here. Let's head back and get started on your rounds."

"Good idea. It's kinda creepy out here. I'm a fan of those true crime shows, but I never in my wildest imagination thought I'd be part of one."

"Someday you might get a call for an interview from one of those shows."

Sandra scrunched her face, then grinned. "I hate to admit it, but that would be kinda cool. The being interviewed part, not the rest." Her grin turned sour.

Louise, herself a frequent watcher of the genre, understood what Sandra meant. Death and murder were, of course, horrible, but at the same time oddly fascinating—until you found yourself a part of it.

Walking back to the cart, Louise shone her light onto the ground near the tree holding the fabric. "Hold up a minute, Sandra. I think I see footprints."

"Well, you were just standing over there. They're probably yours."

"Maybe."

Clouds had moved in, and what little light shone from the moon was now gone. Louise slowed her pace to prevent stubbing her toe, and to avoid stepping in any evidence.

"Here—see these prints? They're too large to be mine." Louise lifted her foot and, using her flashlight, studied the bottom of her shoe, then studied the prints in the mud. "And the pattern on the sole is different. The bottom of my shoe has circles, and this print has waves. Can you shine your light over here?" Louise tucked her flashlight into her pocket, then using her phone, took photos of the footprints. "That should do it. Let's get going—it feels like rain is on the way."

An hour later they completed Sandra's rounds; the animals were fed and watered, their habitats cleaned and locked up, and the flashlights returned to Sandra's office. As they were leaving the trailer, the clouds let loose with a torrential downpour, soaking both of them to the skin.

Louise accompanied Sandra to the back parking area to inform the officer on duty that they were done locking up, and he accompanied them to their cars. Louise headed home, looking forward to a hot shower and another hot chocolate. She thanked God for showing her the footprints that would most likely be gone after that deluge of rain. She could only hope that Alex would be as thankful for her actions when she told him what she'd been up to tonight.

The events of the day once again filled Louise's mind as she drove home, but as she pulled into her driveway, a torrent of butterflies stirred her intestines. What had Daphne said earlier? Alex had a surprise for her, but Daphne didn't know what it was. Louise thought back to conversations she and Alex had had over the past few weeks. They'd talked about taking their relationship past friendship, to more like courtship—if anyone called it that anymore. Alex said the word and Louise laughed at him, thinking he was in one of his goofy moods, but when he looked hurt, she realized he was being serious. Louise was softening to the idea; perhaps it was time to leave past hurts in the past and trust God for the future. Was a romantic relationship with Alex in God's plan for her life?

Louise turned into her driveway and turned the ignition off. A battle waged in her mind as she sat in her car thinking through possible scenarios—good and bad. Daphne and her husband, Joe, were pro-Louise and Alex—of that Louise had no doubt. Her sister, Maryanne, wasn't shy about telling Louise that she'd be happy to have Alex as a brother-in-law.

Louise *pondered*—a word Daphne loved to use—her relationship with Alex. Did she want to risk putting herself into an emotionally vulnerable position by dating a police officer? She shivered at the thought. *Why does this scare me more than dead bodies and fractious animals?*

Her mind on autopilot, she entered her house, where she was greeted by a grumpy, hungry cat who followed her into the kitchen. Oscar gobbled down his food as soon as Louise, his housemaid, set the bowl on the floor. After pouring herself a bowl of cereal, she headed into the living room to check the windows.

The sight of stationary headlights at the foot of her driveway sent bile into Louise's throat. She slammed her back against the wall, placing herself out of sight to anyone outside, then pulled the cord to close the blinds. She wasn't expecting visitors, and it was too late in the evening for a friend to just stop by unannounced. The driveway to the closest neighbours was at least two hundred yards up the road, so it was unlikely to be one of them.

Louise opened the blinds a couple of inches. The car was still there, as its headlights were reflected in the mirror on the far wall. The vehicle hadn't moved. If the occupant was a lost motorist using her driveway to turn around, they'd be gone by now. Louise raised her phone to take a photo of its reflection, but the glare from the lights masked the licence plate and any details about the car. A car that was still there and still not moving, but with the engine running. Had someone followed her from the rehab centre? Why?

Chapter 11

"THIS IS STUPID!" Louise stood up and moved into the kitchen, where she closed the blinds, preventing any lurkers from spying on her through those windows. The car hadn't moved in over ten minutes and she hadn't heard anyone get out. That didn't mean someone hadn't gotten out—they might be in stealth mode.

Louise hurried upstairs to retrieve her baseball bat—it was still on the landing where she had left it earlier that day. How many intruders could a person deal with in less than twenty-four hours? Luckily, the first one was merely an artificial intruder into her peace of mind, but even with the advancements in self-driving cars, there had to be a flesh-and-blood driver operating the one blocking the entrance to her driveway.

She had sent a text message to Alex, but his lack of response at this late hour told her he was likely sleeping. She didn't want to text him again, or call him. If he'd been able to fall asleep after the day he had, that was exactly what he needed.

When she called 911 about the current intruder, they assured her they'd send a car as soon as possible, but because of the shortage of available patrol cars, there might be a delay. The airport was still an active crime scene requiring the presence of multiple officers on site overnight, and those remaining were stretched thin. The operator advised her to ensure that her doors and windows were locked, and to call them back if anyone from the car approached the house.

After she hung up, Louise had sat quietly on the living room floor until her no-nonsense, take-charge persona kicked in and she decided to take control of the situation. After all, she had the home field advantage.

With her trusty wooden friend resting over her shoulder, Louise crept out the back door and made her way into the wooded area to the side of her house. She knew every path, tree stump, and bush in these woods by memory, eliminating the need for a flashlight and giving her the added advantage of surprise if she encountered the car's driver.

Louise advanced several yards into the woods before turning ninety degrees and heading toward the road. Once she was near it, she'd scope out not just the car, but also the driver. She planned to remain outside until the police arrived, and the unusual warmth of the March air agreed with that plan. If the driver spotted her, she would race through the woods to the neighbour's house. It was unlikely someone unfamiliar with the landscape could follow her.

The ground was covered with leaves that had fallen months ago and were soggy from this evening's rain, allowing her to remain silent as she advanced toward her target. Once she was close to the road, Louise squatted down behind a fallen tree and used her binoculars to get a look at the car—one of those European two-passenger models. She covered her mouth to quiet her gasp. The driver's seat was empty. She glanced in every direction. Had she walked into a trap?

Not seeing any movement, she froze and listened for any evidence of company—a foot hitting an exposed tree root, someone walking into a tree trunk, or someone making agonized grunts as a hanging twig poked them in the eye. She didn't have to wait long.

"Oh!" The exclamation was followed by several grunts and the sound of snapping twigs.

There it was—evidence that the driver had ventured into the woods. Had he planned to sneak up to the house and break in? Louise studied the tiny car. How large could the individual driving that car be? Were there two people, or just the one?

The intruder broke the silence of the woods. "Nuts!" The voice sounded feminine.

Louise thought back to the protestors at the rehab centre that day. If someone had followed her from there, it had to be one of the smaller women. There was no way their cranky leader could fit into that car.

Assured that the driver was close to the road, Louise circled back to the house, then to the road a few yards deeper into the woods. As she got close to the road again, she detected movement. Her instincts about the driver of the small car were accurate—the person ahead of her couldn't be more than five feet tall. Louise had at least a four- or five-inch advantage over this woman, not to mention more than a few pounds, and the quick reflexes her profession had instilled in her. This was in addition to the strength she'd acquired from daily wrestling sessions with large dogs. And of course, she had her trusty baseball bat.

Filled with confidence, Louise stepped closer to the intruder. "Hey, you. What are you doing out here? What do you want?"

The woman spun around. Louise opened the flashlight on her phone and shone it into the woman's face.

The frightened older woman covered her eyes and backed up, stumbling over a bush but regaining her footing. "I'm not doing anything. Who are you? Turn that light off."

Louise shook her head at the squeaky, quivering voice. "I own this property. You're trespassing. The police are on their way."

The mention of the police filled the woman with rage. She pulled back her shoulders and lifted her arm to point at Louise. Her movements accentuated her rounded upper back—kyphosis, a condition Louise's grandmother had suffered from. What was this frail woman doing following her at night and wandering through unfamiliar woods?

As Louise drew closer to the intruder, she could see that the woman had to be well over eighty. The obvious dye job to return her short grey hair to a younger brown didn't mask the deep crevices in her face, the sunken eyes, and the excess skin on her neck. Along with the unnatural curvature of her back, she had skinny arms and bowed legs. Not only was she elderly, but she looked as if she'd had a difficult life.

Louise's anger momentarily turned to compassion and pity—until the woman started talking.

"You were at that place." The woman jabbed at the air with her bony finger. "That place. Oh, what's it called?"

"Sydney's Wildlife Rehabilitation Centre?" Louise said. "Or is it Facility?" She rubbed her chin and gazed at the sky. If Daphne had been with her, she would have giggled at Louise's behaviour.

The trespasser had a different reaction. She shook her whole body, starting with her head and ending with her behind, reminding Louise of her canine patients after they'd had a bath. She'd never seen a person do the "shake it all off" manoeuvre and had to suppress a laugh. This woman was obviously in need of help. Louise prayed that the police would arrive soon, hopefully before this person had a medical emergency.

"He told me all about you people and how you hurt the animals. You do it to make money." The woman wrinkled her nose and snorted. "That's terrible. Those poor creatures."

Louise crossed her arms and leaned against a nearby tree. "I believe you've been misinformed."

The tiny woman resumed her finger jabbing as she inched closer to Louise. "It's cruel keeping wild animals trapped in cages. You should let them all out. Let them go home to their families."

Sandra had told Louise that many of the protestors had been lied to about the rehab centre's purpose. This woman was clearly one such person.

"I'm afraid your facts are in error. The rehab centre's reason for being is to treat injured wildlife and ensure that their survival skills are intact before they're released back into the wild."

"That's not what he told us."

"*He?* He who?" There hadn't been a man in the group Louise had encountered. She'd assumed the grumpy woman was the leader, but Sandra did say that some of the regulars weren't present today. Perhaps Madame Grumpy Face was second-in-command. "Does *he* have a name?"

"Of course he does, but you don't need to know it."

"How can I determine the legitimacy of his claims if I don't know who he is? I'd be happy to sit down with him sometime to discuss his concerns." Louise prayed that her tactic would work. What she'd give to have the name of the lead protestor—the head of the ARSE squad.

The little woman appeared to grow a few inches and her face took on an air of confidence. "His name isn't important, because I doubt he'd talk to you. It's unlikely you know half of what he does about animals and wildlife. Those animals should be free to roam."

Where were the police? This conversation was becoming tiresome. Louise decided to change tactics. "Tell me, do you have any animals living in your house?"

The woman's confident look dwindled to a deer-in-the-headlights look of confusion. "I have a cat. Why? I rescued him."

"Rescued him from where? Was he in danger?"

"He was living outside. He kept coming to my door for food, and one day I let him in."

"Did you put him back outside?"

"Of course not."

"Why?"

"Because it's dangerous outside. He couldn't survive. He'd get hurt, or maybe starve."

Louise shifted her weight as she stood against the tree and shook her head. "Really? Because a lot of cats survive quite nicely outside. That's why we have an abundance of stray and feral cats in the area."

The woman's nostrils flared. "It's not the same thing. Cats are not wild animals."

Louise shrugged. "Most aren't, but you make an interesting point about how dangerous it is out here." She extended her arms wide to indicate the wild. "Injured wildlife have a greater chance than healthy animals of starving to death or being killed by other animals. Don't they deserve a chance for treatment and survival?"

The woman's respiratory rate visibly increased, and her raised hand quivered as she struggled to come up with a response.

Louise was relieved to see the flashing lights of a police car approaching. She nodded toward the road. "I think your ride's here."

Chapter 12

LOUISE HOOFED IT up the stairs to the office she shared with Daphne. Daphne's van was already in the clinic parking lot, filling Louise with guilt at being late a second day in a row. How did Daphne, with two small children, always make it to work on time? Louise had been relieved when Mary called at eight thirty this morning to inform her that both of her morning surgeries had cancelled. People were still upset about the explosion at the airport the previous day, and some were reluctant to leave their homes until the police could identify the culprits, or better yet, arrest them.

While Louise understood their fears for their safety, she also felt that letting that fear paralyze society was what terrorists desired. Control via fear. There was no proof yet that the blast was a terrorist act, but she couldn't shake the thought that it was more than an accident.

The explosion was huge, and had occurred at a time that would draw a lot of media attention—during the set-up of a charity event to raise money for the children's hospital. It couldn't be a coincidence. The event had, of course, been postponed indefinitely. The roads to what remained of the small local airport were blocked off to public traffic. Reporters on the morning news were frustrated that they couldn't get closer to the scene. It was deemed a temporary no-fly zone, preventing the use of news helicopters or drones.

With a few hours open in her schedule, Louise decided to check in at the clinic, then head back to SWaRF to check on Sandra and Major. Working with only ten hours of sleep in the past forty-eight hours, she sheepishly snuck into her office and turned on her Keurig.

Daphne wasn't at her desk, and Louise wondered out loud where her friend was. "Probably seeing to patients. How did I get so lucky as to have such a dedicated and patient business partner?"

"I ask myself that often."

Louise jumped, spilling coffee from the mug she'd just picked up. "Ouch!" She turned around to see Daphne laughing in the doorway.

Daphne approached her desk. "Not quite the *same* question. I ask myself how *you* were so lucky as to have found *me*."

Louise shrugged and smiled. Though the words were well founded in truth, she knew Daphne was teasing her.

Daphne bit into the doughnut she was holding, then sat at her desk. "The Morrisons brought snacks and drinks for everyone when they dropped Jack off this morning. He had a good night—no more vomiting or diarrhea. We'll keep him here for the day to keep an eye on him, but he's definitely turned the corner for the better."

Louise was happy to hear that things were looking up for the little dog with parvovirus. "That's great news. What about Perdy?"

Daphne frowned. "We haven't heard from them. Rita called B-REC first thing this morning to ask why we haven't gotten any records for Perdy's overnight stay. Apparently, Perdy was a no-show at the clinic, so Rita tried the Theobalds' number, but no answer. She left them a message asking them to call us back right away. That was over an hour ago." Daphne shook her head and sighed. "I don't understand people."

Louise wiped the coffee that had landed on the back of her hand onto her pants, then took a drink of the hot liquid. She took a moment to embrace the calming effect it had on her nerves, because it sounded as though this would be another caffeine-dependent day.

"Sometimes I think it's best not to try to understand people. What I will try, however, is one of those doughnuts. I'll be right back," Louise said.

She headed into the staff room, where she found Miranda arranging a bouquet of flowers. Louise said, "Those are pretty. Are they from your secret admirer?"

Miranda shook her head as she snipped the bottom off of a yellow tulip before placing it in a vase. "No secret admirers for me these days. These are for Dr. Carling."

Louise opened the doughnut box and snagged a French cruller. "Oh! Daphne has a secret admirer? Don't tell Joe."

Her attempt at humour was met by Miranda's confused look.

"Joe's her husband."

Miranda gave Louise a smile that said "The joke is old and not funny, but I don't want to offend a new employer." Then out loud she said, "right! Anyway, they're from the Morrisons, along with the cookies and doughnuts. They're really nice people, and Jack is so sweet. Such a contrast."

"Contrast? Most of our canine patients are sweet. It's the clients who can be a challenge at times."

"Oh, I get that. That's what I meant. The Morrisons were so friendly and patient, even when it looked like Jack might not make it yesterday. They were just grateful that everyone was doing their best to help him. Then there's . . . you know." Miranda raised her eyebrows and tilted her head. "Perdy's owner. She was so rude to everyone when she picked him up. I'm kinda glad she didn't show up this morning."

Louise nodded. She knew where Miranda was coming from, but sometimes to help the animals, the veterinary team had to deal with some unsavoury humans.

Miranda continued, "I just hope Perdy's okay."

"Me too, but unless they return Rita's call, there isn't much we can do but hope and pray that he hasn't slipped back into a coma, or worse. By the way, shouldn't you be in school? Heidi told me you're in high school."

Miranda scooped up the stem trimmings from the table and tossed them into the trash. She then grabbed a cloth and dried the table. "Not today—it's March break for the high schools. It worked out well, because Mary called earlier asking if I could work this afternoon since Shirley's still not well.

When she told me she'd be on her own this morning, I said I could do the whole day if she liked."

"Don't tell me—she liked?"

Miranda laughed. "I think she did." She lifted the vase and headed for the door. "I'd better get back down there or Mary'll wonder if I changed my mind and escaped out the back."

"Sounds good."

After Miranda left the room, Louise set a double chocolate doughnut on a paper towel and headed back to her office. She wanted to fill Daphne in on the happenings at the rehab centre, then call Alex. He hadn't called her this morning, so she could only assume he was feeling okay and had made an early start on the day. It was only twenty-four hours since the explosion, and the police department was still short staffed.

When Louise returned to the office, she found Daphne bent over at her desk, rummaging through a drawer. "Lose something?" she asked.

Daphne raised her head and Louise had to bite her lip to suppress a laugh.

Daphne's brow furrowed. "What?"

Louise mumbled, "Nothing." She'd decide later whether or not to tell her friend about the coating of icing sugar around her mouth. Daphne was a fan of playing practical jokes on Louise and the staff, so any opportunity to get her back was always welcome.

"Okay. Whatever you say." Daphne pushed the desk drawer closed and tapped on her keyboard. "My next appointment's not for half an hour. I thought I'd get started on organizing some of our tax papers for the accountant, but I might have lost a few of them. Joe keeps nagging me about being more organized."

Daphne's husband was an accountant in a government office. It was a running joke between Daphne and Louise that despite over eight years of marriage, Daphne was still unsure which office he worked for, and what exactly he did. Joe, a very organized person who had agendas for all his different activities, was a direct contrast to Daphne, who tended to leave things to the last minute yet still somehow got everything done.

"How was the show last night? Did you make it on time?" Louise crossed her fingers. She wasn't superstitious, and she knew that fingers had to be crossed before an event, but she did it anyway.

"Barely." Daphne appeared happy for the distraction from her tax-related task. "Ella was already on stage with her class, but they hadn't started their song yet. My heart broke a bit when I entered the auditorium and saw her sad eyes staring at the empty seat beside Joe. I waved my arms and jumped up and down, thankful the entrance was in the back and no one but the kids could see me, but then her little friend Missy spotted me, tapped Ella's shoulder, and pointed. I froze when the roomful of adults turned around and looked at me. Most laughed. Joe didn't."

"He was mad?"

"Let's go with annoyed. He didn't say anything, and by time we got home and got the kids to bed, he was happy to sit and watch a *Star Trek* rerun."

"Good ol' Captain Kirk to the rescue! How was the show? Ella's show, not *Star Trek*."

Daphne stroked her chin. "Hmm . . . a group of kinder-garteners singing 'You Are My Sunshine.' It was fabulous." Daphne beamed at the memory of her first-born in her first performance. "What were you up to last night, dare I ask?"

"I popped by SWaRF to help Sandra out, and to check on Major. That reminds me—I need to call her. We'd talked about bringing Major into the clinic today if he still wasn't eating, but he seemed to be improving as of last night, so it might not be necessary. If things are under control here, I thought I'd head up there since my surgeries all cancelled."

"No more"—Daphne made air quotes—"'incidents'?"

"Not at the centre."

"That's good." Daphne returned her attention to her computer, then back to Louise. "What does that mean, 'Not at the centre'? What *did* happen?"

"One of the protestors followed me home."

Daphne's eyes widened and her jaw dropped.

Louise shrugged. "No big deal. She was harmless." She chuckled. "Really. A light breeze would have knocked the poor woman over. The scariest part was her almost cult-like devotion to who I assume is the leader of their group. She wouldn't even tell me his name, as though saying it aloud would cause the sky to crack. The police told me her name is Beth Gilley. They took her away in a squad car and had her car towed from my driveway."

"What was she doing at the centre that late?"

"Good question. Now that you mention it, it *is* strange. I didn't see her until after I got into my house, so she must have been keeping out of sight at the centre. She wouldn't have known I was going to be there. No one other than Sandra knew I was heading up there last night."

"I can't imagine Sandra had her follow you."

Louise rubbed her forehead. A troubling thought was emerging. "I agree. Sandra wouldn't have had someone follow me, but what if *she* was the intended target? What if the woman was meant to follow Sandra and the only reason this ended without incident is because Beth Gilley realized she'd followed the wrong car?"

Louise grabbed her bag and headed for the door.

Daphne called after her. "Now where are you going?"

"I have to get to SWaRF fast. Sandra might be in danger."

Chapter 13

L OUISE CALLED ALEX several times on her way to the rehab centre, but he wasn't answering. She left him numerous messages, each time pleading with him to call her back, and informing him that she feared for Sandra Kelly's safety. Her fears multiplied when Sandra also failed to answer the phone.

"Where are you, Alex? Where are you, Sandra?"

Louise floored the accelerator and soon found herself flying into SWaRF's parking lot. She white-knuckled the steering wheel when she spotted the same protestors she'd seen the day prior. She scanned the group to see if Beth Gilley was among them. She was, as was the grim-faced woman who, by the way she was standing tall over the others, once again appeared to be assuming leadership over them. The sound of the car drew the hefty woman's attention to Louise, and the two locked gazes for an instant.

"I don't have time for this." Louise pushed the sign-bearing crazy woman out of her thoughts and directed her car to the path Sandra had used to take them to SWaRF's back lot. After parking across the path to block it, Louise grabbed her bag from the front seat, then glanced at her baseball bat that sat perched against the back seat. She'd placed it there this morning in case she was followed again, and now she worried that a protestor might try to follow her down the footpath. However, she was certain she could outrun any of the older, out-of-shape-looking women at the gate, so she left the bat where it was. No need to be accused of wielding a weapon if there was an incident.

Louise, having found Sandra's trailer without incident, was happily surprised to see Alex's navy-blue SUV parked alongside Sandra's golf cart. If they were in a meeting, that might explain why neither had responded to her messages, but what could be so captivating that neither was available for so long? Louise sighed at the thought that they were simply ignoring her messages since they both knew that Sandra wasn't in danger. Or was she?

Had Alex received Louise's messages and raced here to check on Sandra? Her mind scrolled through all the possible scenarios as she made her way to the trailer entrance. She bounded up the stairs, grasped the doorknob, then stopped. What if the murderer was inside the trailer? Or worse, what if he'd already gotten to Sandra, and Louise was too late? Or maybe the murderer had followed Sandra onto the rehab grounds, and Alex was hot on their trail. Or the suspect might have grabbed Sandra and left the property. Alex could be scouring the facility looking for someone who was long gone.

Louise inhaled deeply and summoned from deep within her the courage to open the door no matter what she might find. She turned the knob while pushing on the door, but it was locked. *Nuts!* She contorted her body over the railing of the landing to peek into the adjacent window. To give herself a better view, she pushed up on the railing but lost her balance when she heard . . .

"It's a good thing I have a copper here with me. It looks like we have a peeping Tom."

Louise felt her centre of gravity shift farther to the wrong side of the railing and reached for the mailbox beside the door. Grasping it just in time, she kept herself from falling but couldn't pull herself back onto her feet. She hovered above the hard ground for a few seconds before Alex pushed her back toward the landing.

"Good timing." Having regained her footing, Louise was happy to see her rescuer. Alex and Sandra's sudden appearance had startled her, but the only thing that hurt besides her hand, which had sustained a small cut, was her pride. The insult to her pride quickly subsided—seeing Alex and Sandra alive and well was all that mattered in the moment.

Sandra didn't hide her amusement at Louise's predicament. "What is it you were doing?"

Louise shrugged a shoulder. "Me? Nothing. Just looking to make sure you weren't lying bleeding in your office." She crossed her arms. "I've been worried about you, and neither of you have responded to my messages."

Alex took his phone from his pocket and tapped the screen. "Oh yeah, look at that. Ten texts from Louise and two phone messages." He tapped the screen again. "She's worried that Sandra might be in danger." He looked at Sandra, then at Louise. "She's fine!"

Louise frowned at him. "Ha, ha! Funny man. When I was talking to Daphne earlier, we wondered if the woman who followed me last night might have intended to follow Sandra. Why would anyone follow me? No one would have known I was here last night."

Alex rubbed his chin. "I knew right away you were here last night. Well, I suspected it."

Louise shrugged. "I'm confused."

Alex laughed. "Not as confused as the forensics team was when they got here this morning and found a Ziploc bag in a tree and another on the ground near the pond. Any idea how that happened?"

Louise shrugged again. "I guess someone was trying to be helpful. Perhaps it was about to rain and said person was worried that evidence might get washed away."

"Said person could have alerted the officer we had stationed here."

"Said person might not have known about the officer's presence at the time of the Ziplocking of the evidence." Not remembering if Sandra had told her about the officer before or after their after-dark jaunt to the crime scene, Louise cast a glance at Sandra. The founder of SWaRF remained silent; Sandra wasn't going to give away any of Louise's secrets.

Louise opened the photo app on her phone. "There might have been some evidence that couldn't be preserved with a piece of plastic and would be washed away." She showed the footprint photos to Alex.

His expression changed from amused to impressed. "These

could have been from someone who works here at the centre, or some of the officers who arrived at the scene. When did you take these?"

"Last night, when I was helping Sandra with her rounds. We noticed the prints near the piece of fabric, and they looked fresh. Like from yesterday. They're big, like a man's print, and Bailey wasn't here yesterday."

"Not that we know of. He could have been on site undetected." Alex smirked. "It's hard to gauge shoe size from photos. Too bad you didn't place a ruler beside the prints. You know, like a *real* detective would have done."

Louise knew he was teasing her, but she wanted to kick herself for not thinking of the need to indicate size in the photos. "You're right. I should have used a pen, like we do when taking photos of biological samples after an autopsy."

Alex smirked again. "You mean *necropsy*? It's called a necropsy in animals. Autopsy is used for people."

Louise was ready to slug him. She didn't mind him correcting her when it came to detective work, but she was the medical person in their relationship. "Yeah, I saw that TV show too. The one with the obnoxious scientist who thinks that vets can only do necropsies. Tomayto, tomahto—they both make tasty sandwiches."

Sandra moved forward and mock separated her two companions. "Speaking of tomatoes, what do you say we make our way into the trailer and have a snack? I'm famished." She fished a key ring from her jacket pocket. "And no need to break in, Louise—I have the key."

After the trio had finished their sandwiches, followed by cookies and coffee, Alex excused himself to return to the airport. Louise wasn't convinced his explanation for being at the rehab centre, either today or yesterday, was truthful. She didn't doubt that his concern for Sandra was real, but had he really been called out to the site because of the plastic bags over the evidence? Why would he leave the investigation of an explosion that killed five people, including two police officers, to check out a couple of baggies?

Alex hadn't said it outright, but Louise knew that he knew she'd covered the scrap of fabric and the cigarette butt. He could simply have asked her about it later at their regular Tuesday night dinner and movie. And he'd already been at the rehab centre when she sent him the first message voicing her concerns for Sandra. No, something else was going on. Alex had another reason for being here today, and he was being evasive about it. Louise was determined to find out what that reason was, but first she had one more task to complete before heading back to the clinic.

"Sandra, what do you say we head back to the area where we found the footprints? I have an idea."

Sandra shot up from her seat. "Sure! Let's go. I have to admit, I think I'm catching your inquisitiveness bug." She rubbed her hands together. "Perhaps someday I'll be interviewed for one of those true crime shows, just like we were talking about. I love those shows!"

Amateur detectives that they were, they were soon at the site of the washed-away footprints. Louise showed the photos of the prints to Sandra. "See this twig? I know finding it's a long shot, but it has a distinct shape to it. It's straight for one third of its length, then it kinks at about a one-hundred-and-thirty-degree angle. Just below that, on the long side, is a piece of loose bark. If we can find this twig, we can measure it and figure out the shoe size."

"It rained pretty hard last night, but this ground is fairly flat and there wasn't any wind, so it should be here some-where." Sandra used a larger branch to push away dead leaves that might be covering the twig. Then she stopped and stared into the distance.

Louise turned her head to see what Sandra was looking at, but all she saw was more trees and leaves. "What's up? Did you hear something?"

"I'm just thinking about what you said to Alex earlier." Sandra leaned against a large oak tree. "Do you really think that woman meant to follow *me* last night?"

"It was just a thought. I mean, they didn't know I'd be here. Or maybe it was dumb luck on the woman's part. She might have been passing by, then followed any car she saw leaving, thinking it would impress her boss."

Louise doubted that was the case, but she'd been thought-less to voice her fears in front of Sandra. She should have waited for a chance to speak to Alex alone. Now all she could do was attempt to reassure her friend, but at the same time, Sandra might very well be in danger. How could she simulta-neously caution the target of the protestors to be careful but also assure her there was nothing to worry about? In the last twenty-four hours alone, the number of things to be worried about was steadily increasing.

"Have you heard from Bailey today? Did he show up for work?"

Sandra shook her head. "No, and it's really not like him. I mean, to not even check in? He's always been so conscientious about being on time, and now I haven't heard from him in three days. He hasn't posted anything on his social media accounts, either. He's always posting memes and silly comments. I'm getting really worried about him."

"Did you mention that to Alex?"

"Yes. He said he'd send someone out to Bailey's place to check on him."

"I'm sure *that* didn't take much encouragement." Louise regretted the comment as soon as it left her lips. Bailey was already on the police department's radar as a suspect—any excuse to check out his home would be welcomed—but her tone and choice of words was accusatory toward Alex and his colleagues. Louise had a great deal of respect for the police department, but Sandra didn't know her well enough to differentiate fatigue-induced joking from pointed criticism.

A little backpedalling couldn't hurt. "It's great they're going to check on him. We have one of the best police forces in Ontario. Like Alex always says, everyone's a suspect until they can be cleared by the evidence. If we can find that twig, maybe it will help us clear Bailey."

Sandra bent down to retrieve something, then held it high above her head. "This twig?"

The same twig that lay beside the suspect footprints in Louise's photos. "My dear, I believe you've found it. Good work! Now, do you happen to have a measuring tape with you?"

"Not something I usually carry around."

"Of course not. How about a string?"

"Shoelaces?"

"Perfect!"

Sandra removed her shoelace and handed it to Louise, who then laid it beside the twig that had been returned to it's location on the ground. She placed one end of the shoelace at one end of the twig, then tied a knot where it met the twig's other end.

As she was finishing her task, Officer Wayne approached them. "Hi, Louise. Anything I can help you with there?" The look in his eye told her that, like Alex, he was suspicious that she was interfering with the investigation.

"Hi, Wayne. As a matter of fact, you could give me a hand up."

Wayne offered his hand, then pulled her to her feet. "What's that you're doing with the shoelace? If that was here on the ground, you need to leave it there."

"No worries. This is Sandra's. We used it to measure that stick there." Louise pointed at the piece of evidence with her toe. "You might want to bag it."

Without another word to Wayne, Louise threw her arm around Sandra's shoulder. "Let's go, Sandra. We have work to do."

Chapter 14

AFTER MEASURING THE shoelace with a ruler Sandra found in her workshop, they started making their way back to Louise's car. Mary had contacted Louise, asking when she expected to return to the clinic, because clients were calling to rebook previously cancelled appointments, and some asked if they could see her that afternoon.

Louise was happy that some people once again felt safe to leave their homes and go about their daily routines, but she also had to wonder how safe anyone was. Someone might have set off a bomb in a public place, and now the detective on the case was rushing to a seemingly unrelated location to look at Ziploc bags.

Despite Alex's repeated warnings to her about the dangers of interfering with a police investigation, Louise's determination to get to the truth was increasing. In their normally quiet town, a dead body had been discovered the same day there was a deadly explosion at the airport, and now Bailey Nelson was unaccounted for. Louise wasn't willing to accept that these three unusual events were merely coincidental. Was Bailey a victim, or a suspect?

Louise stopped herself from voicing that last thought out loud. Sandra had enough to worry about, and suggesting that one of her employees might have met the same fate as the woman in the pond wouldn't be helpful. The police were looking for Bailey, and they had probably already scoured the rehab's property and surrounding lands with their police dogs. If there was another body within two kilometres of Sydney's Wildlife Rehabilitation Facility, it would have been found already. Louise scratched her head. *Where are you, Bailey?*

". . . like I was saying, Sydney came to us after she'd been rescued from a wolf sanctuary." Louise returned her attention to her companion in time to see Sandra make air quotes when she said the words "wolf sanctuary."

What had they been talking about before Louise became lost in her own thoughts? *Think Louise, think. Oh, right. You asked Sandra about the origins of the centre's name.*

"Rescued from a sanctuary? Aren't those the places rescued animals are taken to?"

"That's the general idea, but unfortunately no matter how good their intentions are when they start out, some of them get in over their heads. Like us, they rely on donations, but when they have poor management or lofty ideals that don't mesh with reality, things can go south rather quickly. Sadly, when that happens, it's the animals who suffer. Sydney and her pups are only one example."

"We read about animals getting sent to sanctuaries, but I can't honestly say I've seen any reports of these places failing. You don't hear much about rehab centres either. The consensus seems to be 'Sanctuaries good, everyone else bad.'"

"Sad, isn't it? The name on the sign is meaningless. The reality is, it takes a lot of money, and a huge time commitment on the part of management, staff, and volunteers, to care for the animals. That's why we're a fix-and-release organization. We can't house and care for an indefinite number of animals for an indefinite amount of time. Once our animal visitors are capable of returning to the wild, that's where we send them. For some reason, that's not a feel-good story for the media. Getting the public fired up about a case of animal mistreatment sells more papers, or gets more clicks, than educating people about what we're doing behind the scenes to care for the animals."

Louise kicked a pebble off the path and watched as it rebounded off the corner of a large rock. The pebble bounced twice, then with a small splash landed in its final destination, a muddy puddle. Life wasn't unlike that puddle. What might look like a refreshing place of respite—cooling water on a hot, humid day—could eventually be exposed to have a dirty reality, like disease, or, as in the case yesterday, a murder victim.

Sandra continued. "When Sydney came to us, she was pregnant, emaciated, and full of parasites. My head tech, Leanne, and two volunteers took Sydney on as their special patient. They gave her round-the-clock attention to make sure she was eating and healing. Our previous vet provided the dewormers we needed. Thankfully, once the parasites were cleared, she began to gain weight, and by time she was ready to give birth, she was healthy enough to do so. Sadly, one of the pups didn't survive, but when we consider what shape Sydney was in when she came to us, three viable pups out of four is a successful outcome. Had she given birth at the sanctuary in the state she was in, I'm certain neither the pups nor Sydney would have survived."

"Wow. That's quite the story, and one that does need to be told. Where's Sydney now?"

"We couldn't release her into the wild because she was raised as a pup in a private home." Sandra blew out a breath and rolled her eyes skyward. "We don't know where they got her—they might have found her as a pup in the wild. Anyway, she was taken away when she became too wild for the people to handle." She *tsk*ed. "Imagine a wild animal becoming wild? Sheesh!" Sandra paused to tie her shoes, having replaced the shoelace in her office. "From there she was sent to the sanctuary, but eventually it was closed down due to multiple health code violations, on top of animal neglect."

Louise noticed dark clouds rolling in. The temperature was dropping, giving the familiar feeling of a winter storm on the way. It was the middle of March, only a few days away from the official start to spring, but that didn't mean winter storms were out of the question. Louise was thankful to find her winter gloves in her pockets and she swiftly put them on.

Sandra put her own hands into her pockets and started walking again toward the end of the path, and Louise's car. "We found a good forever home for Sydney, where she and her pups are spoiled. They have a large area to run, play, and hunt, as wolves are meant to do, at a stable facility that doesn't rely only on public donations."

"Where's that?"

Sandra smiled at Louise. "Here we are at your car. Thanks for checking in on Major again. He's back to normal today as far as behaviour and appetite are concerned. We'll keep an eye on him for another week, and if he continues to do well, we'll release him in the same area he was picked up at. If he doesn't, you'll be hearing from us."

Sandra's reluctance to reveal the location of the other facility wasn't lost on Louise. They were still getting to know each other, and caution about who you shared information with was no doubt a lesson Sandra had learned over years of caring for wildlife and dealing with self-appointed animal saviours. Louise didn't need to know where Sydney was located, but she was happy to know it was a Sandra-approved location.

The protestors Louise had seen earlier were still at SWaRF's front gate. Louise shook her head at the foolishness of it. They were in an isolated area with very little traffic, so who were these women intending to influence by being here?

As she opened the door to her car, she watched the women, who stood huddled in a circle, bouncing like children in an inflatable castle, their arms crossed tightly against their chests. They were unprepared for the weather—they were obviously cold, but none of them were wearing hats or gloves.

It wasn't outside the realm of possibility that their presence might be for reasons other than protesting animal rights. The fact that they hadn't yet noticed Louise's return told her they weren't on the lookout for people to share their concerns with. What were they up to? Louise retrieved her phone and took a few pictures of the group. Their apparent leader, Madame Grumpy Face, was facing Louise but was too wrapped up in her group's discussion to notice she was being photographed.

The ground had dried since the previous night's downpour. Louise sighed—she would have loved to have gotten photos of their footprints. She played with the idea of finding a hose and spraying it on the ground around the sign carriers, but time was ticking and she was expected back at the clinic.

She was about to enter her car when a gust of wind pulled the door handle from her grasp and slammed the door closed. She now had the full attention of Madame Grumpy Face, Beth Gilley, and friends. Pointing at Louise, Madame Grumpy Face whispered to one of the other women, a plump individual who was wearing a plum-coloured pantsuit and had large-framed glasses and short brown hair. Louise guessed she was in her late sixties.

Plump-in-Plum was carrying a sign that said Stop the Imports and held it in front of her chest as she approached Louise with a fierce, no-nonsense frown.

Stop the imports? That was a new sign—Louise hadn't seen it the day before. Why would they be protesting imports at a facility that cares for domestic wildlife?

Now standing face to face with the protestor, Louise checked the time on her phone. She didn't have much time to spare if she was going to get back to the clinic on time for her first appointment. "What can I do for you?"

The woman frowned. "With what you're up to in there, you people should be ashamed of yourselves."

"What are we up to in there?" Louise genuinely wanted to know.

"You know exactly what's going on. You were in there for over an hour."

While Plump-in-Plum was ranting about perceived atrocities taking place on the grounds of SWaRF, Madame Grumpy Face approached, waving her hands in the air. "Why are you bothering my friends?"

Louise held back a chuckle. She hadn't approached this woman's friends—it was they who'd approached her. She was practical minded, and loved a good exchange. "Because *you're* bothering my friends?"

That was an unwelcome answer, and Madame Grumpy Face pushed Plump-in-Plum aside to get closer to Louise. Louise backed up. She was well versed on how to deal with a one-hundred-pound, poorly trained aggressive dog, but this woman was far scarier. Louise glanced at the back seat of her car, wondering if she could get to her trusty bat before Madame Grumpy Face reached her throat.

"The police are still on site. I suggest you back up or I'll be forced to give them a call," Louise said.

Madame Grumpy Face laughed. "Go ahead. By the time dispatch calls the cops that are here, we'll be long gone."

Louise smiled a gotcha smile. "That would be true if I didn't have one of the officers in my contacts list. We attend the same church."

Madame Grumpy Face backed up. Sandra had reminded the protestors yesterday that if the police had to be called again, they could all be arrested for trespassing.

"Now, if you'd be so kind as to remove yourselves from around my car . . . I have an appointment to get to."

Plump-in-Plum started to move aside, but Madame Grumpy Face grasped the woman's arm, preventing her from leaving. "Going off to make some money, I suppose. That's all you people care about, making money."

Louise doubted that this cranky lady knew she was speaking to a vet, but still the accusation stung. Those in the veterinary profession were often accused of "being in it for the money."

"Actually, you're right. I'm going to work to earn some money. It's how I pay my bills."

Madame Grumpy Face glared at her. "We're here on our own time, trying to save lives. I don't suppose you'd understand that."

"I'm very happy for you all that you've no need to work to pay your bills." Louise was growing tired of the conversation. Would she be able to manoeuvre her car around these two without making contact? "Some of us, however, do have to work. We can't spend all day bothering other people—working people."

Plump-in-Plum's face took on a glow, as though she'd just discovered the theory of relativity. "Joan works. In fact, she works at—"

Madame Grumpy Face's hand swiftly went from Plump-in-Plum's arm to her face. Louise was astonished at the boldness it took for one grown woman to slap her hand over another woman's mouth. If Louise had been the victim of that behaviour, Madame Grumpy Face would have a palm full of teeth marks, but Plump-in-Plum retreated into herself as though suddenly aware she'd made a huge error.

Louise was happy to have the first name of this group's leader, but a last name would be more useful. "So, Joan—I assume that's your name. Joan what?"

Joan wasn't budging on revealing the information. She

pushed her subordinate away and glowered at Louise. "That is information you do not need to know."

With the women out of the way, Louise could open the car door. She hopped in and started the engine, happy that the lunatic women had enough sense to move out of the car's path when she placed the vehicle in drive. As she drove away, Louise promised herself she'd get to the bottom of what was going on here.

This was the second time she'd been told she didn't need to know the name of an ARSE member; Beth Gilley had said it last night too. Who were these people? They were protecting their names, protesting in an isolated area where no one would see them, and claiming that SWaRF was importing animals.

Louise thought over the events of the past day and a half. If someone was importing animals, they could have been using the airport to do it, but what did that have to do with the rehab centre? Bailey Nelson worked at SWaRF, and he was missing. Louise floored the gas pedal. She had appointments to get to, and after that she would drill Alex for answers.

Chapter 15

LOUISE LONGED TO get off her aching feet, but the client in front of her was in no hurry to finish up the appointment and be on her way. She smiled at the older woman as she started on another conversational diversion from her pet's problem. Normally Louise enjoyed spending time with Mrs. Cable, a sweet octogenarian with an equally sweet senior cat named Tyson, but her sore feet and heavy eyelids kept her from concentrating on the Cable family history.

"Mary tells me Tyson has been meowing more at night. Is that right, Mrs. Cable?" Louise was unsuccessful at suppressing a yawn.

"Oh, my dear." Mrs. Cable leaned across the table and

scanned Louise's face. "You do look tired. Are you getting enough sleep? You young people keep the oddest hours. I guess it's because of all the things available to keep you entertained these days. I remember when I was your age, we only had two TV channels, and my goodness, the internet hadn't even been thought of. Not by the average person, anyway. I suppose the folks who invented it might have been thinking about it back then." Mrs. Cable rubbed her chin and scrunched her nose. "I wonder who that was?"

Louise forced her eyes to stay open. "Who what was?"

"The person who invented the internet. Do you know?"

Louise shook her head. "No. Sorry. Now back to Tyson. He's meowing more than usual? In cats his age, that can often mean an overactive thyroid or high blood pressure." As soon as she said it, she knew what was coming.

"High blood pressure? Oh dear, my George had that. Poor man. Do you know, we were married almost fifty years before the diabetes took him from me?"

Louise offered a sympathetic nod. She remembered George Cable well. A tall handsome man who had always accompanied his wife for Tyson's checkups. The Cables first brought Tyson to the Black Creek Animal Hospital a few months after Louise and Daphne opened it. The then ten-year-old black-and-white domestic shorthair had had a urinary infection and was urinating around the house. After they took a culture to select the appropriate antibiotics, he responded rapidly to treatment. That was nine years ago, and sadly, since then Mr. Cable had passed away.

"How are you getting along, Mrs. Cable? It's been . . . Is it two years since Mr. Cable passed?"

"Yes, dear. Two years. You have a fabulous memory, even when you look like death warmed over."

Had this come from anyone else, Louise might have been insulted, but Mrs. Cable had always been kind and polite, even if her compliments were occasionally graced with an unpleasant yet accurate observation.

"I'm doing well. My grandson, the single, handsome one who lives out west, is coming for a visit next week. I was going to wait to see you until he could come with me . . . You're still single, I believe." She gave Louise a sly smile. "I don't know if Mary mentioned it, but Tyson's been meowing a lot lately. I wonder if his bum needs, you know . . . cleaning."

Tyson had had issues with his anal glands years ago, a problem that had embarrassed but also fascinated Mrs. Cable, as she repeatedly brought it up even though he'd never had any recurrence of the problem.

"I believe Mary did say something to that effect. Why don't I take Tyson to the back so that Heidi and Jenny can get a blood sample?" Louise planned to also check his blood pressure, but she didn't want to say this in case another mention of hypertension brought on another comment about Mr. Cable.

"That sounds fine, dear."

Louise scooped Tyson into her arms but only made it halfway out the door before she heard Mrs. Cable's voice. "While you're back there, dear, perhaps you could check his blood pressure too. It's a terrible thing, that high pressure, and I don't want him left untreated if he has it."

Louise, grinning like a Cheshire cat, kept moving. "We'll be sure to do that. We won't be long."

When she arrived in the treatment area, she found Jenny and Eric cleaning Jack Morrison's paws with a wet cloth.

Eric was the youngest of their veterinary technicians, having graduated from college only a couple of years ago. He'd overcome a few challenges in his teen years and was now a valuable part of the team.

Raising the cloth in the air, Eric waved when he saw Louise. Her heart sank, as there were brown marks on the white towel. "He didn't have diarrhea again, did he?"

Thus far, Jack had responded well to his treatment for parvovirus, and Daphne had planned to send him home later today. If he'd had another bout of diarrhea, they'd have to reconsider that plan and place him back on IV fluids to prevent dehydration.

Eric's face cast the smile of a Grand Prix champion. "Nope! He did pass some stool, but it was normal." He made a playful frowny face. "Then he walked through it."

Jenny rubbed the little pup's head. "Silly puppy." She shrugged. "But a messy puppy is better than a sick puppy."

Louise quietly agreed. "Is Heidi around? I need to get some blood from Tyson and check his blood pressure."

Eric tossed the dirty cloth in the laundry hamper that sat in the corner. "She just ran upstairs to grab a cola. Should be back in a minute or two."

"Perfect." Louise sat Tyson on the exam table opposite the one Jack was sitting on. She then used the ophthalmoscope to examine Tyson's retinae. "Just as I thought. Retinal hemorrhages. Just a couple, and they're small, but it goes along with hypertension."

As if it had been scripted, Heidi entered the treatment room and approached Louise and Tyson. "Hey, Ty, how's it going, buddy?" She squeezed the older cat's face playfully and was rewarded with a purr and a head butt.

Louise explained her concerns about Tyson's meowing to Heidi, who then set up the Doppler blood pressure unit. After confirming hypertension, Louise left Heidi to get the blood sample with help from Jenny or Eric once they were done cleaning up Jack.

"I'll be up in my office." Louise typed into the treatment room computer. "I've put in a script for Amlodipine for Tyson. Let Mrs. Cable know to start it once she gets home, and I'll call her tomorrow with the blood results."

Heidi took a gulp of her pop. "Will do, boss. Lucky for Mrs. Cable, Tyson's one of the rare cats who's easy to pill."

When Louise arrived at the office, she went straight to her coffee maker and turned it on. She then opened the desk drawer that held her stash of chocolate and grabbed the nearest treat. After swallowing a generous helping of a nut-filled delight, she put milk in her mug, then collapsed into her office chair. She sipped her coffee, crossed her arms on the desk, and laid her head down.

From the corner of her eye, she could see Daphne staring at her as she said, "Tired? Running around sticking your nose where it doesn't belong will do that to you."

"I don't know what you're talking about. I had to go to Sydney's last night to check on Major, and again today. What I really want to do is go to the airport."

"*That's* what I'm talking about. Other than Alex having been there when the explosion happened, what's your motivation? What are you hoping to find out? The news says the place is swarming with police. The side roads to the airport are still closed to the public."

"But I haven't gone to the airport, so technically, I'm not sticking my nose where it doesn't belong." Louise knew she deserved Daphne's accusation. After all, she'd almost been killed a few months ago after getting herself trapped on a yacht with a band of criminals. She crossed her heart. "I promise I'll never get onto any boats with strangers ever again."

Daphne shook her head and returned her attention to her computer monitor. "Same goes for planes, I hope."

"No worries. Sadly, there won't be any planes taking off from Tobin Memorial Airport for a while. And even if there were, I've no intention of getting on one."

"That's good news!" Alex was standing in the doorway of the office, frowning at Louise.

"How long have you been standing there?" Had he heard her voice interest in what was happening at the airport? Of course, even if he had, it shouldn't surprise him that she'd be curious. Everyone in the region, if not the country, was probably wondering what was going on with the investigation into the explosion.

"Hey, how's your friend . . . Sorry, what was his name?" Louise took a sip of coffee, hoping it would wake her enough to remember. It seemed to work. "Norman? How's Norman?"

"He's doing well, thanks." Alex sat on the chair in front of Daphne's desk and struggled to get comfortable on the lumpy, well-beyond-its-prime piece of office furniture. "You really do need to replace this thing."

"You say that every time you're here."

"And I'm right, every time."

"You're the only one who ever sits there." Louise looked at

Daphne. "Maybe we should throw it out. It *is* an eyesore, and it's taking up room."

"And get a new one!" Alex readjusted his position and rubbed his back.

Louise shook her head. "Sorry, not in the budget, but we could perhaps make a deal."

"Something tells me I won't like this deal." Alex scratched his chin.

"You tell me the *real* reason you were at SWaRF this morning, and I'll see if I can talk Daphne into putting a new guest chair in the budget."

Alex let out a sigh. "I was there to check on the evidence. Good job, by the way, of not overly tampering with it."

"What do you mean, 'not overly'?"

"Putting baggies over it *is* tampering. A good defence attorney could get the evidence thrown out. With any luck, once we find the culprit, they won't have a good defence attorney."

"Isn't a lousy attorney often the reason criminals get a new trial?"

"Good point." Alex moved to the windowsill and used it for a seat. "Exactly why you shouldn't be tampering. I know you're trying to help, but there are things I can't tell you—because not only could you unwittingly compromise the case, but you could also be in more danger than you can imagine."

"More dangerous than gun toting thugs and the threat of a watery burial?" Daphne was probably trying to be funny—to lighten the mood—but the look on Alex's face unnerved Louise. Without speaking, he conveyed that the danger was real.

"I can tell you this." He got up and closed the office door. "It can't leave this room until after the press conference later today. The explosion wasn't an accident—it was a deliberate act. Bomb residue was found and the hypocentre appears to have been the staff room that is . . . I mean *was* . . . adjacent to the field where the fundraiser for the children's hospital was being set up."

Daphne whispered, "Oh my," then clapped her hand over her mouth. Her normally pink complexion turned white. "You mean someone might have been trying to hurt the children? Or the volunteers?" Her hand began to shake.

"Not necessarily. The event wasn't scheduled to start until today, and the bomb appears to have been on a timer. The bomb squad think it *was* meant for yesterday. It's possible that those responsible didn't know that the volunteers and coordinators would have been at the airport yesterday. It's possible that the culprits didn't expect the casualties."

"Do they suspect one of the event coordinators? Or someone else involved with the event, like a vendor?" Daphne opened Louise's desk drawer and withdrew a handful of tiny chocolate bars. She ripped them open and shoved all of the chocolate into her mouth.

Louise couldn't remember seeing Daphne this uptight before, but it didn't surprise her. Daphne had already been showing signs of stress, and now she had images of children in danger in her mind.

"No. And again, not a word of this is to leave this room." Alex returned to the windowsill. "The bomb was most likely in one of the lockers used by airport staff. That area is only accessible to a small number of employees, and a security badge is needed to gain access."

Louise felt stomach acid hitting the back of her throat. "An inside job?"

Alex nodded. "The question is, why?"

"And what does it have to do with the murder at the rehab centre?" Louise knew he wouldn't answer that question. Staring into his eyes, she was fishing for a reaction. He didn't flinch. The man was a true professional. She'd have to try a different tactic later—perhaps he'd be more open to questions after the public update. "What time did you say the press conference is?"

"Soon." Alex glanced at his watch. "In fact, I'd better get going." It was now his turn to hold Louise's gaze. "Remember what I said—don't get mixed up in either investigation." He turned to Daphne. "If there's more work you can find for your associate here, please do so."

Louise frowned. "We have plenty of work to keep us busy, thank you."

Alex left without responding. Daphne grinned.

Louise hugged her coffee cup with both hands and sipped slowly. "He's not funny. He's hiding something."

"No, he's a detective who's trying to solve two serious crimes and doesn't want a civilian"—Daphne pointed at Louise—"that's you, to get hurt. And he doesn't want you to mess up either case when they eventually go to court."

"I've already found evidence. Sandra and I determined the shoe size of the prime suspect."

"The prime suspect? You mean *your* prime suspect?"

"Okay, sure, *my* prime suspect. I don't know who it is yet, but I'm sure it's a man—the shoe size is eleven and a half. Give or take an inch." Louise shrugged. "The twig was bent."

"The what?"

"I'll explain later. In the meantime, I need to think of a way to get more information about what's going on at the airport. I'm sure there's a connection between the bombing and the murder at SWaRF. They're trying to pin the murder on one of SWaRF's employees, a guy named Bailey Nelson. He does their maintenance, and according to Sandra he's always been a reliable employee, but he's been a ghost for three days."

"Missing persons cases, along with bombs and murders, definitely sound like something that should be left up to law enforcement."

"Unless they're focusing on the wrong person. I have a few more appointments, and then I'll call Sandra to see if she's heard from Bailey yet." Louise turned to leave, then stopped and turned back to Daphne. "Speaking of ghosts, have you heard anything yet from Perdy Theobald's owner?"

Daphne frowned and her eyelids drooped. "No. Not a word. Rita has called them numerous times, but nothing. I don't understand it."

"People are odd. In fact, some use up more than their fair share of yeast."

Daphne's brow wrinkled and she tilted her head. "Yeast?"

"Yup!" Louise nodded. "She has so much excess yeast in the dough that is her brain that not only does she—figuratively speaking, of course—have an unnaturally large head, but also an overinflated sense of self." Louise smiled, proud of her new allegory, though unsure if that was the correct terminology. "In other words, she has an ego bigger than she deserves."

With a twinkle in her eye, Daphne pressed her lips together, then said, "That's an unkind remark."

As Louise left the room, she was sure Daphne added, "No matter how accurate it is."

Chapter 16

T WO PUPPY VISITS, a post-surgery recheck on a cat who'd had an abscess, and three itchy dogs kept Louise busy for much of the afternoon. She had hoped to get a chance to do a facial recognition search for Joan Grumpy Face and Plump-in-Plum, but her investigation into the rehab protestors would have to wait, as Mary had just informed her that a retching dog was on its way in.

The clients, Mr. and Mrs. Lee, had called about a half an hour earlier to say that after a trip to the park, their dog, Flip, was retching and her back was hunched.

Mary entered the doctors' office, a file folder in hand, followed by Daphne. "The Lees just called. They're around the corner. Should be here in a few minutes." Mary handed the file to Louise, then returned to the front office.

Flip was a two-year-old female Great Dane who'd been spayed at a spay and neuter clinic the year prior. While many clinics offered tacking of a Dane's stomach during ovariohysterectomy, commonly called a spay, to prevent twisting of the stomach, the local spay and neuter clinic was set up to do high volume at low cost. To Louise's mind, this wasn't a bad idea—as long as they offered pain medication, IV fluids, and close monitoring during the procedure. However, extras, like preventative stomach tacking, weren't offered.

Great Danes and other deep-chested dogs were at risk for a condition called gastric dilatation-volvulus (GDV), in which the stomach rotates and causes fluid and gas to become trapped. If not dealt with quickly, the tissues can become necrotic and the patient could die. For Louise, this condition was second only to dog spays as far as scary things vets have to deal with in day-to-day practice.

"Thanks, Mary." Louise opened the file and frowned. She looked at Daphne and gave her best attempt at a sad, pitiful face.

Daphne shook her head. "Sorry, Louise. If it is a GDV, she'll probably need surgery. I have to get out of here on time today—otherwise I'd do it for you. You've done a few of them already with no issues, and the techs are all here to help."

"Hey, no problem." Louise waved her hand in the air. "Anyway, maybe she just has a tummy upset, or a foreign body obstruction."

"Maybe. You never know. I promised Ella I'd be home early today and we'd go out for a special mom-and-daughter dinner, just the two of us. I'm feeling a bit guilty for being late to her concert last night. She was so excited when I suggested it this morning that . . . well, I can't disappoint her again."

"Of course you can't. Don't worry about it. I've got this." Louise put on a brave face, but the surgery was scaring her more than chasing an intruder through the woods at night. Flip was going to need much more effort than the swinging of a baseball bat.

Mary's voice came over the intercom. "Flip and the Lees are here. She's not looking so good."

Louise raced to the treatment area to find Heidi and Eric placing an IV catheter in one of Flip's front legs as the big dog lay on the exam table. She did a quick exam; the dog's mucous membranes were pale and her capillary refill time was slow. Her heart and respiratory rates were elevated.

Jenny soon appeared with the emergency cart and removed a sterile surgical pack that held a large tube. She removed the packaging, placed the tube on the exam table, then retrieved a stainless steel bucket and placed it near Flip's head.

A roll of tape, placed between Flip's canine teeth, was used to guide the tube into the big dog's mouth, past her epiglottis and down the esophagus, where it was met with resistance. Louise applied more pressure, but the resistance at the esophageal hiatus was unyielding.

"Let's move her onto her sternum and try again."

The team worked together to position Flip on her chest, and Louise repeated the attempt at gastric decompression but was again unsuccessful.

"Nuts." Louise shook her head, then flung the tube behind her. "I'll decompress with a needle. Then we'll get her into surgery right away." She scrounged through the emergency cart, then held up a long needle. "Perfect." She glanced at Jenny.

"Normally I'd ask why we have a two-inch fourteen-gauge needle, but right now it's like finding a nugget of gold."

Flip was laid on her right side, and Heidi tapped on the left body wall. When she located a hollow-drum sound, she clipped and scrubbed the area.

Louise donned a pair of surgical gloves and removed the plastic cover from the large bore needle. She repeated the tapping motion, and once she located the point Heidi had found, Louise plunged the needle through the dog's skin and into the stomach. She smiled as a hissing sound met her ears—she'd gotten the tip of the needle successfully into the stomach lumen.

As the trapped air left the stomach, she pushed her fist into Flip's abdomen to maintain the position of the needle. Decompressing the stomach in this manner wasn't ideal, but it bought the team time to prepare for surgery to detorse Flip's stomach. Reducing the pressure in the dog's stomach prior to surgery reduced the risk of necrosis to the tissues, and also reduced the risk of inadvertently incising the stomach while opening the body wall.

Heidi obtained a blood sample, and Jenny set up the ECG to monitor Flip's cardiac health.

Eric set up the surgical suite while Melanie monitored Flip's heart and respiratory rates. Melanie, a recent high school grad and former co-op student at the clinic, was working as a technician's assistant in the interim before starting college in the fall.

The blood results assured Louise that Flip's liver, kidneys, and several other parameters were okay. The ECG revealed that the deep-chested dog had the occasional irregular heartbeat but was overall stable in the cardiac department.

The three veterinary technicians transferred Flip to the surgery table and did a final surgical prep on the surgical site. After Melanie helped her gown up, Louise nervously took a deep breath, said a heartfelt prayer, and headed into the surgery suite.

One hour later, Flip's stomach had been returned to its normal orientation in her abdomen and had been tacked to her body wall to decrease the risk of another GDV event. Once Flip had recovered sufficiently from the anaesthetic to have the endotracheal tube pulled, Louise left the young dog in the capable hands of the clinic techs, who would take turns monitoring Flip's vital signs until she was fully recovered from the anaesthetic.

When Louise returned to her office, in need of a large dose of caffeine, she was surprised to find Daphne sitting at her desk.

"What are you still doing here?" Louise turned on her Keurig and fell into her desk chair. She flipped her running shoes off and retrieved a snack from the chocolate drawer.

Daphne inhaled so deeply Louise wondered if she'd get a caffeine high from the scent of the brewing coffee. "I was just about out the door when Mrs. Theobald called. She's on her way over with Perdy, and apparently she's on the warpath."

Louise squeezed her eyes closed and held her breath as she suppressed a mental image of Mrs. Theobald breaking out in a nasty case of ringworm. Daphne was a committed and skilled veterinarian, always offering the best care possible while being compassionate and understanding of her clients' situations—financial or otherwise. Louise often wondered at the patience

Daphne had for some of their nastiest clients; she had the ability to see beyond the surface and feel for them.

No matter how much she tried to emulate her friend, Louise wasn't blessed with that same level of patience and empathy in the face of entitled, rude behaviour. If people were going to behave horribly toward others, Louise found it difficult to behave well toward them. It was something she'd been working on for many years but continued to struggle with.

"Flip is doing well and the rest of the schedule is light, so I can handle Mrs. Theobald. Head home and take that beautiful girl of yours out for dinner."

Daphne pursed her lips and tapped her chin with her finger. "Are you sure?" She eyed Louise's shoeless feet. "You look like you're in need of a rest."

Louise jumped out of her seat and stood in front of her friend. "No worries. Off you go. I could use a good confrontation, but hopefully Perdy's doing okay and the warpath is a figment of Mary's imagination." Louise knew this was unlikely; Mary was skilled at assessing a client's level of agitation, whether that agitation was warranted or not.

Daphne gathered up her things. "Thanks. I'll see you tomorrow." Before Louise could respond, Daphne was down the stairs and on the lower level.

Louise made herself a second cup of coffee, then wandered down the hall to the staff room to see if any sweet treats were available. She was excited to see a box of cookies, but as she dug out a couple of the crunchy delights, she realized she hadn't heard from the reception desk yet. Daphne had been gone for over fifteen minutes and had said Mrs. Theobald was expected soon. Louise returned to her desk and buzzed Mary.

"Is Mrs. Theobald here yet?" It wouldn't have surprised her if the difficult woman was either pulling a no-show or deliberately taking her time to arrive.

Mary's voice crackled over the intercom. "Yes. She caught Daphne in the parking lot and insisted that Daphne check Perdy. He's worse than he was when she brought him in yesterday. Daphne and Heidi are in the back working on him. Mrs. Theobald is in the parking lot screaming into her phone. I don't know who's at the other end of that wave of viciousness, but I'm happy she's not in here blasting me."

Louise tossed the cookies onto her desk and shoved her feet into her shoes before racing to the treatment area. Daphne was supposed to be heading home, and every muscle in Louise's neck tensed at the news that her friend had been corralled by an unruly client. Louise would take over Perdy's treatment and have Eric escort Daphne to her van. Maybe he could drive the van around to the side door so Daphne could sneak out.

She flung the treatment room door open, ready to let Daphne know she'd take care of Perdy, but the sight before her told her there was no need. Heidi was removing the oxygen mask from Perdy's head, and Jenny was disconnecting the intravenous line that had been used in an attempt to rehydrate the poor feline.

Seeing Louise, Daphne shook her head and frowned. "There was nothing we could do. We tried, but it was too late. Poor little guy was comatose when he came in."

"He was so cold, his temperature didn't register on the thermometer." Heidi retrieved a clean towel to place Perdy's body on. "And his blood pressure was practically non-existent. It's a wonder we got a catheter in at all."

Louise wasn't surprised by the skill of Heidi and their other technicians at placing IV catheters in the most challenging cases, but she was surprised by the state of the patient on the table. Even after almost a decade in practice, she continued to be astonished by the lack of some people's common sense. Mrs. Theobald had been told repeatedly how serious Perdy's condition was. She'd been told the importance of continued care at B-REC, yet she hadn't followed through and taken him there. Rita had been trying all day to reach her, with no response. What could possibly have been so important that she ignored their advice and attempts to reach her? If it was a financial issue, Louise could understand not going to B-REC, but not the ghosting.

"He responded so nicely yesterday. I can't believe this! Poor little guy." Daphne sniffled, then walked toward the door that would take her to the front office. "I'll let Mrs. Theobald know that Perdy didn't make it, then get going."

Louise followed her friend but remained inside, watching through the window as Daphne talked to Mrs. Theobald—ready to intervene if the client misbehaved. To Louise's surprise, the woman whose pet had just passed away said a few words, threw her hands in the air, shrugged, got in her car, and drove away.

Daphne re-entered the building. "All I can say is wow. Apparently, she felt that he was fine after we released him, so she took him home instead of going to the emergency clinic. When they got there, she opened his carrier and he crawled under the bed, and that was the last she saw of him until this morning. When she woke up, she found him soaked in urine and lying on the bathroom floor. She wiped him with a towel, closed the bathroom door, then went to work. When she got home, he was just lying there, not moving, barely breathing. He hadn't touched the food or water she'd left out for him, so she brought him back to us since we didn't"—Daphne made air quotes—"'fix him properly' yesterday."

Louise frowned. "So, no food or water since he left here yesterday?"

Daphne lowered her head. "No. I have no words." She inhaled deeply and pinched the bridge of her nose. "I hate leaving right now—the staff are pretty upset about this—but I have to get going. If I hurry, I can still get home before Joe feeds Ben, and Ella thinks I'm not going to make our mother-daughter date."

Chapter 17

AFTER DISCHARGING ONE bouncy Jack Morrison to his delighted owners, Louise checked on her post-op GDV patient, Flip. The young dog was sitting up in her kennel with her tongue hanging out the right side of her mouth and her head tilted to the left. When she noticed Louise, Flip moved to the front of the kennel and pressed the side of her face against the door, which resembled a chain-link fence.

Without having to lean down, Louise scratched Flip's chin. "You're looking amazing, my girl. Your folks should be here soon to pick you up."

Rita had informed Louise earlier that the paperwork for the Great Dane's transfer to B-REC had already been sent to the emergency clinic. The Lees were to arrive just before the Black Creek Animal Hospital closed at 7:00 pm to pick Flip up and drive her to the twenty-four-hour facility.

Assured that her emergency surgical patient was on her way to a complete recovery, Louise headed to the staff room to hunt down more of the cookies she'd spied earlier. Rita and Heidi were sitting at the dining table. The wall-mounted TV was turned to the news channel, and a familiar face was on the screen. Alex's press conference had been a few hours earlier, but this channel replayed the lead stories of the day in a continuous twenty-minute loop.

"You're not watching that again, are you?" Louise headed for the box of cookies but was disappointed to find it empty. She'd forgotten about the ones she'd tossed on her desk earlier. "Anything new since they first aired the press conference?"

Louise could feel her staff members staring at her, but she didn't turn around. She hadn't brought lunch, was now famished, and the cookies were gone. It would be over an hour before she met with Alex for dinner. *How far is the nearest sandwich shop, and can I get there before the Lees arrive?* She took a deep breath, half hoping the air would fill her stomach as well as her lungs.

Hearing giggling behind her, she turned around.

Heidi held up a plate. "Looking for these?" It was a beautiful plate of cookies.

Rita pointed to the fridge. "And there are still doughnuts. I put them in the fridge to keep them from going stale."

Louise helped herself to a doughnut, then sat at the table and grabbed a cookie. "If I keep this diet up, I'll have to go shopping for new pants again."

"Stress eating. I understand it well." Rita helped herself

to another cookie. "I've made two trips to the store today to restock the goodie cupboard. I think Mrs. Theobald has stressed us all out more than we thought, and add to that the explosion yesterday and a GDV surgery." Rita shook her head, then finished her cookie.

"I still can't believe that someone set a bomb off at the airport. It's one thing to hear about it when it's far away, in other places, but . . ." Heidi cracked open a can of cola. "Well, don't get me wrong. It breaks my heart for the people affected in those faraway lands, but . . . this was so close. Right in our own backyard—literally."

Louise wasn't convinced Heidi's use of the word "literally" was completely accurate, but it was close enough. While the explosion wasn't in the clinic's backyard, it was geographically near enough to put everyone on edge.

Heidi sipped her drink. "They're just replaying Alex stating that the bomb was placed in the staff room and they suspect a timer was used. I'm guessing the bombers used it so they wouldn't be on site when the explosion happened. Cowards!"

Heidi's expression changed when she said "cowards," and Louise was in full agreement with the sentiment. If you have a point to make, speak up, show your face, and go through the proper, peaceful channels. Don't hurt innocent people and hide. "The timer will make it more difficult to identify the suspect. The bomb could have been there for hours, days, or weeks. I'm not sure how they determine when it was placed on site, if they even can."

"One new piece of information scrolled by since Alex spoke earlier." Rita was referring to the text bar that ran along the lower-left corner of the screen. "Two planes were parked in the hangar attached to the office building. Evidence was found near one of them that might be linked to the motive for the bombing, but it didn't say what the evidence was. The plane was destroyed, but they think the evidence was blown from the plane into a wall."

Louise scrunched her face. "I'm surprised they released that information."

Heidi shrugged, finished her cola, and stood. "Maybe there's a leak in the department."

Rita laughed. "Oh no, Heidi. You're starting to have a suspicious mind like Louise. Maybe you need a holiday."

Heidi smiled. "Maybe I do. But first, I'll finish getting Flip ready for discharge. The Lees should be here any minute."

After Heidi left, Louise flopped down into the newly vacated chair and leaned across the table toward Rita. "And just what exactly is wrong with being suspicious?"

Rita laughed again. "I hear it can get you into all kinds of trouble." She picked up the bag beside her and rose. "I'm heading home. My work here is done for the day."

After wishing Rita a good evening and turning the TV off, Louise headed to her office to get her own things ready to leave. Alex was due at her place for dinner, and she didn't want to waste one minute that could be used to drill him for information.

Chapter 18

LOUISE TRANSFERRED THE precooked, store-bought lasagna into a casserole dish and placed it into the oven to warm. She then folded the box and shoved it down to the bottom of the blue recycling bin. She placed the utensils she'd used for the transfer on top of a frying pan she'd put in the sink. If Alex didn't look too closely, he might assume Louise had cooked him the dinner from scratch.

She slapped her forehead. "Nuts! I forgot to pick up garlic bread." She threw open the spice cabinet and was thrilled to see powdered garlic. Her luck, however, ran out when she looked for bread to spread some butter and garlic on. "Oh well, it's doubtful he would have believed the homemade dinner bit anyway." Louise retrieved a box of cheesy crackers from the cupboard and dropped it onto the kitchen island. "Next best thing!"

She rinsed the frying pan and returned it to its tomb in the lower cupboard.

"Your turn, Oscar," Louise called out to her furry housemate, then plugged in the can opener. The speed with which Oscar appeared from anywhere in the house when she turned on the can opener made her laugh. "I keep meaning to look for that transporter you've hidden away, bud." She scooped a serving of Oscar's favorite food into his bowl. He purred as he ate; Louise was aware that it was an autonomic response, but she liked to think it was his way of saying thank you for the meal.

Alex arrived a few minutes later, and Louise sat unusually silent during dinner. She had questions about the cases, both at the airport and at the rehab centre. She was certain they were related but couldn't figure out how. She needed more information, and the best—and worst—source of that information was sitting across from her gorging on pasta, cheese, and tomato sauce. Whenever she was trying to get information from him, whether work related or personal, he was a hard nut to crack.

Every Christmas Louise attempted to squeeze clues about what gift he'd gotten her from her detective friend, but each year she was as unsuccessful as the last. He hadn't even mentioned this new surprise he had for her—the one Daphne had spoken of yesterday. Louise hoped that the extra hamburger in this "meat-lovers" version of the lasagna might soften him.

She could start with the surprise and see if he was in a sharing mood, but what if it had to do with a subject she didn't want to discuss, like their future together? No, this wasn't the time to get into an in-depth discussion about that. Or was it? Could she use it as a distraction to throw him off balance and get him to open up about the bomb and the murder? Louise shook her head. No, that would be unfair, and risky. As much as she wanted to know what was going on regarding these events, she didn't want to use their relationship to trick him.

Alex stared into Louise's eyes. "What's on your mind?"

She straightened in her chair and leaned back. "What do you mean?"

He narrowed his eyes. "You're unusually quiet, randomly shaking your head, and seem to be lost in thought. So, either you've picked up a case of ear mites at the clinic or something's on your mind."

"Not possible. Ear mites are species specific." Louise excused herself and went to the kitchen. She scooped up the box of crackers and returned to the table. "Sorry. No garlic bread."

"Is that what's on your mind? The missing garlic bread?"

Think Louise, think. "Any word on the woman who followed me home yesterday?" That was an innocent enough question. Why shouldn't she ask about a potential stalker?

Alex scooped up a forkful of pasta and shoved it into his mouth, chewing only once before swallowing. How he didn't choke or at the least get indigestion from his barbaric eating habits was a mystery to be solved another time.

"Her full name is Beth, short for Elizabeth, Gilley. Retired secretary. Widowed. Her husband worked for the local hydro-electrical supplier until he retired. One grown son who lives out west. No record."

"The officer who responded to my call last night told me her name, but did the woman say why she was following me?"

"Nope. She denied everything. She claims she was heading home and got turned around because of the fog."

"There wasn't any fog last night. Well, not in the atmosphere—I can't speak to what was going on in her head."

"That was mean-spirited." Alex squinted at Louise. "Are you feeling okay?"

"No, I'm not." She couldn't disagree that her comment was unkind. What he didn't know was that in the past couple of days, her unspoken thoughts about others were becoming less and less kind. "I chalk it up to stress, worry, and lack of sleep. I know she was intentionally following me. She's one of those protestors at SWaRF. She was there earlier today after I met up with you and Sandra. She avoided eye contact, something I wish ol' Madame Grumpy Face had done. I could have lived the rest of my life quite happily without interacting with that woman."

Alex, about to place another forkful of food into his mouth, stopped mid-way to his lips. "Madame Grumpy Face? I assume that's not her real name?"

"No. That's what Sandra calls her. She appears to be the group's leader. The other women bow down to her—I think out of fear more than respect. One of them called her Joan, but I don't have a last name. Did you see them when you arrived at SWaRF?"

Louise was tempted to show him the photos she'd taken of the protestors to see if he had information on Joan. But even if he did, he was unlikely to share the names of the protestors, and certainly not any details about their occupations, so she decided not to. After Alex left she'd use facial recognition to see if she could identify the women. If not, she could always send him the photos later.

Having successfully reached his mouth with his fork as Louise was talking, Alex swallowed, then washed the lasagna down with a swig of ginger ale. "No. I went in through the back roads. Sandra had told me the protestors were out there, and I didn't have time to chat with them before heading back to the airport." He grinned like a toddler who'd just snagged a lollypop. "Besides, I figured you'd interview them for me." He scraped the last vestiges of his dinner off his plate, then wisely left the room to put the plate in the sink.

Sitting alone at the table, Louise eyed Oscar, who'd been sitting quietly on the windowsill. "He thinks he's so funny. Wait until he finds out there's no dessert. Then we'll see who's laughing."

Clocks had been moved an hour ahead the second week of March, marking the beginning of daylight savings time. With the longer days and temperatures warmer than normal for this time of year in southern Ontario, Louise suggested that she and Alex have a sit-down on her wraparound porch.

The dashing police detective helped Louise clean up the few dishes before turning on the coffee maker, then went outside to his favourite Adirondack chair. Louise intended to follow him out, but just as she pushed the door open, the phone rang and she saw Daphne's name on the caller ID. She called out to Alex, "I'd better see what Daphne needs. I'll be out in a minute with the coffees, and I'll see if I can find some cookies."

When Louise arrived on the porch a few minutes later, she dropped the tray with the mugs onto the table. The cups rattled, spilling the hot liquid, which soaked into the napkins.

Alex jumped up from his seat. "What's that?"

His heightened reaction to the noise startled Louise; she'd never seen the normally calm police officer acting jumpy. She mentally palmed her forehead. *Of course he's jumpy, Louise—he was almost killed by a bomb blast less than two days ago.*

"Are you okay?" she asked.

Alex shrugged and sat down, then wiped the sides of one of the mugs before taking a sip. "Sure. I guess you're not the only one with a wandering mind this evening. I was watching those rabbits by the fence playing and thinking about how fast things can change. Norman and I had been joking around, and then before we knew it, we were lying under a pile of rubble."

"How's he doing?"

"He's coming along. Word is his wounds are healing nicely and he'll probably be transferred to a rehab facility next week."

Louise was excited to hear that Norman's physical wounds were healing well, but after observing Alex's reaction to the sound of the tray hitting the table, she wondered about both officers' mental health. The injuries she'd seen at the hospital—not to mention the nauseating smell of burnt flesh—were horrific. What had Alex and the others at the airport seen, heard, and smelled? Would those memories haunt them for a lifetime? Louise shook the thoughts out of her mind. Alex needed her support; they couldn't both crumble.

She had already been determined to get to the truth about the bombing and murder, but seeing that Alex's mental health, as well as his physical health, had been threatened, she was more determined than ever. *I'll help you figure this out, Alex, whether you want my help or not.*

"I'm sure Norman's wife is relieved he's on the road to recovery. My heart breaks for the families of those who didn't make it."

"Mine too." Alex sipped his coffee, then looked at the tray, disappointment in his eyes. "No cookies?"

"Sorry. Guess I need to go to the store tomorrow."

"Those with injuries have a long road ahead of them. Burns and penetrating injuries from flying debris. Three people lost limbs in the explosion, and more are at risk of needing an amputation. We need to pray that God gives wisdom to the doctors and surgeons."

Louise squeezed Alex's hand. She'd been praying for the victims and their families since the bombing, and she knew Alex had been too. Had she been praying enough? The past couple of days had been a whirlwind of stressful events, and she hadn't spent much time talking to God.

"I was surprised that something about possible evidence of a motive was revealed to the public," she said.

Alex inhaled deeply. "So was I, as was everyone else at the station. There are so many agencies involved in this investigation, it's hard to say where the leak came from."

"What other agencies?"

"Border security showed up today . . ." He eyed Louise. "How's Daphne doing? That was her on the phone, right?"

"It was." How abruptly he'd changed the topic wasn't lost on Louise. Alex mentioned border security but stopped before giving any details. Why would they be called into a case involving a small airport—one that didn't handle international flights?

"She wanted to let me know that she got home in time to take Ella for their mother-daughter dinner. Ella was so excited that she'd insisted Joe help her get dressed up for the occasion. When Daphne arrived home, Ella was wearing her finest princess dress and a tiara. She was the best-dressed customer at Swiss Chalet."

Louise held her phone up to show him the photo Daphne had sent while they were talking. They shared an "aww" moment, swooning over the adorable goddaughter they shared, even though they weren't married. They hadn't been dating when Ella was born, and they weren't dating now. Or were they? Louise was more confused than ever about her relationship with Alex. After yesterday's events, which had her thinking briefly at the hospital that she'd lost him forever, she knew that life without Alex wasn't something she wanted to consider.

She couldn't expect him to be her *friend* forever, as someday he'd find someone who would give him the companionship he was hoping for. Someone who'd give him more than a trip to the movies and store-bought lasagna. Louise knew that he longed for a wife, and even a gaggle of children, if that was in God's plans for him.

She shook off her thoughts of the future and returned her mind to the present. Louise filled him in on the happenings at the clinic, including the contrast in behaviour between Mrs. Theobald and the Morrisons. "The world is made up of all kinds of people."

Using his leg, Alex dragged a footstool closer, then put his feet up, crossing his ankles. His relaxed look was completed when he intertwined his fingers behind his head. "It sure is."

The clouds in the distance were changing to a brilliant red

orange as the sun set behind them. The sky appeared to be on fire, yet it was beautiful, not scary. Louise wondered at God's artwork and the subtle ways in which He reminded people of His presence each day.

Alex would need to get going soon, so she leaned back and relaxed, feeling safe by his side. He rarely stayed out late when he had an active case, and now he had two cases that might or might not be related.

The calm of the moment was lost when Louise remembered that she still had questions she wanted answered. "I've told you about my day—how was yours?"

"I know you're trying to get information out of me, and I should be irked, but honestly, talking about what's happened is better than thinking about what might have happened. Just remember, I can't reveal any details about an ongoing investigation."

"Of course not." Louise rubbed her chin. "Any updates on the fabric or cigarette butt found?"

"No."

"I see. I can ask all the questions I want because you aren't going to answer them anyway."

Alex moved his hands to his lap and looked at her. "No, I'm telling you the truth. There are no updates on that evidence. The fabric is only useful if we have something to compare it to. If we find a suspect wearing a shirt of the same material with a matching piece of it missing, we can say, 'Aha! You were at SWaRF and ripped your shirt on a tree.'"

"Wasn't there any blood on the fabric?"

"Don't know yet. It's still at the lab."

"What about the cigarette butt?"

"Same thing. We can do DNA testing, but that takes time."

"Oh." Louise felt like a tire someone had poked a hole in. "Any word on Bailey Nelson's whereabouts? What about the footprints? From the size of them, we know they're a man's."

"Size can't be determined from a photograph."

"Sure it can, give or take an inch." Louise related how she'd ventured into the wooded area of the rehab centre to retrieve the twig seen in the photograph. "It's definitely not from an average woman's shoe."

Alex pursed his lips and tilted his head. "You may be on to something there. Did you move the twig?"

"Of course not. I showed it to Wayne—he was the officer on duty—and asked him to, well . . ." Louise shrugged. Sandra had picked it up, but they'd been careful to put it back where it was found. "I don't know. To do whatever he needed to do to document it."

He smiled. "That's actually helpful information."

Louise felt her tire refilling with air. "Ha! See?"

"I do see. I see that we're looking for a man whose shoe size is eleven and a half—give or a take an inch—who was at SWaRF sometime before it rained last night. What's Bailey Nelson's shoe size?"

Louise hadn't thought of that. If she could find out his size, maybe she could help clear him of the crime . . . or help convict him. Sandra was certain Bailey wouldn't be involved in criminal activity, but Louise didn't know him. In fact, she didn't know Sandra that well either, so trusting Sandra's judgment about a SWaRF employee was unwise. The fabric she found could be from Bailey's shirt. And there was the cigarette butt. Sandra said Bailey didn't smoke, and that even if he did, he wouldn't smoke on SWaRF property. But if he was capable of murder, he'd have no qualms about breaking a no-smoking rule.

After Alex finished his coffee and left for home, Louise sent a text to Sandra. *Do you know Bailey's home address? I think we should check something out.*

Chapter 19

S ANDRA WOULDN'T BE available for an hour, so Louise used the time to look for the protestors' names using facial recognition. She hadn't used this technology previously and had no idea if it was possible to identify someone this way. After browsing multiple sites that claimed to provide the needed software, Louise downloaded a program that looked promising. It was costly, but the first five searches were free. She had photos of three of the women who were at SWaRF earlier today.

Louise started with Joan since she appeared to be the group's leader. She dragged the first of three photos she'd taken of Madame Grumpy Face into the software's image window and clicked on *Continue*. No matches. The second photo on

Louise's phone had a motion artifact, so she skipped it, loaded the third photo, and crossed her fingers.

When a list of matches with accompanying links to online articles appeared on the screen, she threw her fist into the air. "*Yes!*"

Oscar, who'd been sleeping on a chair by Louise's desk, flew from his perch and ran upstairs. "Sorry, buddy."

The first article showed a picture of Joan with a group of other women. Louise recognized Plump-in-Plum but none of the others. Sandra had mentioned that those at SWaRF during the past few days were mostly new faces.

All of the women were looking toward the camera but not at it. They appeared to be gazing at an individual who was wearing a hoodie and whose back was to the camera. They were not only looking at Hoodie, but also listening intently, their facial expressions making this obvious.

Free of emotion but with wide eyes, their faces reminded Louise of a documentary she'd watched recently on cults. The followers had been brainwashed into believing that their leader was an all-knowing, superior being. When he was speaking, they gathered in a semicircle and listened intently, their faces blank as though they had no thoughts of their own. Was Hoodie a cult leader?

"Who are you?" Louise squinted at the store window in the photo's background, hoping to see Hoodie's reflection. "Nope. That only works on TV."

She read the article that accompanied the photo but was disappointed at the lack of identifying names. The journalist referred to the group as ARS members but didn't identify them.

"No *E* at the end—I guess this was before you all became environmentalists."

Louise closed the page, clicked on the next link, and found a similar scene. Joan and many of the same women were holding up signs and looking at Hoodie, whose face was again not visible. Her spirits lifted when she noticed that this article named several members.

Joan's last name was listed as Williams, Plump-in-Plum was designated Erica Cotton, and a middle-aged woman with shoulder-length brown hair and glasses was Tina Purcell. Two women and a man were standing behind those three. The man's name was Patrick Howard, but the two women beside him weren't named. Louise was sure that none of the three in the back row, nor Tina Purcell, were in the group she'd encountered at SWaRF.

She glanced at the time on the laptop; she'd have to leave soon to meet Sandra at Bailey Nelson's home, but there was plenty of time to open one more article.

Another photo with Joan Williams and her friends appeared. This time Hoodie wasn't the focus of their attention but could be seen in the background, looking at a man who was sitting on a bench near the women.

"What is it with Hoodie? Is she deliberately position-ing herself so she can't be identified?" Hoodie was farther away from the lens in this photo, allowing an estimation of her height and weight. "You look to be about as tall as Plump-in . . . I mean Erica Cotton, but your sweater hides your build."

Louise scanned the article to see if it would reveal Hood-ie's name. Hoodie wasn't identified, but the man on the bench was. Louise's adrenalin soared to record highs as she read his name. The man, whose face was partially obscured by a base-ball cap, was identified as Bailey Nelson.

"What are you doing with ARSE?"

The article was dated January of the current year and had been taken near Tobin Memorial Airport.

Bailey Nelson lived in a mobile home on the east side of Rural Route 17. Louise was familiar with this area—a few months earlier, she'd found herself breaking into a client's home here while searching for a missing employee. She had since heard that the client moved out west. The little brick house, with a weathered For Sale sign swaying with the wind, looked deserted.

Bailey's address was about one hundred yards farther up the road on the other side of the street. Louise pulled into the deserted house's driveway, then swung her car around to the back of the house. She fought back memories of finding a photo in the residence that reminded her of darker days in her own past. Days that preceded her faith in God, as well as her friendship with Alex, Daphne, and Daphne's husband, Joe. Her fiancé at the time, Zack, had been ripped away from her in an instant. The grief was still there, and now she'd almost lost Alex as well.

Louise shook off the memories as she threw her car in park, exited the vehicle, and crept toward the road, hoping the neighbours wouldn't see her. A mailbox up the road, lit by a streetlight, proudly proclaimed the name of the blue-and-white mobile home's owner: B. Nelson. This was the right place. A dark blue pickup truck sat in the driveway. The truck implied Bailey was home, but no house lights were on. It was early for a young single man to be in bed, but Bailey had called in sick. Was he sleeping soundly, unaware of what was happening at his workplace?

Once she reached the edge of his driveway, Louise could see two newspapers wrapped in clear plastic on the DIY front porch, still lying where they'd landed after the paper delivery person tossed them at the small home.

Was Bailey too ill to retrieve the papers, or . . . ? Louise's heart skipped a beat, a surge of urgency and caution overcoming her when she thought of alternative explanations. What if Bailey had been sicker than he let on to Sandra? He might have passed away from his illness. Or was he another murder victim? He'd been with the protestors at the airport a couple of months ago. Was he one of them? He might have been the person who gave them access to the back pond, and maybe they'd killed him to keep him quiet. But why would they need access to the pond? There was nothing there.

Despite the warm evening air, Louise felt a chill run through her. Alex had Bailey listed as a suspect. She couldn't ignore the possibilities that the SWaRF employee was hiding out in his mobile home, had been killed by accomplices, or was on the run.

"This is nuts. I don't know this person, or how dangerous he could be. Time to head home and call Alex."

Louise turned to head back to her vehicle but stopped when Sandra's car drew up beside her.

Sandra waved at her, parked beside Bailey's truck, and exited her car without closing the door. She peered into the passenger side of the pickup truck, then leaving her hands on it, frantically circled it, scanning the passenger seat and the empty, uncovered truck bed. "This is weird." Sandra clasped her hands while staring into the cab.

"In what way?" Louise had convinced herself they shouldn't proceed to check out Bailey's home on their own, but Sandra had clearly just discovered something out of the ordinary.

"The truck is clear of clutter, like someone cleaned it out. Bailey's a great guy and a great worker, but he's not so good at being tidy. I'm always ribbing him about the mess of fast-food containers on his passenger-side floor."

A normally messy person wouldn't start cleaning while sick, adding to Louise's concern that Bailey's illness was a rouse. That he was somehow involved with ARSE.

"You're sure he didn't clean it out before you last saw him?"

"No. The last time I saw him was the end of his shift last Friday. That was four days ago. He'd forgotten a hammer and wrench he needed to borrow from our tool shed. I noticed them on the counter in the staff room just after he'd left, so I ran the tools out to him. The truck was as messy as usual." Sandra gulped in the night air, then frowned. "It was late in the day, so no way did he drive home and then clean out the mess before heading to bed. The next morning, he called in to say he was too sick to work. This doesn't make any sense. First that Tina woman dead on my property, now this."

Louise agreed that things weren't adding up. If Bailey didn't clean out his truck, then who did, and why?

"Does he have a girlfriend who may have gotten tired of the mess? Maybe someone who borrowed his truck over the weekend? His mother?"

"No girlfriend. I think his mother passed away a few years ago, and Bailey would never let anyone else drive this truck. He told me he had to save for a long time to buy it, and I believe it—he treats it like his child. She even has a name,

Blue Belle." Sandra marched toward Bailey's porch. "We need to get inside and make sure he's okay."

Louise followed behind, but something Sandra had just said tickled her brain. She matched Sandra's pace, then placed a hand on Sandra's shoulder to get her to stop walking. "What did you just say about the woman in the pond? What did you call her?"

"Tina. I think that's what Officer Wayne called her. Tina Pur . . ." Sandra tapped her forehead with the palm of her hand. "What was it?"

They stood silently in the darkness for a few minutes. Louise thought back to the ruined badge the woman had been wearing when they found her. ". . . ell? . . . cell? Pur . . . cell?"

"Yes! That's it! Purcell. Tina Purcell. They called me to see if I knew who she was—if she was a SWaRF employee or volunteer. She wasn't either. I've never heard of her."

Louise *had* heard of her. When searching the internet, she had emailed the articles about ARSE to herself. She opened the email app on her phone and clicked on the link to the last article she'd read.

"Look at this." She turned the phone to show Sandra. "Here's a photo of Madame Grumpy Face, whose real name is Joan Williams, by the way." She used two fingers to enlarge, then reposition the photo. "And this woman must be Tina Purcell. The names are listed under the photo." Louise shrank the photo to its original size so the names would appear.

The light from the phone's screen lit up Sandra's face. Louise watched as her companion examined the photo and the names listed below it. Would she notice what Louise had noticed earlier? If so, would she be honest about it, or pretend not to notice? Louise soon got her answer.

Sandra's eyes widened and she stomped her foot. "That's Bailey! What's he doing with ARSE? I don't believe this. He has a lot of explaining to do!" Sandra's nostrils flared. She whirled around and pounded on Bailey's door with her fist. "Open the door, Bailey!"

"Sh!" To shield the light, Louise dropped the phone into her pocket, then grabbed Sandra's hand before she could hammer the door again. "You'll alert the neighbours that we're here. If Bailey's inside, he may be injured, or . . . Well, we have to be cautious. The last thing we need is to become suspects if something's happened to him."

Sandra's voice softened. "What are you saying?"

"I'm saying we don't know where he is, we don't know why he's in that photo, and we don't know why his normally messy truck is now neat and tidy. I'm not so sure anymore that we should even be here. Bailey might be working with ARSE. I should call Alex." Louise reached for her phone.

Sandra touched Louise's arm. "No, please don't. We're here already. Why don't we just look around a bit and see if we can find anything? I won't do anything that could draw attention to us, or make us suspects."

Louise eyed the pickup truck. "It might be too late for that. Your fingerprints are all over a recently cleaned truck. You couldn't even claim that your prints are from the other night when you delivered Bailey's forgotten tools, because not only has the truck been cleaned, but it's also rained a lot since then."

Sandra stared, wide-eyed, at Louise.

"Sorry, Sandra—I'm sure you're not a suspect." Louise knew that wasn't completely true. Now that the police knew that the victim was a protestor, Sandra was probably at the top of Alex's suspect list.

Louise pulled some latex gloves from her pocket. "Put these on before touching anything else. Hopefully you take medium—we were all out of large at the clinic."

"Do you always carry exam gloves around with you?"

Louise tilted her head and smiled. "I never leave home without them." *Not when I'm snooping where I'm not supposed to be snooping.*

Louise tried the front door. As expected, it was locked. "Sandra, you head that way, and I'll go this way," she said, pointing. "Look in the windows as you circle around to the back. We'll meet up there."

They parted ways. As Louise rounded the north corner of the mobile home, she spotted a cheap plastic patio chair against the wall under a window. Seeing the chair filled her with excitement and fright at the same time. She could use it to see into the window, but was this how an intruder could have accessed Bailey's home? Louise shook off the conflicting thoughts and headed for the chair.

She placed one foot on its seat, avoiding the crack down the middle, and grasped a plant hanger adjacent to the window. She used the hanger to pull herself up, but as she did so, the crack widened. Feeling the chair give way below her, Louise held on tightly to the hanger. She was stuck, hanging from the side of the mobile home. How did she get herself into such situations twice in one day?

Louise thought through her options. If she let go, she'd fall to the ground, potentially hurting herself on sharp pieces of plastic. With her free hand, she pressed on the window; it was securely in place and locked. She'd have to release her grip and hope she landed gracefully and injury-free.

"Do you hang around like this often?" Sandra said, looking up before she bent over laughing.

"Only when I'm with you." Louise joined in the laughter, but her tiring muscles reminded her of their situation. She placed her finger over her lips. "Remember, we need to be as quiet as possible. Did you happen to see anything else I could stand on? Another chair? A table?"

"There's a bunch of clutter out back on a table. True Bailey style. I'll grab something. Hang on—pun totally intended."

"Ha ha!"

Louise counted only seconds before Sandra returned, but SWaRF's founder was no longer in a laughing mood. She looked as though she'd seen a ghost.

Sandra placed the table under Louise's dangling feet and held it steady.

Louise placed her feet on it, then sat on the table, facing Sandra. "You don't look so good, Sandra. Are you feeling okay? You're not sick, are you?"

"When I was clearing the junk off the table, I found the wrench Bailey borrowed. It has a piece of tape with SWaRF written on it, so I knew it was ours."

Louise leapt off the table to the ground. "That's great—it tells us he was here. If the wrench was in the backyard, he must have taken some time to work on his project."

Sandra shook her head. "No, you don't understand. The wrench was there, but on the ground, it looked like . . . It was red and . . . there was a lot of it." Sandra inhaled and held her stomach. "I think I'm going to be sick."

"Please don't do that." It wasn't the appropriate time to tell Sandra that if she vomited, Louise probably would too. "I think we need to get inside and see if there are any signs of a struggle. Did you notice if there's a back door?"

"There is."

Louise followed Sandra around the corner to the back of the home. Relieved to find the back door unlocked, she turned on her phone's flashlight, then slowly opened the door and crept inside. It was as quiet as it was dark, and very creepy.

"Have you been here before? Do you know the layout?" Louise asked.

Sandra shook her head. "No, not to this home, but one like it. If it's the same, then this door opens into a kitchen. The living space is that way." She pointed to the right. "And the bedrooms are the other way."

Louise, Sandra close behind her, walked through the kitchen and turned left. They went to Bailey's bedroom first.

Sandra called out, "Bailey, are you in here?"

Not getting an answer, Louise shone her light around the room. Bailey wasn't there. The mess, an unmade bed with sheets thrown around and clothes littering the floor, made it difficult to tell if there'd been a struggle in the room.

Louise went to the next room. "A lot of people who live alone will use the spare room as a home office."

The smaller bedroom was set up with a filing cabinet, a desk with a computer and printer, and a table with assorted electronic devices, including some neither Louise nor Sandra could identify.

"Wouldn't the police have already searched here? If they think Bailey's responsible for the murder, wouldn't they be allowed to search his house?" Sandra asked.

"I'm not sure, but I think they need probable cause." Louise wasn't aware of what that might be in this case, but it sounded good. "And they might be waiting on a search warrant. We don't need a warrant. You're simply a concerned employer and friend."

"And you?"

Louise lifted her phone. "I have the flashlight."

"I'm pretty sure I have one of those too. In fact, I think everyone does."

"Do they? Who knew?" Louise touched the computer mouse and the monitor flickered on.

In front of them was a spreadsheet with the title: *ARSE Movements and Motives.*

The spreadsheet was a detailed listing of protest locations over the past two years. Louise scrolled down. Near the end of the list was mention of the airport and the wildlife rehabilitation centre.

"Why would Bailey have this?" Sandra lowered herself into the desk chair.

Louise shook her head. "Don't know. He was either one of them and this is the itinerary they sent him, or—"

"Or what? I can't believe that the man I know as Bailey Nelson, trusted employee and friend, would betray me by joining ARSE."

"Unless he was a member before he joined SWaRF." For Sandra's sake, Louise didn't want to believe it, but she couldn't get the image of him sitting by the group at the airport out of her head. "We have to look at all angles, Sandra. He was at the airport with ARSE members a mere few weeks before the bombing. Then the dead body of an ARSE member showed up in his workplace. And . . . *poof!*, he's gone." Louise regretted the "poof," but she was becoming more and more certain that Bailey Nelson wasn't who he portrayed himself to be.

Chapter 20

"I F I CAN make a copy of that document"—a green light on the printer indicated it was already on—"then later I'll do a background search on the protestors' actions. It'd be interesting to see if any crimes were committed while they were in the areas listed here."

"Well, that's easy to do." Sandra moved the cursor over the file tab, clicked, then moved it to the print option.

Louise, who stood beside her, placed her hand over Sandra's. "Wait. The printer has a memory key. If we print something, we might wipe out important evidence. We don't know what the last thing Bailey printed was."

"No problem." Sandra reached across the desk and pushed

the memory button. The printer spat out a copy of the spreadsheet open on the computer.

"Good thinking." Louise retrieved the paper and folded it
before putting it into her pocket. "So, Bailey printed the ARSE
schedule before he took off. Why?"

"I don't know, but you have it all wrong. Bailey didn't '*take
off.*' I think that was blood on the ground in the backyard. What
if someone grabbed him? He could be injured somewhere, or .
. ." Sandra took a big breath and released a sound like that of a
whimpering puppy.

"Sorry. I'm sure the police would have seen the blood if
they entered the property yesterday. Like I said, I think they'd
need a warrant to come inside, but I'm not sure about the backyard." Louise didn't know if they'd been to Bailey's yard. She'd
call Alex to let him know about the blood on the tools, because
Sandra was right, Bailey could be injured somewhere—or on
the run after injuring someone else. She'd keep that last thought
to herself for now.

Sandra got up and Louise took her place at the computer.
She clicked on the file icon on the lower taskbar; the window
listing Bailey's files came in to view. There were multiple files
with innocuous labels: *Recipes, Photos, Family History, Work
Schedule, Tax Documents*, and *Passwords*.

Louise clicked on the *Passwords* file. It was password protected. She nodded. "Thought so. I do the same thing."

Next, she clicked on the *Photos* file to see if Bailey had pictures of the ARSE members. More importantly, he might have
pictures that would reveal he was friends with the group. Pictures that could prove he was one of *them*. For Sandra's sake,
Louise hoped there would be no such photos.

As she scrolled through the images, Louise was temporarily

relieved that there were no incriminating images, but if Bailey was a smart guy, he wouldn't keep incriminating evidence in such an obvious place. No, he'd bury it somewhere else.

Louise scratched her head while she stared at the list of files. "Sandra, does Bailey cook?"

"Never." Sandra, who'd been looking through Bailey's closet, stood beside Louise at the desk. "I told you. He lives off fast food. I don't think he even knows where the grocery store is. Why?"

"Why would a guy who doesn't cook have a file for recipes?" Louise clicked on the file.

"I guess that's why." In the *Recipes* file were several more folders, all labelled *ARSE*, then a subtitle. *ARSE—Photos, ARSE—Locations, ARSE—Members, ARSE—Newspaper, ARSE—Social Media.* "I think we hit the jackpot."

"I guess that depends on what game you're playing, and who the winners and losers will be. I really hope Bailey won't be the loser here."

"Me too, Sandra, but we need to find out what's going on. If he's innocent, hopefully we can find something here to tell us where he is. If he's not . . ." Louise paused. She knew this was difficult for Sandra, but they couldn't avoid the possibility that Bailey wasn't who he'd been pretending to be. "If he's not . . . well . . . he needs to be stopped."

"Even if he turns out to be a member of ARSE, it doesn't mean he's a criminal."

Louise was impressed by Sandra's quick resolve to forgive Bailey. She seemed willing to accept that he might be an ARSE spy, yet wanted to defend his honour when it came to more dastardly deeds.

Louise attempted to open the ARSE files, but the only one

that wasn't password protected was *ARSE-Photos*. She double-clicked and was rewarded with multiple pictures of various ARSE members Louise had seen in the newspaper articles and on site at SWaRF. "Do you recognize any of these people?"

Sandra shook her head. "Just the ones we've already identified." She pointed at two women standing together in the background. "I think those two have been to the rehab centre, but they haven't been around the past couple of days."

Joan Williams was in all of the photos. Beth Gilley and Tina Purcell were in a few of the later ones. "That's odd," Louise said.

"What's that?" Sandra squatted down and rested her elbows on the desk, her fists beneath her chin.

"The hoodie-wearing person is in most of these photos too, but like in the other pictures, her face is obscured or her back is to the camera."

Sandra tapped the screen with her finger. "Not in this one. The person is facing the camera—we can't see the hood, but I'm pretty sure that's a hoodie. Look at the pocket on the front. And the zipper."

The photo had been taken from a distance, making it difficult to make out the person's face.

Sandra slapped Louise on the shoulder. "And I don't think that's a woman."

Louise squinted at the picture. Her lack of sleep over the past couple of nights was seriously affecting her ability to focus on fine details. "Why do you say that? Most of the other protestors are women, so I just assumed—"

Sandra tapped on the screen with more vigour this time. "Because *that*, my dear, is a beard."

Louise squinted again. "You're right. Too bad he's wearing sunglasses and a hat. And it's taken from such a distance, if we enlarge it, it'll probably just go grainy. Unlikely we can use photo recognition to identify him. Have you seen him before?"

Sandra cocked her head from side to side. "Maybe? But other than the beard, it's impossible to make out any other features."

Louise snapped a photo of the screen, then moved over to the table with the assortment of electronic devices. "What do you think this equipment is for? It looks like something out of a sci-fi movie."

Using her flashlight, she scanned the room, thankful that there was no one living directly across the street who might notice a moving light. *We don't need any concerned neighbours calling the police on us.* Among other things, there were two other monitors on an adjacent table, as well as modems and Wi-Fi cameras. A multitude of cables running along the floor resembled a spiderweb designed by an intoxicated arachnid.

"This is a crazy set-up, and this equipment must be worth a fortune." Louise looked at Sandra and tilted her head. "How much do you pay Bailey?"

Sandra stared at the equipment. "Not this much. Where did he get all this? And why does he need it? Gaming?"

"If he has this much equipment for gaming, where's the chair? Don't serious gamers have a special chair?"

Sandra shrugged. "I have no idea."

"There's one scenario we haven't thought about."

"What's that?"

"Any chance Bailey's a spy?"

Sandra frowned at Louise.

Louise clapped her hands together. "Think about it. He's got photos taken from a distance—surveillance photos. Why? Because he didn't want to be seen by the people he was photographing. He's stored the photos in a secret file. He has all this equipment." Louise raised her palms. "Think about it."

"Well, if we found his secret files this easily . . . I hate to say it, but if Bailey's a spy, he's not a very good one."

Louise's shoulders dropped. "True!"

With no clues in Bailey's office as to his whereabouts, they searched the rest of his home. Louise took the kitchen and living room, while Sandra volunteered to check his bedroom and bathroom. Louise was still uncertain how much she could trust Sandra's judgment when it came to Bailey's innocence or guilt, but the fact that the wildlife rehabber was willingly searching a single man's bedroom, never mind his bathroom, boosted Louise's confidence in the woman's objectivity.

When they were each satisfied that they'd covered their assigned areas, they met at the back door, but before they opened it, a noise came from the backyard.

"What was that?" Sandra asked, clutching Louise's arm.

Louise felt Sandra's trembling hand and was sure the woman could feel Louise trembling too. Louise put her finger over her mouth. "Sh. Duck down and stay still." Luckily, they hadn't turned on any of the home's lights, and Louise had already turned her mobile flashlight off to avoid drawing attention when they exited the house.

It sounded as if someone was looking through the mess of tools Sandra had discovered earlier. The bloody wrench was still there—Louise hadn't wanted to disturb it in case the police hadn't investigated Bailey's yard yet. Now she regretted not removing it. What if the noisy intruder was here to retrieve that very weapon? Had they used it to harm Bailey? Or was Bailey himself returning to the scene of the crime to remove incriminating evidence? No, if it was him, he wouldn't sneak around.

On the other hand, this person, whoever they were, couldn't be described as "sneaking around" with all the noise they were making.

Louise said a prayer and hoped one of the neighbours would hear the commotion and call the police. Getting caught in Bailey's house was preferable to being smashed with a wrench.

Sandra began to get up, as though she intended to sneak a peek out the window. Louise placed her hand on Sandra's shoulder and gently pushed her back down. Louise rapidly shook her head and whispered, "No, stay out of sight."

When silence returned, Louise waited a few minutes, then crawled to the front window and risked a peek out. A small figure wearing a hoodie ran across the street to a waiting car. The person jumped into the passenger side, and then the car sped off.

Louise took a deep breath and felt her neck muscles loosen. "He—or she—is gone."

"You didn't get a look at them?"

"I saw someone in a hoodie. I assumed at first that it was the man in the photos, but this person was small. Petite, even. Like"—Louise thought back to her encounter with an intruder the night before—"Beth Gilley! The one who followed me. Man, that woman has nerve."

"You're sure it was her?"

"Sure? No. But I'm sure she had an accomplice this time. They drove off together. It wasn't the car Beth was in last night. This was a normal-sized four-door sedan. I think it was grey . . . maybe."

"That could be anyone."

"True." Louise rose to her feet. "Could you give me a drive

to my car? I parked across the road and I'd rather not walk that far. I have to admit, I'm a bit shaken."

"Maybe we should stay in here and call the police. There could be more of them out there, watching the house."

"Something tells me that this Beth woman is a pawn, and most likely so is the person who was driving the car. You know—weak-minded individuals who do the dirty work while the ringleader keeps his hands clean. If I had to guess, the leader of ARSE is sitting at home with someone who can provide an alibi."

Louise followed Sandra out the back door, then turned the lock to the on position and pulled it tight. "In case they come back and try to get in."

"Why didn't they try to get in just now?"

Louise shrugged. "No idea." She almost walked into Sandra when the woman stopped suddenly.

"Maybe that's why." Sandra pointed at the mess of tools. The wrench was gone.

"Good thing you noticed it earlier. We can let Alex know that it was here and someone came back for it."

Sandra drove Louise to her car behind the empty brick bungalow. A large garage that the owner had converted to a dog kennel caught Louise's eye. "There's a light on in the garage. That's odd."

"Was it on when you arrived earlier?"

"I can't remember."

Sandra frowned. "You're not going to check that out too, are you? I really want to get out of here."

"No worries." Louise patted her on the back. "One mystery at a time. It was probably left on by the last realtor who was showing the place."

Chapter 21

THE MORNING APPOINTMENTS at the Black Creek Animal Hospital were filled with the typical spring concerns: puppy and kitten checkups, heartworm tests, dogs who had diarrhea after ingesting thawing grass and mud, and animals with various other weather-related issues.

Mrs. Hancock had called in a panic about her nine-month-old female cat, who was screaming. The worried owner was assured that her feline companion was showing signs of being "in heat"—a common term for a dog or cat in estrus and looking for a mate to breed with, but the clinic offered an examination to confirm it.

Louise assured Mrs. Hancock that her suddenly noisy and

excessively friendly cat was indeed in heat, then escorted her and her furry companion to the front desk to schedule an appointment for surgery.

"Mary, can you take care of Mrs. Hancock? Let's try to get Dahlia in for a spay in the next week or two." Louise handed Dahlia's file to Mary, then turned to the client. "There's no charge for today's visit. I'm happy Dahlia isn't sick. Her behaviour may last a couple more days, and in the meantime, be careful not to let her get out of the house. We don't want any unexpected surprises in nine weeks."

Louise had one morning appointment left and hoped to get it done quickly because she needed to call Alex about what she and Sandra had discovered last night. She'd tried to call him first thing in the morning before heading to the clinic, but his phone went straight to voice mail.

Louise remained unconvinced he was free of undiagnosed internal injuries, so when she couldn't reach him, she called the police department to check up on him and verify that he wasn't lying unconscious in his bed. She was being foolish, clingy even, yet she couldn't shake the fear that she'd almost lost him. The overwhelming dread and grief when she'd first looked into his hospital room and thought he was gone forever was still raw.

The explosion had been about forty-eight hours ago, and so many things had happened since. Louise was relieved when the dispatcher assured her that Alex was fine and had gone out to the airport before sunrise. The dispatcher let it slip that there had been some developments but stopped short of telling Louise what they were.

"Not so fast, Dr. Miller." Mary's voice brought Louise's thoughts back to the present. "Sandra called. She sounded worried about Major and wants you to call her back as soon as you can."

Louise's heart sank. Yesterday Major had been acting normal, and they believed that whatever was ailing him had resolved on its own. Why was Sandra worried about him today? Was he off his food again? Vomiting? Lethargic?

Louise went into the exam room and brought the schedule up on the computer. Her next appointment was a recheck on a dog spayed the week before, and then she was free for the next two hours; on Wednesdays, they usually had staff meetings during that time.

After Mary escorted the client into the room, Louise asked how the patient was doing, then checked the suture site. All was normal, so she asked Heidi, who'd been in the pharmacy area behind the exam rooms, to remove the sutures.

With Heidi finishing up the last morning appointment, Louise raced up to her office to call Sandra. Her fears were confirmed—Major was off his food again. The blood work and urinalysis done initially had been normal, and Louise had wanted to do an ultrasound, but that was made impossible two days ago by the protestors. She needed to head back to SWaRF immediately, re-evaluate Major, then arrange for his transportation to the clinic for radiographs and an ultrasound.

The ultrasound machine she and Daphne had purchased was small and could be used at SWaRF, but they could neither anaesthetize Major nor take radiographs there. The radiography equipment at the clinic wasn't mobile, and purchasing a mobile unit for SWaRF wasn't affordable. If the funds were available, it would be ideal to set up a hospital at SWaRF that would allow the veterinary team to treat the animals, including carrying out surgical procedures on site, but sadly the actions of the protestors, combined with a poor economy, had negatively impacted donations.

Louise took a couple of deep breaths to control her rising anxiety. The protestors claimed to be fighting to protect the animals, but they were making it difficult for the caretakers to care for them. What was their end goal? It seemed that some of them preferred to see injured or orphaned animals suffering in the wild rather than being cared for by humans.

Daphne agreed that Louise should head to SWaRF rather than stay for the staff meeting. Daphne and Rita could handle things; the Morrisons had called earlier to say that Jack was continuing to grow stronger, and Flip was resting comfortably after returning to Black Creek Animal Hospital from B-REC. The big dog was doing well and would be discharged later in the day.

As she drove to SWaRF, Louise couldn't shake the feeling that despite Daphne's calm demeanour, something was bothering her friend. She'd try to get back to the clinic before afternoon appointments started so she and Daphne could talk. Louise prayed that Joe and the children were well. Daphne had made it home on time last night for her dinner out with Ella, so that couldn't be what was troubling her.

In Louise's opinion, Daphne was both an amazing veterinarian and an amazing mother. She wondered how people with young families balanced the needs of children with the day-to-day stresses of a career. *I can barely feed myself and Oscar, and that's thanks to his constant reminders that his food bowl needs filling.*

Louise turned into SWaRF's front parking lot, realizing she still hadn't gotten directions on how to get to the back entrance. She'd have to do that today. That thought was reinforced when she saw a group of protestors camped outside the front gate. *Why are they back again?*

She scanned the group. Beth Gilley and the two unidentified women from the photos were there, as were Erica Cotton and Joan Williams. Louise followed the direction of the women's gaze and clapped her hands with delight. The man in the hoodie was there. If she could find out who this guy was, perhaps she'd be that much closer to discovering the group's true motives.

Hoodie Man was standing among the women, and the way they were listening so intently to him confirmed he was the group's leader. Even Joan Williams appeared to be a follower, not the leader she'd made herself out to be yesterday. *Madame Grumpy Face must be second-in-command.*

Louise estimated Hoodie Man to be just over six feet tall and approximately fifty years old. In Bailey's photos, the man's features were masked by the distance and sunglasses. She now had a full view of this mystery man. What really stuck out was his curly salt and pepper hair and beard that were so tight to his head and chin that they looked fake, like the hair of a plastic doll. With his hands on his hips and his shoulders pulled back, he stood in front of the women, who were gazing at him as though he was their supreme leader. The zipper of his hoodie was open, exposing a belly that strained against his too-small shirt, its middle button threatening to lose its hold on the bulging mass.

As Louise eyed him and his followers, she wondered what his story was. Did he legitimately care about the well-being of the animals, or was he simply another narcissistic leader who fed on the vulnerability of his followers? Beth Gilley was also wearing a hoodie, adding to Louise's suspicions that she was the one at Bailey's house the night before. To please this man, Beth had been willing to follow a stranger home at night and wander through darkened woods. Louise shook her head at the thought of the tiny frail woman not only confronting a stranger for this man, but also returning to a crime scene to retrieve evidence.

Before she was noticed, Louise grabbed her phone and snapped a few photos of the group. Hoodie Man wasn't wearing sunglasses, giving Louise a full-face photo she'd be able to use in the facial recognition software she'd found yesterday.

Besides the hoodie and bulging buttons, something else about the man's attire caught her attention. He was wearing a green-and-blue plaid shirt! Louise opened her photo app and scrolled back to the picture she'd taken of the torn fabric. It was plaid, but red and green. Louise studied the photo. A person could have more than one plaid shirt. He was wearing green and blue today, but he could have been wearing red and green a couple of days ago. Or had the fabric been green and another colour initially? Was that red dye and a part of the pattern, or was it blood?

The sudden disappearance of the sunlight shining on her face impelled Louise to raise her head. She jumped back. Hoodie Man was standing directly in front of her, his spooky grin revealing cracked, yellow-stained teeth. Was he a smoker? There'd been a cigarette butt at the crime scene.

Louise gulped. This man was very close and much larger than she was, and he had an army of followers behind him. If he was a murderer, would he hesitate to take another life? Would he do it in front of these women? How dedicated to him were they?

The questions raced through her mind as she tried to think

of a way to escape. Her car was right behind her. She could grab the door handle and try to jump in, but the man could easily grab her arm and pull her back out. Louise looked down at his feet and was momentarily distracted by wondering what his shoe size was.

She raised her head and looked him in the eye. "Hi." She could think of nothing else to say. He didn't smell of cigarette smoke, but it might be masked by the strong, cheap cologne he was wearing. The chemicals entered her nostrils and lungs, inciting a cough.

Louise coughed several times. The man backed up. *Afraid of germs, are you?* She faked a few more coughs. Once he was a comfortable distance away, Louise scooted away from her car and moved toward the clearing that would take her to Sandra's office.

Hoodie Man returned to his group and spoke to Beth Gilley, who then approached Louise. Louise's instincts about the man were right. *He keeps his own hands clean while getting pawns like Beth to do his dirty work.* Beth's small stature, short legs, and curved spine kept her pace slow. As the woman drew closer, Louise kept her eyes on Hoodie Man and Joan Williams, now in a heated conversation.

Beth shot her twig-like finger into Louise's face. "You need to leave. We know what you're up to."

Louise shook her head at the repetition of the same nonsense she'd heard yesterday from Erica Cotton. "What are we up to?" She recalled the sign Erica had been holding. "You do know that this centre is here to treat injured and orphaned *local* wildlife, don't you? They don't care for imported animals. No exotic animals. You've been misinformed."

Beth pushed her hands into her hips. "I don't think so.

Keith knows all about what's going on in there. He has sources that keep him informed."

"Informed of what?"

"Animals shouldn't be kept in zoos. It's not the natural order of things."

"That's a fairly subjective statement. Who determines what the natural order of things is? You? Your leader? What did you call him? Keith? Keith what?"

Beth's eyes widened and she shot a look over her shoulder. The fragile woman was obviously nervous that she'd just revealed her leader's first name. "You should go." The bony finger returned to pointing in Louise's face.

"I will go, as soon as my work here is done." Louise pushed the finger out of her way, then lowered her face closer to Beth's. "Take your own advice. Go. Get out of here, away from those people over there. Something tells me they're up to more than they're telling you."

"Don't be foolish. Keith has done more for animals than anyone else ever has. If it wasn't for him, lots of species would be wiped out already, including bees and butterflies."

Louise let out a spontaneous laugh at the foolish comment. "Is that what he told you?"

She stared into Beth Gilley's eyes, unsure if the woman really believed her own words. Sadly, Beth appeared convinced that this poorly dressed, poorly groomed, noxious man was the ultimate champion of the animal kingdom. *I guess that's how cults start.* Louise felt a pang of pity for Beth and the other women. What was missing in their lives that they were so easily taken in by a self-proclaimed saviour?

Chapter 22

LOUISE CHECKED THE time as she pulled into the clinic's parking lot. The schedule allocated noon to two every Wednesday for a staff meeting, giving the veterinary team time to discuss ongoing cases, client concerns, and other topics that might have arisen since the last meeting. Team members were encouraged to share issues that came up in their departments, but also to share positive stories to lift each other up.

Louise had managed to return soon enough to participate in the last ten minutes of the meeting. As she made her way to the staff room on the upper level, she hoped there was pizza left—a staff meeting must-have—because she'd forgotten to pick something up on her way back from SWaRF.

Rita's voice was audible in the hallway. "There's still some pizza here. Let's get it eaten."

Louise went from a natural pace to a trot. "Save some for me!"

When she entered the meeting, Rita was holding out a plate with two slices of steaming pizza and smiling. "We saw you pull up and heard you on the stairs. I knew the thought of missing out would get you running."

Louise feigned a grumpy face, then laughed. "Funny girl." She took the plate from Rita. "Thank you!"

As she gobbled up her first slice of Canadian pizza, over-flowing with bacon and mushrooms, Louise knew she'd regret it later when the spicy tomato sauce activated her gastric reflux, but currently it filled her need for a full stomach. After eight years as a veterinarian, the stress of the job was getting to her physically and antacids were her new best friends.

Shirley, who'd been off sick the past two days, was seated beside Louise. The married mother of two teenagers was the younger of the two full-time receptionists. Once her kids had been old enough to take care of themselves after school, Shirley was eager to get back into the work force.

With a full mouth, Louise whispered, "Nice to see you back. Is everything okay?"

Shirley put on a half-smile and shrugged.

Oh no. Louise didn't like that reaction. Shirley had been with them a few years now and was an outstanding reception-ist, but lately she'd had to deal with more than her fair share of cranky clients. Being a receptionist in any business was dif-ficult; you were on the front lines, the first to deal with clients or customers. Being a receptionist in an emotionally charged environment like a veterinary clinic took a special type of strength. Louise made a mental note to talk with Shirley as soon as she had a free moment.

Rita announced the clinic hours for the upcoming Easter long weekend—not this weekend but the next. As usual, they'd be closed on Good Friday as well as on the Saturday, allowing everyone a three-day weekend. Cheers and clapping followed.

Rita continued. "As usual, we'll refer all urgent cases to B-REC from Thursday evening to Monday morning over the long weekend. The outgoing voice message will be set to inform clients that any needed medication refills should be taken care of by Thursday. Our social media pages will also have that information."

Rita looked at Daphne and held her gaze, then did the same with Louise. Her pursed lips told Louise that Rita was upset about something. "Speaking of social media . . . Daphne, Louise, we should chat in your office after we're done here." Rita shook her head. "Anyway . . . Louise, any updates on Major?"

Louise swallowed her last bite of lunch, then wiped tomato sauce from her cheeks. "Major's off his food again and now he's vomiting. I've arranged his transfer here this afternoon. He'll be given an oral sedative before the trip, and when he gets here, we'll top that up as needed so we can get an IV line into him. He'll need to be under full anaesthetic for the rads and the ultrasound."

"Jenny and I can help out with that." Heidi opened a can of cola and took a drink. "Eric is on front office this afternoon. Melanie can help him with the heartworm tests."

"Sure, that'll be way more fun than helping with a coyote." Melanie gave her a mock frown.

"Hey, working with me is always fun!" Eric tapped his chest and threw his hands in the air.

"Oh yeah, I forgot." Melanie playfully rolled her eyes.

"Will Major make it to us this time?" Daphne was sitting on the far side of the room, under the window, with her feet on a stool, and her legs crossed at the ankles. "Any more issues with the protestors?"

Louise slowly shook her head. "I don't anticipate any issues. The police are still there investigating the murder scene. They'll make sure Sandra and Major get out of SWaRF without an issue, so we should be good to go this afternoon." She said a silent prayer that this would be the case.

"Everybody has a cause these days. In my fifty . . . um"—Mary cleared her throat—"plus years, I've never seen so many protests about so many things than in the past couple of years. It's one thing to have a passion for a cause, but some of the people are just crazy."

Louise appreciated Mary's honesty and couldn't argue with her about the unhinged behaviour some protestors displayed nowadays, but she was reminded of Alex's comment about her own behaviour of late. Her thoughts and words were becoming less kind as she allowed her many frustrations to take over. "I suspect most activists start out with admirable goals, but somewhere along the line, their passion takes them to places they never intended to go. No doubt some of it's due to misunderstandings—people read things on the internet without knowing the facts. And I'm sure some people have been misinformed by stronger personalities, or they honestly think they know more about a situation than anyone else."

Louise thought back to her encounter with Beth and Keith. "And who knows, they might have been influenced by a cult-like leader—a narcissistic personality. It's scary to think that a person with little knowledge about a subject can talk with great confidence and convince others that he knows everything." Louise was thinking about the ARSE leader, Keith, and how Beth Gilley claimed he was all-knowing.

"The good ol' Dunning-Kruger effect." Daphne intertwined her fingers and rested the back of her head in her hands.

"Exactly." Louise, who had no idea what the Dunning-Kruger effect was—she'd have to look it up later—saw no reason not to agree. Daphne had taken philosophy in college and often came up with insightful tidbits of information.

Louise continued her observations. "Of course, there's also the profit motive. If you support a cause that can garner a lot of sympathy, especially from wealthy people who want to show a positive public image, you can bring in a lot of money. Where does that money go? Does anyone care? I'm sure some do, but others are merely virtue signalling to build up their own status."

"Wow, Louise, you've given this a lot of thought." Heidi tossed her cola can into the recycling bin across the room.

"I've been doing a lot of driving the past few days, so I've had a lot of time to think."

Jenny, their resident artist who always sketched during meetings, closed her notebook and shoved it into a backpack. "Roger says some of these protestors are actually criminals. Terrorists even." She chuckled. "Terrorists—right. I think he's been inhaling too much fishy lake air." Roger, Jenny's long-time boyfriend, worked at the Bathurst Region docks unloading cargo containers from ships. "He told me that security is getting tighter at his work all the time because of all the illegal imports."

The doorbell alerted the group to their first client, or possibly a delivery. The clinic entrance was locked during their staff meetings, and a sign was posted on the front door informing clients that they reopened at 2:00 pm, along with a phone number to call in case of an emergency.

Rita looked at the wall clock. "Looks like we've gone a few minutes over. I think we've covered everything."

Without saying a word, Mary rushed downstairs to let the bell ringer into the building.

As the rest of the team flowed out of the room, Louise remained seated. Erica Cotton, otherwise known as Plump-in-Plum, had been carrying a sign yesterday that said STOP THE IMPORTS. Louise wondered what imports the sign was referring to, as SWaRF didn't import animals—nor did they rehab exotic animals. If exotics were brought into Sandra's rehab centre, the animals were transferred to a facility better equipped to care for them.

Was this a case of misinformation, or was someone importing exotic animals and using SWaRF as a cover? Bailey Nelson had a complicated network of computer equipment in his home, had access to SWaRF, and he was now missing. Was he importing exotic animals and transporting them via cargo ships? Louise pondered the complexity of getting a live animal on and off a cargo ship that carried hundreds of containers from all over the world. It would be a risky venture in two ways: you could get caught by the authorities, and the chances that the animals would be alive on arrival were very low.

The other option for smugglers would be the airport. Louise's heart started to race. She wondered if she should get in touch with Alex ASAP, because if Bailey had been using the airport, that would be a connection between the murder and the bombing. She jumped out of her seat, ready to call her detective friend, but stopped short of hitting dial. She was expecting him to drop in later, and besides, the Tobin Memorial Airport was for short-haul domestic flights only. If Bailey was using that airport to smuggle exotic animals into the country, how was he doing it?

Chapter 23

LOUISE'S HEART DID a flip-flop when she found Rita and Daphne sitting together at Daphne's desk, both of them staring at the computer monitor. Daphne's hand was over her mouth, her head slowly shaking while Rita rubbed her back in a supportive, reassuring manner. *Now what?*

"Should I even ask what's going on?" Louise held her breath, hoping she'd misinterpreted their body language.

"It's a head-scratcher. I can't believe someone could be so hateful and mean. We did everything we could for Perdy, and now this!" Daphne stood abruptly and raised her fist at the computer. "I almost missed two important nights with Ella . . . and this is . . . I don't even know what to say." She flopped back down.

Rita stood and moved the guest chair she'd been sitting on out of the way so Louise could see what the women had been reading.

Louise read the entry on a social media review site, then hit the keyboard, closing the window. "Why, that ungrateful . . ." She looked at Rita. "When did this show up?"

"This morning. I check the reviews before staff meetings in case there's something we should discuss. There rarely is, but you never know. Now this." Rita rolled her eyes. "I didn't want to bring it up at the meeting."

"Can we report it and have it taken down?" Louise eyed Daphne while speaking to Rita. With everything that had happened in the past couple of days, a nasty review on social media, especially one personally attacking Daphne, was the last thing they needed.

Rita pulled her chair closer, started to sit, then aborted the plan. "You really should replace this old thing. It's horrible on the back. Anyway, I'll try to get the post removed, but it can be difficult with some of these sites, and it can take a few days, if not weeks." She looked at Daphne and attempted a smile. "But you know, people don't pay attention to stuff like that. Our loyal clients will know that the review came from a bitter person and has no basis in reality."

Daphne wiped her eyes. "I know. I shouldn't be worrying about the words of one angry person, but we tried so hard to save that poor cat. Mrs. Theobald did nothing for him, and now she's claiming his death is my fault."

Louise made fists. "Can we post a response? One that doesn't break client confidentiality rules but lets readers know that the woman's lying?"

Daphne sniffled. "That could be tricky."

"Let me work on this. I'll get the post removed, or figure out an appropriate response." Rita backed toward the door. "I didn't want to upset you, Daphne, but I thought it would be better if you and Louise knew it was there before a client mentioned it."

"For sure, Rita. Thanks. Let us know what you come up with." Louise settled into her chair as she watched Rita leave the office.

"We really should replace that chair." Louise hoped that the change in subject would take Daphne's mind off Mrs. Theobald's vitriolic words.

"I've been saying that for months." Smiling, Alex appeared in the doorway, but once he looked at Daphne, his smile disappeared. "What's going on?"

Daphne shook her head but remained silent.

Louise, sensing Daphne was done talking about the review, waved her hand dismissively. "Nothing." When Daphne turned her head away, Louise whispered to Alex, "I'll tell you later."

He pursed his lips and nodded in an "I understand" manner. "I got your text about some information you had for me about the missing employee."

Louise rejoiced at the perfect timing. Watching Alex's annoyance with Louise over her interference with his investigation was bound to get Daphne's mind off the nasty review. "Sandra Kelly and I took a trip to Bailey Nelson's home last night." Louise studied Alex's face for a reaction. Nothing. If he was upset, he gave no hint of it. "Sandra was worried about him, so I offered to go with her to check on him."

"Offered? Or suggested?" Alex crossed his arms, his face remaining neutral.

Louise shrugged. "Tomayto, tomahto."

He frowned. "Not really, but go on."

"The back door was unlocked—we didn't break in or anything."

"Hmm."

Louise held Alex's gaze. He was behaving as though he already knew they'd been there. "When we first got there, we were going to leave, but then Sandra was concerned that Bailey's truck was too tidy."

"Too tidy?" Alex remained expressionless.

"Yeah. I guess he's normally messy. Anyway, there was no answer when we knocked, so we made our way around the back. Like I said, the back door was unlocked, so we went in to see if he was inside, and if so, to make sure he was okay."

"Was he there?"

"No, but he did have a big assortment of computer equipment, and . . ." Louise stopped herself. She didn't want to get Bailey into trouble by telling Alex that he might be linked to ARSE, but she also didn't want to withhold information if Bailey was in trouble and needed help. She'd share bits of information and see what direction the conversation went. "There was a bloody wrench in the backyard."

Alex inhaled and frowned again. "What do you mean *was*? Where is it now?" He leaned his back against the window ledge. "The warrant to search Mr. Nelson's home came in early this morning. Julie Corridor, the lead agent from the Forensics Investigation Unit, reported a large quantity of dried blood on the grass and back patio, but her team didn't find a wrench."

"We didn't take it, if that's what you're thinking, but while we were inside, someone entered the backyard. Sandra and I stayed out of sight until she left. We noticed afterwards that the wrench was gone, so she must have taken it. She didn't try to get in the house, so we assumed she came just for the wrench."

Alex uncrossed his arms and stood up straight. "*She? She who?*"

Louise shrugged. "I can't be one hundred percent positive, but I'm sure it was Beth Gilley. The intruder had the same build and was wearing a hoodie. Beth was wearing a hoodie when I saw her at the rehab centre today."

Daphne, who'd been sitting quietly watching the exchange, spoke up. "You told me that Beth Gilley was a tiny frail woman. You think she whacked someone with a wrench, then returned for it?"

Louise shook her head, then filled her Keurig with water. "No. I can't imagine Beth would have the strength the hold a wrench above her head, never mind injure anyone with it. I mean, she'd have to whack someone hard enough to make them bleed a lot. You know"—Louise lifted a spoon above her head and swung her arm down to demonstrate hitting someone with force—"like that! I think she was cleaning up after someone else."

Daphne scrunched her face. "Oh, that's awful."

Louise hadn't thought about the amount of blood at the scene until this moment. When she and Sandra had been at Bailey's home, it was too dark to see the surrounding area clearly. If there was a lot of blood and it was Bailey's, he probably needed medical attention quickly—if he was still alive.

Louise shot a worried look at Alex. "It was too dark when we were there. If I'd seen a lot of blood, I would have called

911 right away. Was there a blood trail? Do you think someone could have survived that type of injury?"

"From what Julie told me, it's possible, but there wasn't so much blood that they could be certain the victim succumbed to the injuries." Alex paused briefly. "I'm not happy that you went over there last night, but I guess if you hadn't, we wouldn't know that a possible weapon's now missing. And we wouldn't know the description of the person who retrieved it. Julie's team collected samples for DNA testing, and they fingerprinted the whole scene. I suppose I'll have to let them know your prints may turn up?"

Louise smiled. "No worries. We wore gloves." She scratched her head. "Well, there might be a few of Sandra's prints on the truck."

Alex produced a notepad and pen and jotted down some notes. "Did you find anything else in the house I should know about?"

Louise stared at the ceiling, then turned away from Alex to finish setting up the coffee maker. "Nothing your team won't find on their own."

"Good to know." Alex popped the notepad into his jacket pocket. "Daphne, can you let Joe know that I won't be at the men's Bible study tonight? Between the bombing at the airport and the murder at the rehab centre, the police department is swamped. Every able body is doing what they're able."

Louise was pleased that he felt well enough to make corny jokes. "How's Norman Talbot doing?"

"On his way to *human* rehab in a few days. He's expected to make a full recovery."

"That's good news!"

Alex approached Louise's desk, and now it was his turn to

hold her gaze. "Do I need to remind you to stay away from Bailey Nelson's home now that it's considered a crime scene?"

Louise flopped into her chair and shuffled the files that were on her desk. "No. You don't. I promise I won't go back there."

He frowned at her, then turned and left the office. She knew he didn't believe her, but she was telling him the truth. She and Sandra had thoroughly investigated Bailey's home, and she was certain there was nothing more to be found. Besides, the crime scene team would find anything they'd missed.

The intercom buzzed and Mary said, "Sandra called to say that they're about fifteen minutes away with Major. I'll let you know when they pull into the parking lot."

Louise hit the talk button. "Thanks, Mary." She opened her internet search engine and typed in *Causes of vomiting in wild coyotes.*

She was assaulted with a list of various infectious organisms, canine viruses such as parvovirus and canine distemper, and assorted poisons. Louise's heart sank. None of those could be diagnosed via radiographs and ultrasound, and the lab work they'd already done was normal. As per his blood results, Major's kidneys, liver, and other abdominal organs were healthy.

When the young coyote was first found by a couple of hikers, he was severely dehydrated and almost non-responsive. He was weak enough that Sandra's team at SWaRF could easily transport him to the rehab centre.

"What is going on with you, Major?" Louise tapped on the edge of the keyboard as she rested her hands over it, hoping the search engine would suddenly shoot out the answers she needed. It didn't. "I guess we'll have to resort to good ol' medical diagnostics to get the answer. Imagine that—the internet doesn't know everything after all!"

She laughed at her own joke and glanced at Daphne to see if her friend was smiling. They shared an odd sense of humour; the things that made them laugh were often lost on others. Daphne's weakness for Louise's bad jokes was one of the many things Louise appreciated about her. While others might give Louise a confused look, she knew that her best friend would crack up in a fit of laughter.

She was disappointed to see Daphne staring at the computer, not even a slight curve to her lip. The distraction of Alex's visit was a short one; Daphne was thinking about the negative review again.

Louise said, "I'm tempted to suggest that Mrs. Theobald functions surprisingly well for someone with so much air in her head, but Alex pointed out last night that some of my comments lately have been less than loving."

Without looking away from the monitor, Daphne said, "I can't say I disagree with either of you."

Before Louise could respond, Mary buzzed again. "They're here!"

Looking at Daphne, Louise cocked her head. This was indeed unusual behaviour for her business partner and friend. They needed to talk, but first she had to get to Major before the sedatives he'd been given at SWaRF wore off. They'd top them up with either more sedative-laced treats or an injection, depending on his level of alertness in the van.

Louise swung her stethoscope over her neck and picked up her life-giving cup of caffeine. "Hey, why don't we do something this evening? Doesn't Joe take the kids to his mother's house on Bible study nights? We could do dinner. Maybe a movie?"

"Sure." Daphne forced a smile.

On the way to the treatment room, Daphne's response to Louise's comment about Mrs. Theobald played in Louise's head on a continuous loop. Daphne not only agreed with Alex that Louise's comments were becoming mean-spirited, but also that Mrs. Theobald was an airhead. Earlier, Daphne had agreed with Louise that the same client was a dough-head. It was unlike Daphne to support this kind of joking, giving Louise alarm that her friend was teetering on the edge of burnout.

She said a prayer for Daphne before heading out to the van that housed her wild patient, hopefully still heavily sedated.

Chapter 24

AFTER TOPPING UP Major's sedation with an intramuscular injection, crew members from SWaRF and the Black Creek Animal Hospital worked together to transfer the young coyote safely into the clinic. Once in the treatment room, Heidi and Jenny intubated Major and administered gas anaesthetic before transferring him to the radiology room.

Setting up for the ultrasound in the adjoining room, Louise heard the familiar beep of the X-ray machine, followed by Heidi's angry voice. "That's maddening."

Louise glanced down at the tablet beside her that showed an image of the coyote's radiograph. A fish hook was clearly visible in Major's stomach.

"Humans suck." Heidi continued. "Some lazy person tosses his garbage on the ground after a day of fishing instead of using a garbage can, and this poor little creature suffers for it."

Louise peeked around the corner in time to see Jenny nod in agreement as Major was moved onto his back for the next radiograph. Because Louise wasn't wearing protective gear, she retreated back to the ultrasound room before Jenny stepped on the paddle to get the second X-ray.

"This view confirms it's still in his stomach. Let's move him back onto his side." Jenny could be heard saying. "Sometimes the hooks are still in the fish, and when it dies and washes up on shore, the scavengers get hooked while enjoying a meal. Last summer a dog in Georgetown died after swallowing a fish hook. I don't remember the details, but there was a big call to have more garbage cans available in popular fishing areas. I don't think it helped, though. I've been down there since, and it's not unusual to see garbage on the ground right beside an empty garbage can."

Heidi called out. "Louise, we're done with the rads. As I'm sure you heard, there's a fish hook in the stomach. Do you still want to do an ultrasound?"

Louise joined the techs in the X-ray room. "I saw the rads on the tablet. We'll proceed with the ultrasound. That fish hook might be the cause of his recent inappetence and vomiting, but it's possible it's been in there a long time. Sometimes the body will deal with a foreign object by walling it off with the equivalent of scar tissue. And if it's the fish hook causing his issues, it may have perforated and led to peritonitis. It's best to know what we're dealing with ahead of surgery, and we still can't rule out pancreatitis."

Heidi and Jenny transferred Major to the small ultrasound room, then clipped the fur on his belly after placing him on his back in a soft trough. Louise started the scan at his bladder, then worked her way around his abdomen, checking all of his organs, including his kidneys, spleen, liver, and gastrointestinal tract. She finished with his pancreas. "Other than the metal in his stomach, everything looks good. I hate to think how long that thing's been in there causing him pain—his body condition tells me it might be weeks. Thank God the hikers found him when they did."

Louise wiped the gel from the ultrasound probe and her hands before giving Major a chin rub. "We'll take him into surgery right away. There's no point in allowing him to wake up, then stressing him again tomorrow to re-anaesthetize him. Daphne can probably stay later and cover the appointments—Joe and the kids will be out tonight."

Louise had mixed feelings about asking an already stressed Daphne to cover so Major could have his surgery. It would be ideal if Daphne could have a quiet evening at home to relax, but they didn't have any other choice—it was too late to cancel the remaining appointments. They'd been looking for a new associate veterinarian since their last one had gotten himself into some serious legal trouble, but the veterinary community was experiencing a shortage of vets.

Louise tied the last skin suture, then used a gauze square to wipe off the small amount of blood around the wound. "That does it. Thankfully, the hook came out without needing to remove any of the stomach wall. The intestines are a healthy pink colour—I gave them a good massage to get them moving." She pulled off her surgical gloves and gown and tossed them into the garbage and surgical laundry respectively. "We'll need to recover Major in his transport kennel, and once he's awake enough to stand, we can send him back to SWaRF. Sandra's on standby to pick him up."

Heidi grinned. "I don't suppose the gang at B-REC would appreciate us sending them a wild coyote."

"Nope. Ideally, he'd have twenty-four-hour monitoring at a fully equipped veterinary clinic, but the rehab centre does have an RVT on staff who's offered to stay with him overnight. Sandra and another staff member will sleep in the staff quarters in the trailer, and I'll be on call if there's something they can't handle. That's the best we can do until the funds are available to set up a hospital ward on site. They have the room, but they can't afford the equipment right now."

Major soon started swallowing, and the endotracheal tube was removed. Louise helped Heidi and Jenny situate him comfortably in his transport cage, and then she headed to the front desk before going to her office to write up the surgical report. She was reminded of how Shirley had acted at the staff meeting and wanted to see what they could do to keep her from quitting.

"Oh, I'm not quitting, Louise. Why would you think that?" Shirley's face said she was bewildered by the thought.

Shirley had seemed upset at the meeting, and Louise immediately assumed it meant she was leaving the clinic. "I'm glad to hear it. You're an important part of our team. We'd have a difficult time replacing you. You've had your fair share of cranky clients lately, so I guess I worried that it had finally gotten to you."

"No." Shirley flipped her hair back. "Well, of course, there are a few 'special' clients." She laughed as she made air quotes around the word "special." "But most are fabulous, like the Morrisons. Mary tells me they brought snacks for everyone as a thank you for caring for Jack."

"And then there's Mrs. Theobald." Louise rolled her eyes to the ceiling.

"True, but clients like that are rare. And besides, I wasn't here to deal with her." Shirley laughed again.

"I'm glad you have a healthy—or should I say positive—perspective on things."

"I'm not quitting, but I will need to take a few days off next month. I was so sick the past few days. The doctor says it's . . . some kind of colic. I thought that was a horse thing, but it has to do with my gallbladder. It needs to come out."

"Biliary colic?"

Shirley pointed into the air. "Yes! That's it."

"Well, I'm relieved. Not that you have to have your gallbladder out, but that you're not leaving. Just let Rita know what you need and I'm sure we can accommodate it." She was so relieved Shirley wasn't quitting, she would have okayed a month off with pay if Shirley had asked for it. Luckily, Louise didn't say that out loud and Shirley didn't make the request. Louise was also grateful for the reminder that most of their clients were amazing people.

She found Daphne enjoying a brief break between appointments in the staff room. "Hey, there you are. I can cover the rest of the appointments if you want to take off. I'm still game for a movie and dinner if you are, but if you want to go home and see the kids before they head to Grandma's, I've got you covered."

Daphne stirred her tea, then added more sugar. "Joe's already dropped them off. It's almost five thirty."

Louise looked at the clock on the wall. "How did that happen? I guess I was in surgery longer than I thought. How are you doing?"

"I'm okay. Still thinking about that nasty review, but Rita assures me she'll take care of it. I know I shouldn't let it get to me, but—"

"But nothing. We're all human, and being treated badly by someone you're trying to help hurts." Louise rummaged through the cabinets, looking for a snack. "Hey, why don't we skip the movie and head up to SWaRF later? Sandra should be picking Major up soon. We can check to see how he's getting settled, and I can show you around the place."

"Isn't it still a crime scene?"

"Just the pond area—they still have the yellow police tape up. That's in the back of the property. Sandra's office and the animal habitats are on the other side of a small wooded area."

Louise was offering the trip to SWaRF as a distraction for Daphne, but what she really wanted to do was visit the airport.

"Oh no. What are you thinking?" Daphne knew innately when Louise was scheming.

"I'm just thinking that after we hit SWaRF, it's not that much farther to the airport."

"Oh no."

Louise understood Daphne's concern. After all, Alex had repeatedly warned her to stay out of the investigation and away from the airport, but something was eating away at her. There was a good possibility that the bombing at the airport and the murder at the rehab centre were connected. She wouldn't interfere, she'd just get as close as possible and see what she could see. And it wouldn't hurt if an officer or two she knew were around; she could milk them for information.

Louise's heart fluttered as she focused on her new objective. "Come on—there's nothing to worry about. The police are still all over the place. How much trouble can we get into?"

Chapter 25

DINNER OUT CONSISTED of a burger and fries purchased via a Wendy's drive-thru.

"We can eat out next Wednesday. I'll even treat again." Louise had a twinge of guilt. She didn't want to cheat Daphne out of a nice meal, but she couldn't shake the urgency to get to the airport. "I thought we'd be at SWaRF longer, but now we have lots of time to see if we can get close to the area where the explosion happened." Louise plucked a stray piece of bacon that had dropped from her burger and tossed it into her mouth. She crumpled the foil wrapper and tossed it into the back seat.

"Eating out next Wednesday sounds good to me. Especially the part about you paying." Daphne covered her mouth as she talked and chewed. "But you're insane if you think you'll get anywhere near the blast site."

When they'd arrived at Sydney's Wildlife Rehabilitation Facility, they found that Major, who was already resettled into his habitat, was clearly more comfortable than he'd been earlier that day, as demonstrated by his straight back and steady gait. He was no longer walking tip-toed with his abdomen hunched up. Louise instructed Sandra to offer him small amounts of water frequently but to withhold food until the morning so the incision in his stomach wall would have some time to start healing.

Louise had decided to forgo giving Daphne a tour because Sandra was busy getting things ready for their overnight coyote-monitoring session. And as well as feeling the stress of a sick animal on site, Sandra was still stressed by Bailey's disappearance, and finding Tina's body in the pond. Daphne agreed that it wasn't an appropriate time for a tour.

Louise and Daphne ate their dinner and chatted in the car as they made their way to Tobin Memorial Airport, approximately thirty minutes west of the rehab centre. As usual when they spent time alone, their conversation wandered from their current objective to random speculation.

Daphne emptied the container that had held her fries, folded it up, and tossed it into the back seat.

Louise gave her friend the side-eye. "Hey!"

Daphne shrugged. "*You* tossed your garbage back there. I was just being polite and following my hostess's lead."

"Fair enough." Louise turned on her left turn signal as they approached a four-way stop. She waited for the two vehicles that had been waiting their turn to proceed, then turned onto the street that would take them to their destination. "Did Joe say what tonight's Bible study is about?" She was fishing for information—she wondered if part of Daphne's stress was related to anything happening at home. If so, perhaps she'd open up and talk about it on their drive.

"Something about the Good Samaritan, I think. He's been a bit of a good Samaritan himself the past couple of weeks. One of the men in the young adults' group has been struggling with some of his first-year college courses, and Joe's been trying to help him. I think it was statistics, but honestly, it just sounded like a lot of gibberish to me."

"Statistics? Gibberish? I can see that. I forgot most of what we learned in that class the day after I completed the final exam."

"Right? Why was statistics a pre-vet requirement, anyway? The only word I remember is probability. That's it." Daphne's tone didn't give any indication she was stressed outside of work. In fact, she'd been more like her normal self since they left the clinic parking lot.

"And don't get me started on complicated maths like calculus. I had over ninety percent in that class, but I couldn't tell you a sine versus cosine now." Louise playfully slapped her forehead.

Daphne rubbed her chin. "Um, I think that might be trigonometry, not calculus."

Louise shrugged and laughed. "I'm not going to argue."

Daphne straightened up in her seat and leaned toward Louise. "And what was up with physics?"

There was a moment of silence as they pondered the point of the physics requirement in veterinary medicine.

As the sun disappeared behind a row of tall maple trees on a hill, Louise removed her sunglasses. She was relieved that the rainy weather they'd seen over the past few days had moved on, and clear skies were predicted for the remainder of the week.

Daphne rolled down her window and inhaled deeply. "Ah! The smell of the country."

Louise giggled and shook her head. She could count on Daphne to say that very same thing every time they passed a pasture. Initially, Louise was disgusted by the odour, but if pushed, she had to admit that the smell of a cow field was a pleasant reminder of a peaceful country drive.

As a theory about the course requirements came to her, Louise tapped her lips with her forefinger. "I suppose if a vet is examining the back end of a cranky horse, she could calculate the force with which the hind leg of the animal might contact her torso. And taking into account the distance to the barn wall and the velocity with which she might be propelled toward said wall, then the force . . ." She turned to Daphne. "Is that the correct term?"

Daphne shrugged.

Louise returned her attention to the road and continued. "She could then deduce the probability of having a fractured vertebra upon contact with the wall. I'm sure there's some mathematical formula you could use that involves the horse's weight, the distance to the wall, and the veterinarian's body mass."

Daphne nodded and slapped her knee. "That's it! It makes complete sense now. That's why we had to take all those courses."

"I'm glad I was able to clear that up for you."

Louise was thrilled to hear Daphne let loose a belly-fuelled, hard-to-catch-your-breath laugh as they pulled into the airport's overflow public parking lot. The lots closer to the hangars and terminal were still inaccessible to the public, as indicated by multiple signs warning drivers they were off limits.

Beyond the temporary security fencing that, according to Alex, had been erected within hours of the explosion, Louise counted a minimum of six vans and SUVs marked with the logos of the Ontario Provincial Police, the Canada Border Services Agency, and the Canadian Transportation Agency, as well as two RCMP Tactical Armoured Vehicles. There were also several Bathurst Region Police Department squad cars, which explained why the local force was still stretched thin.

She was transfixed by the sight before her. "Alex wasn't kidding when he said there were multiple agencies involved. There's a box van over there with the Government of Canada logo on it." Louise looked over at Daphne. "Do you think there's a high-ranking politician here?"

Daphne's lips twisted as she thought about the possibility. "Travelling in a van? I'd think they'd have a nice car, maybe even a limo."

Louise nodded. "You're probably right. So what . . . ?" She retrieved a backpack from the back seat, then pulled out a set of binoculars. "There's another logo on the body of the van— CITES. I wonder what that is."

"I don't know." Daphne sighed. "Remind me why we're here?" She released her seat belt.

Louise thought about her response. Her reason for including Daphne was to distract her from Mrs. Theobald's social media review, but Louise didn't want to share that with her. "I know we can't enter the secure areas, but it doesn't hurt to walk around and see what we can find." She pointed into the distance. "There're some photographers over there. Probably waiting for the big-money shot they can sell to the media. Maybe we can blend in with them?"

"Shouldn't be a problem. I'm sure no one would question why we're using phone cameras rather than professional ones."

"Hmm . . . good point." Louise unbuckled her seat belt and opened the door. "We'll have to play it by ear. At least the surrounding roads aren't taped off anymore. I didn't think we'd get this close."

Louise flung the backpack over her shoulder, then she and her fellow veterinarian-turned-amateur-sleuth headed toward the photographers. Louise stopped abruptly when she noticed that a young officer she'd met at one of Alex's work-related barbecues was standing guard about fifty feet from a clearing in the trees. He was keeping a close eye on the photographers and didn't notice Louise as she approached him.

Louise was tempted to sneak past him, under the tape, and then make her way closer to the explosion site, but she didn't want to get him into trouble. Stephen Mack, sporting a day's-growth beard and short brown hair, had been on the force for two years. Louise wondered if he'd recognize her. She didn't have to wonder for long.

"Dr. Miller, what are you doing here? Are you looking for Detective Hines?"

"No. I'm sure he's busy." In an attempt to look innocent, Louise pressed her index finger to her lips. "To be honest, Stephen . . . Sorry, Officer Mack."

"Stephen's fine." He looked at the ground, then dug the toe of his shoe into the long grass.

Was he naturally shy? Or was he intimidated by the lead detective's friend? Or is it girlfriend? Louise's mind railed again, like a surfer riding a wave. She remained uncertain about what she and Alex were to each other. Friends, of course, but was there more to it?

Daphne tapped her on the shoulder. "You okay?"

Louise jumped. "What? Of course." She looked over Stephen's shoulder to see if the airport buildings were visible from this vantage point. They weren't.

"Hey, Stephen, any word on the evidence found in the plane? You know . . . What was it again?" She glanced back at Daphne, hoping Stephen would assume that she and Daphne already knew what was found.

"The . . . ?" Stephen put his hands in his pockets and squinted at Louise. "I don't believe that information has been released to the public."

Louise wasn't going to get any more information from him. He was still fairly new to the job, but he was well trained and a quick thinker.

Stephen's attention soon turned to the group of photographers. "Hey, you can't go over there. Get back!" He ran toward the paparazzi as one of them was lifting a section of the yellow police tape.

Louise and Daphne looked at each other, then at the tape. Daphne grabbed Louise's arm and dragged her in the opposite direction. "Don't even *think* about going under that tape."

Louise frowned. "Stop reading my mind. Anyway, I have a better idea. Let's walk around the periphery of the airport and see if we can spot anything interesting. We won't go beyond the yellow tape, or any security fences." Louise, backpack still on her shoulder, marched away from the photographers and Officer Mack.

Daphne rushed to meet Louise's pace. "What's in the back-pack?"

"A few essentials. The binoculars, of course, as well as a couple of black jackets, black gloves, and black toques."

Daphne froze. "Excuse me? What would we need that stuff for?"

Louise quickly surveilled the immediate area for anyone who might have overheard Daphne. They were out of earshot of Stephen and the photographers, and she didn't spot anyone else. "In case we need to blend in if it gets dark before we leave. It'll work to our advantage—trust me."

Daphne's eyebrows met in the middle. "Hmm."

They'd wound their way around what Louise estimated to be half of the barricaded airport before she spotted anything interesting. The hangar and office building that had borne the brunt of the explosion were situated in the northeast corner of the property. Louise had parked in the overflow lot in the southwest corner—the only area open for public vehicles.

They had gone west, Louise theorizing that the bulk of the investigators would be on the east side of Tobin Memorial Airport. She appeared to be correct, as they'd walked around the fencing without encountering anyone.

"Just because we didn't see anyone doesn't mean they didn't see us," Daphne said.

"True. But if the guards objected to us being here, they would have stopped us, don't you think?" Louise stretched her hand out behind her, her palm up, indicating that Daphne should halt. "Look closer at the pile of garbage over there."

Beyond the wire fence, a pile of fractured building material covered a large area in front of an intact hangar.

"That must be where they're moving the debris while they sift through the wreckage," Louise said.

"It looks like metal, plastic, insulation, and drywall. It's too far away to see anything specific."

Louise covered her nose with the palm of her hand. The odour reminded her of the smell of burnt flesh in the hospital the other day, mixed with the acrid stench of burnt building materials.

Daphne's scrunched nose told Louise that her companion had also picked up the scent. "I can only imagine how big the blast was, and the fire afterwards, if jet fuel was ignited."

Louise thought back to the scenes at the hospital. Burn victims with bandages around their heads and limbs. Some with bandages ending where limbs should have been. She sighed.

"It's going to be dark soon. Maybe we should head back to the car." Daphne's voice trembled. Was it nerves or the dropping temperature?

Louise waved her on. "If we keep going in this direction, we'll get back to the car, but first let's try to get a closer look at the pile. See over there? There's a gap between that hangar and the building beside it, the one marked MECHANICAL ROOM."

Daphne's shoulders dropped and she followed Louise toward the two buildings, both of them staying close to the fence line. Louise felt another pang of guilt. *Should I have dragged her out here? What if it's dangerous?*

As they passed the first of the two buildings, Louise turned and faced her friend to let her know she was going to give up and head straight to the car—no more snooping—but just as she did, a wooden crate grabbed her attention. She couldn't turn away from it.

"What are you looking at?" Daphne asked.

"That crate over there. Do you see it?" Louise dropped the backpack to the ground, pulled out the binoculars, and handed them to Daphne. "On the ground, to the right of the smallest pile of drywall and wood."

Daphne put the binoculars up to her face and scanned the area. "I see it. How did you spot that from here?"

"I'm sure I've seen one like it recently. Are there holes in it?"

"I think so. Odd. Why would a transport crate have holes in it?"

"For air!" Adrenalin flooded Louise as she thought back to the sign Erica Cotton had been holding at SWaRF. "What if it's for . . . ?" She pushed on Daphne's shoulder. "Duck!"

As they crouched down out of sight, two guards in uniform exited the back door of the hangar.

The taller of the two popped something into his mouth, then started chewing. He offered something to his co-worker, who shook his head.

Tall Man brushed his hand through his hair. "It's going to take weeks to get through all of the debris. What a mess."

Small Man nodded, then sat on a rusted green utility box. "It's amazing more people weren't hurt, or killed. Man, if that bomb had gone off the day after it did—"

"Not something any of us want to think about. I just hope they catch the person responsible."

As the two men stared at the debris pile in silence, Louise noticed that the sun was on the horizon. She was hoping they wouldn't need the dark clothing to hide them in the dark, and that they'd make it back to the car before the need for flashlights arose. She was about to motion to Daphne to start walking again when the men resumed their conversation.

"Did you hear any more details about what was found in that damaged plane?" Tall Man asked.

"Damaged is an understatement. The owner will be beyond mad, but it seems they can't locate them. Something about the name on the documents being fake."

"Not surprising, considering the cargo they were hauling. Whoever was involved with that operation are low-life scum. I can't figure out how they got them this far undetected."

Louise's heart rate sped up to a trot when Tall Man asked about the findings, then progressed to a full gallop as the men provided details about the plane and its contents. Her knees were starting to ache, but she couldn't move and alert the guards to her and Daphne's presence. If the men thought they'd been overheard, they might arrest Louise and her fellow eavesdropper.

"Have you ever heard of those things? I haven't. I tried to look them up on the internet last night, but the spelling messed me up."

Small Man shrugged, then spit on the ground. "Nope. Not me. I just hope we got them all. One of the border guys was saying that one of the crates was empty. Might be bad for our . . . What did she call it? Ecosystem?"

Eyebrows raised and mouths open, Louise and Daphne whipped their heads around and stared at each other. As though they'd practised, they scoped the area around them in a synchronized fashion, looking for signs of life.

The sitting man stood, then returned to the hangar with his partner.

"What do you think they're talking about?" Louise stood up quickly and wiped off her legs and buttocks, concerned about what might be attached. "Spin around."

Daphne did as she was asked. "Now you."

Louise followed suit. "I don't see anything on you."

"Nor me on you. Can we get out of here, please?"

"Good idea. They have to be talking about animals. Crates with airholes, one possibly escaping."

"And something neither of them had ever heard of. What if it's venomous?" Daphne wiped down her shoulders and legs.

They headed back the way they'd come, and as they approached Louise's car, she said, "Let's go back to SWaRF to check out something I saw the other day when Sandra was showing me around the property."

Daphne's shoulders drooped. "Tonight?"

Louise patted her gently on the shoulder. "Of course. Besides, it doesn't hurt to check on Major again. I'll text Sandra and let her know we're on our way."

Daphne sighed. "Should we call Alex and let him know what we're up to? And don't you think Sandra will need to get some rest? We left SWaRF earlier because you were worried about her needing rest. Remember?"

"Sandra will be fine. She's a strong woman, and she wants to get to the bottom of all of this as much as we do." Louise sent a text.

"I don't believe *we* is the correct pronoun here. *I*"—Daphne pointed at Louise—"as in *you* would be more appropriate."

Still concerned about foreign creatures, Louise dusted off her clothes a second time, then hopped into the car. "I'll hold off on calling Alex for now. First I'll see if my memory is accurate, and if so, I'll fill him in about what I found at SWaRF. There's no point in bothering him if I'm imagining things."

"Are the police still there?" Daphne got into the passenger side and fastened her seat belt.

"I'm not sure. Why?" Louise pushed the button to start the engine.

"Because we're returning to the scene of a murder. Hanging out at murder scenes is becoming old hat for you, but it's new for me."

"I'm sure we'll be fine. There hasn't been any further suspicious activity within the rehab grounds, and I know how to get to the back lot so we don't have to deal with the protestors if they're there tonight."

"I don't know." Daphne went silent for a few minutes as Louise turned onto the main road. "Tell me, did you ever buy that gun you mentioned a few months ago?"

"A gun? What would we need a gun for?"

"Oh, I don't know. Protection against a murderer?"

Louise waved a hand in the air. "No worries. I have my trusty baseball bat in the back seat." She indicated it by nodding over her shoulder.

"I'm not convinced that would be of much help."

Louise chuckled. "Would you really want me handling a gun?"

"Now that you mention it, you and a gun *would* be a bad idea."

The sun had set by time they left the airport, and Louise hoped she could find SWaRF's back entrance in the dark. Sandra had responded to her text, saying she'd meet them by the trailer.

Louise stopped at the four-way intersection and waited her turn to go. "We're all set. What could possibly go wrong?"

In her peripheral vision, she could see Daphne staring at her. "You know, Louise, you say that a lot, and every time you do . . ."

Chapter 26

SANDRA MET LOUISE and Daphne at the office trailer as promised, and then they all walked to the woods surrounding the pond where Tina Purcell's body had been found.

"This is kinda creepy." Daphne, scanning for unseen dangers, directed the beam of her flashlight through the trees in every direction. "But exhilarating at the same time."

"The police aren't here anymore, but they did leave the tape up around the pond. They cautioned me that the area was still off limits. And Louise . . ."

Louise, who'd been leading the way, paused and turned to look at Sandra. "Yes?" She knew what was coming.

Sandra wore a large grin. "Officer Hines specifically mentioned you when saying that no one was to cross the boundary."

Louise shrugged. "No worries. I have no interest in the pond this evening. No, I'm more interested in the brushy area you showed me the other day behind the old barn." She pointed to the right with her flashlight. "It's over this way, if I remember correctly."

"You remember correctly."

They walked cautiously over rocks, fallen leaves, and tree stumps before spotting a small barn that had once housed sheep but was now used to store tools and an ATV.

"It was around the back, between the barn and the fence." Louise hurried along the side of the building, doing her best to avoid the puddle that remained despite the lack of rain.

"It's always swampy in this area." Sandra paused and sniffled. "It was the next project on Bailey's to-do list. He wanted to fill in the . . . whatever he called it, so the building's foundation wouldn't be compromised. The barn's not in great shape, but it does what we need it to do for now. We can't afford to replace it." Sandra paused. "I just hope he's okay."

Louise felt a tug at her heartstrings; it wasn't long ago that one of her employees had gone missing under mysterious circumstances. "We'll find him, Sandra."

"Hey, guys, is this what we're looking for?" Daphne's voice came from behind the dilapidated structure.

"How did you get back there?"

"I went around the other side. It's dry over there."

Louise and Sandra looked at each other, and Sandra's frown turned into a smile. "I see why you brought her."

"Yes, I'm often reminded how beneficial it is to have a

friend and business partner who has more common sense than I do."

They joined Daphne, who was shining her light on a crate very similar to the one they'd seen at the airport. "Is this what you were looking for, Louise? It's the same colour, and the airholes are in the same position as the one we saw."

"That's it. Good job, Daphne. You're becoming quite the amateur detective."

Daphne frowned. "No thanks. I'll stick to investigating animal illnesses."

Louise addressed Sandra. "Do you use crates like this?"

Sandra shook her head. "Never. We wouldn't put the animals in something like that. We have humane kennels for transporting them." She pointed at the wooden box. "That thing is *not* designed for the benefit of the animal."

"Did the forensics team check this area out? 'Cause I think they would have made note of the crate if it's the same as the ones at the airport, and taped this area off."

"The airport?"

Louise had spoken without thinking. She hadn't intended to tell Sandra of her suspicion that the airport bombing and Tina Purcell's murder were connected.

"Daphne and I went by the airport before coming back here. I wanted to have a look around, and when we spotted a crate in the debris pile, it got me thinking about this one. I noticed it the other day when you were showing me the grounds. I didn't think twice about it at the time, but—"

"But you think it's related to the explosion? Why?"

"One of the protestors, the one who wears that plum jacket, was carrying a sign saying Stop the Imports. At the time I thought she was misinformed—"

"She *is* misinformed." The volume of Sandra's voice increased dramatically. Louise stepped back in fear. Sandra flung her hand in the air. "We don't treat exotic animals, and we certainly don't *import* them." Her brow furrowed.

"Of course not, but as you've said yourself, many of these protestors are misinformed. What if someone *is* importing exotic animals, and for some reason ARSE believes that it's SWaRF, even though it's not true? That might be why they've been hanging out here lately."

Sandra deeply inhaled the cool night air and held her breath for a few seconds before releasing it. "I'm sorry. Dead bodies and missing people—I'm afraid it's all getting to me."

Louise put her arm around Sandra's shoulder. "I'm sure it is. Don't worry about it. We're all on the same team here. Let's think about this. Bailey is missing the same day we find a body in the pond he's been working on. Later we find evidence on his home computer that he's been tracking ARSE movements, and that he was with them."

Sandra's brow furrowed again, and Louise backtracked. "I mean, not with them as in *working* with them, but in the same area at the airport. At least one protestor thinks you're importing exotic animals, and there's evidence at the airport that someone's actually been doing that." Louise paused, then shone her flashlight at the crate. "And here we have a crate that's very similar to the one Daphne and I saw at the airport."

Daphne, who'd been listening quietly, spoke up. "I've been wondering, though . . . If the crate at the airport is evidence of a crime, why was it thrown into a debris pile?"

Louise scratched her head. "We've been calling it a debris pile, but maybe it's a pile they intend to go through later. Those guards did say it would take a long time to sift through everything. Or maybe it was tossed there before they knew its significance."

"Or maybe it has no significance at all." Sandra sat on a tree stump and dropped her head into her hands. "This is all making my head hurt."

"There *is* a difference between this crate and the other one. This one has wires wrapped around one corner." Louise shook her flashlight to highlight the green and red wires that protruded from one airhole, wrapped around the adjacent corner, then disappeared into another airhole. "Maybe the wires are used to hold it closed."

"Um, I don't see why they'd need a wire tie since there's a latch on the other side." Daphne drew closer to the box, then leaned over to shine her light on the corner. She pointed at the latch. "See here. There's even a lock on it. It's a locked box with wires poking out of it. Odd!"

Louise grabbed Daphne by the back of her shirt and yanked her away. She then pulled Sandra up by the arm. "Run!"

Louise peered out the window of Sandra's office. The night sky was lit up by flashing lights from multiple police cars. One of the RCMP armoured vehicles was positioned between the trailer and the entrance to the woods that led to the barn; Alex explained that it would lessen any impact and shield them from flying material if the bomb went off.

After they'd fled the wired crate, Louise had called Alex while Daphne called 911. Sandra sent out a general alert to the staff, a system she'd put in place after the facility had a forest fire threat. When Louise reacted to the possible bomb,

Sandra hit the emergency button on her phone, alerting all staff to head to the back parking lot.

All SWaRF staff were accounted for, but the animals they were caring for couldn't be evacuated from their habitats. When Alex entered the trailer, Sandra rushed over to him and said, "The animals are still out there. We have to get them to safety."

Alex placed his hands on her shoulders. "It's okay. The bomb squad checked the crate out, and everything's under control."

Sandra's shoulders relaxed. "So, it wasn't a bomb?"

Alex eyed Louise, then looked back at Sandra. "I didn't say that."

Daphne's hand flew up and covered her mouth. "Oh my. We were . . . We were right there. I almost touched it."

Alex glared at Louise. His expression told her he was clearly unhappy with her snooping around, but his annoyance with her behaviour paled compared to her own. She could have gotten both Daphne, her best friend and the mother of two small children, as well as Sandra, killed. Louise's head drooped. What had she been thinking?

Alex redirected his gaze to Daphne. "It was a dud. The bomb guys tell me that whoever tossed it there didn't have it set to go off. And that the responsible party either left quickly, or someone threw it over the fence in an attempt to scare you."

Sandra wiped her brow with her sleeve. "Well, they succeeded. I've never been so scared. I need to let my staff know that there's no danger. Can we go check on the animals?"

Alex rubbed Sandra's arm, then positioned himself in front of the trailer's door. "Sorry, not just yet. By all means let everyone know that there was no bomb behind the barn, but we need to sweep the entire property to make sure nothing else is out there. It may take all night."

Panic in her eyes, Sandra looked back at Louise. She then returned her attention to Alex. "But Major, the coyote. He had surgery today and we have to keep a close eye on him. He's in the building closest to us—I could slip in and out real quick."

"We'll be starting the sweep here at the trailer and working our way to the other side of the facility, but I can't let you go past the armoured vehicle. If there's something else out there, well . . . it would be too dangerous." Alex placed a reassuring hand on Sandra's shoulder. "Once we've cleared the area around that building, I'll check with the bomb squad to see if we can allow someone to check on him, but no guarantees. If there's another bomb out there, we have no idea how big it is and what area could be impacted until we find it."

"Or it goes off," Louise said.

They all stared at her.

"I'm not trying to be funny. Once they've cleared the building Major's in, I'll be the one to check on him." Louise tossed her car key fob to Daphne. "You should get out of here. Go home."

Daphne's eyes watered and her lower lip quivered. "But what about the rest of you?"

"I'm with Louise on this, Daphne." Alex tapped Daphne's shoulder. "You get going. The officers outside will escort you to the car." He addressed Sandra. "And we'll send you and your staff off too. We don't want anyone here who doesn't need to be. One of the cruisers will escort your vehicles down the service road away from the area and to the main road. Then you can make your way home."

Daphne rose to her feet and straightened to her full height, the look on her face showing how unhappy she was with the plan. "Why is Louise staying? She needs to leave too."

"I'll stay and check on Major as soon as I'm allowed," Louise said. "You need to go home and check on your family. Besides, if I'm here all night, you'll have to be awake enough tomorrow to manage things at the clinic."

Daphne hugged Louise. "I don't like this."

Alex opened the door to the trailer allowing Daphne and Sandra to exit.

Chapter 27

LOUISE CREATED A wear pattern from one end of the trailer to the other while she paced, waiting for Alex to return. It had been twenty minutes since Daphne, Sandra, and the staff left the facility, and shortly after that, Alex left to check on the progress near the building that housed Major.

To keep her mind from wandering to the worst-case scenario, Louise counted her lengths as though she were swimming in a pool. Once she tired of that, she counted scuff marks on the floor and spiderwebs on the ceiling, which didn't take long, as the trailer was clean and well maintained.

Where are you, Alex? Louise didn't want to call him—he was busy with the investigation. What she really wanted to do was find him and get involved, to help with the search, but her offer to help wouldn't be welcomed by the law officers currently scouring Sydney's Wildlife Rehabilitation Facility.

Louise wandered to the refrigerator, helped herself to a bottle of cold water, then settled in Sandra's office to wait. A filing cabinet stood against the wall to her right. One of the drawers was labelled Staff. *I wonder if there's anything in there about Bailey that might be useful.*

Rummaging through someone else's files was questionable behaviour, but she might find something to help them track down Bailey. He could be in trouble and in need of help. Surely that justified a little snooping.

Louise stood up and stared at the grey metal cabinet. "Did you give a secondary address when you applied to work here? Maybe a cottage where you're hiding, somewhere with poor cell service? That would explain why you haven't contacted Sandra or the police. Or maybe you have a relative who's keeping you safe. Or a friend."

Through the partially opened window, voices were audible in the distance. Louise couldn't make out what they were saying, but they didn't sound alarmed or agitated. It sounded as if they were simply shouting out locations and directions. Some of the terrain was rough, as Louise knew from her hikes through the facility. Other areas were swampy, like the patch of ground near the ATV barn. Louise prayed for the officers' safety, and prayed there'd be no explosives out there. There had already been enough death and injuries this week. The lives of so many had changed in an instant when that bomb went off.

She rested her hand on the top of the cabinet. The metal was cold, a reminder that they were still in that time of year when temperatures bounced from hot to cool throughout the day.

Louise gazed out the window above Sandra's desk. "What could be so important that it would justify hurting so many people?" She turned her attention back to the drawer labelled Staff. "Were you involved in the bombing, Bailey? For Sandra's sake, I hope not, but . . ." She yanked on the handle. The cabinet tilted forward, threatening to fall over, but the drawer remained closed. "Nuts! It's locked. Of course it is—private employee information needs to be kept secure. I wonder how hard it would be to pick the—"

"Find anything?"

Louise released the handle and whirled around. "When did you come in? How long have you been standing there?"

Alex was leaning against the door frame. "Long enough to witness an attempt to break and enter."

"I was just thinking out loud. I wouldn't actually try to pick the lock or look at someone else's files."

Alex crossed his arms. "Really? Didn't you do that very thing at Mr. Nelson's home last night?"

Louise met his gaze. "No. As I've already told you, his door was unlocked, and his computer was turned on. We didn't"—she mimicked his voice—"'break and enter.'"

Alex laughed. "Sure, we'll go with that—for now." He stood up straight and clapped his hands together. "I've got some good news. The bomb squad has nearly completed clearing the area around the building with the coyote in it. Once they give the word, I'll escort you over and we can check on him."

Louise retrieved her water bottle from the top of the filing cabinet and sat on the edge of Sandra's desk. "That *is* good news, and we can use all we can get. I have to admit, I'm getting pretty tired and would like nothing more than to verify that my patient's well, then head home to bed." She glanced at the clock on the wall. "Poor Oscar. He's been alone all day."

Alex sat in one of the guest chairs. "He'll be fine. It wouldn't hurt him to lose a few pounds, anyway. He's a bit on the pudgy side lately."

Louise glared at him. "He's fine! And that's not how we take weight off cats, by withholding food. It's dangerous to do that. They can get a fatty liver if—"

"I was kidding. Trying to lighten the mood a bit. Sorry. I'm tired too. These cases are keeping the entire force on call night and day. Until we find those behind the bombing and Ms. Purcell's murder, the whole community will be on edge."

"So you think there's a connection between the two?"

"I didn't say that."

"Not outright, but you haven't denied it either." Louise shifted from sitting on Sandra's desk to her chair. "Two major crimes on one day in a small town, the crates, a possible bomb here at SWaRF . . . How can they not be connected? It's too much of a coincidence."

"How do you know about the crates at the airport?"

"It was on the news."

"No. The information about the plane was leaked to the news media, but the information about the transport crates was not."

Louise glanced around the room, willing for a reason she'd know about the crates to appear on the wall. She didn't want to reveal to Alex that she'd gone to the airport. Even more than that, she was reluctant to let him know that she'd put Daphne in danger more than once this evening. He already knew she'd come close to getting her best friend blown up, and now she'd blown her own cover by mentioning the crates.

Not finding an excuse on the walls, she glanced at the floor. "Daphne and I might have taken a little drive to the airport. She's been really stressed lately, and we got this horrible review online from a less-than-stellar client, and Joe and the kids were out for the evening, so I thought a distraction would be good for her."

Alex shook his head and his brow furrowed again. "Nothing like getting killed to get your mind off a bad review."

Heat rose in Louise's face. "No one was going to get killed. And you don't understand—reviews can be very hurtful."

Alex stood and pointed at the water bottle. "Any more of those?"

"In the fridge, down the hall."

Louise sat with her head in her hands as she waited for him to return. She was having a hard time reading him. When he returned to the trailer, he was teasing her, but now he was chastising her as though she was a misbehaving child. They were friends—who was he to treat her like a child? On the other hand, he was a detective working two serious cases, and she had interfered. She was foolish to be upset with someone who was genuinely worried about her safety.

She knew she should back off and leave the detective work to the detectives, but she didn't know if she had it in her to do that. She was as worried about Alex's safety as he was about hers. However, the right thing to do was clear; she'd promise Alex that she'd step back and stop interfering with the investigation.

Alex was typing into his phone when he re-entered the room. Louise waited for him to finish his text and take a seat before assuring him she wouldn't play detective anymore.

After he was settled, she attempted to restart the conversation, but he beat her to it.

"I was just talking with the head of the operation, and I've been given permission to fill you in on a few things. I'm not sure how happy I am about this, but we're thinking that keeping you in the loop might be safer for everyone than having you running around town doing your own investigation. Besides, finding that crate behind the barn was crucial to the case, and we wouldn't have known about it if you hadn't gone to the airport."

Louise's lower jaw dropped.

Alex continued. "And if you hadn't gone to Bailey Nelson's, we wouldn't know about the bloody wrench."

Louise smiled.

"This doesn't give you free reign to interfere and go into secure areas. If you get it into your head to check something out, I want to know about it before you go. And in exchange for our leniency, we expect you to avoid areas we ask you to stay away from. Deal?"

"Deal."

"We can't let you in on everything we know, as you're still a civilian and we have to protect evidence that could be vital to a court case. I assured my superiors I can trust you to keep what I tell you to yourself. Can I?"

Louise threw her shoulders back. "Of course." She thought back to conversations she'd had over the past couple of days with Daphne and Sandra. She had unintentionally revealed things to each of them, but that was before it became official that she wasn't to share information with those outside of the investigative team. She could do this.

"Great." Alex pulled his notebook and pen out of his

pocket. "Your encounters with the protestors at SWaRF—let's start there. Anything jump out at you as suspicious?"

"What *isn't* suspicious about that crew?" Louise rolled her eyes.

"Goofy and suspicious aren't the same thing."

"True. So besides Beth Gilley following me home the other night and then sneaking around Bailey's place, she seems harmless. I think she's doing someone else's bidding."

"Any idea who's?"

"First I thought that Madame Grumpy Face—that's what Sandra calls her, but her real name is Joan Williams . . . At first I thought she was the group leader."

"Joan Williams? That name's familiar." Alex flipped through his notebook. "Hmm."

"Well, who is she?"

"Someone who's been evading a police interview."

Louise leaned forward. "And?"

"And we're interviewing everyone. We were given her name by one of Tina Purcell's co-workers."

"I see." Louise frowned. Alex had official permission to discuss the case with her, but he wasn't going to provide any more than the basic information he needed to get information from her.

"How did you get her name? You told me they were all very secretive."

"Facial recognition."

"Seriously?"

"Yup! I took their photos, found the software I needed online, then voila—suspects identified. Easy."

"Clever."

"Thank you." She was happy to receive the compliment. "Where did Tina Purcell work?"

"Airport."

Louise's jaw dropped again. "Are you saying that Joan Williams works there too?"

"Yes. But remember, that information goes no further than this room."

"I won't say a word to anyone." Louise hoped she could keep that promise; she didn't want to get Alex into trouble with the force, and it wasn't just the Bathurst Region Police Department involved in this case. In addition to the OPP and RCMP, multiple government agencies were involved. How serious would the consequences be for Alex, or for her, if she shared the wrong information with the wrong person? "Really, Alex, my lips are sealed."

"I'm counting on it. Anything else you can tell us about the protestors?"

"Well, the other women do what Joan Williams tells them to do without question. There's one called Erica Cotton who seems fearful of Joan." Louise thought back to when Joan clapped her hand over Erica Cotton's mouth. "Madame Grumpy Face is not at all a nice person, but despite her treatment of the other women, I don't think she's the true leader. There's a man called Keith that even Joan seems to look up to."

"So you think this Keith guy is the head of their group? Do you have a last name?"

"No last name yet. And yes, he's got to be their group leader, but I think he's more than that. Watching how the others look at him and listening to how they talk about him . . . well, it's creepy, like they're involved in some kind of cult. Not a real cult, like one involving brainwashing and giving all your worldly possessions to the head guy, but he does have an unnatural hold over them."

"That's interesting. I'll get Officers Tomlin and Carter to see if they can find his full name and check out his background. Keith? Hmm." Alex scratched his chin. "That name hasn't come up yet in the investigation."

"I'm not surprised. When Beth Gilley said his name in front of me, she acted as though a bolt of lightning would strike her down."

"What about this other woman? Erica Cotton, you called her? What's her story?"

"I don't know her story, but she had a sign that said Stop the Imports. That's one of the things that got me thinking the issues at SWaRF might be related to the airport explosion. But then I wasn't so sure because it's not an international airport."

Louise opened her water bottle and took a big gulp. "It's dry in here when the heat clicks on."

Alex's phone vibrated. "It looks like the bomb squad is satisfied that it's safe to check on your patient."

"Perfect." Louise recapped the bottle and jumped to her feet. "One more thing before we head out, though." She cocked a thumb at the photo of the bird behind Sandra's desk. "It's an Amazon parrot. Sandra's first rescue, and her *only* exotic rescue. If I remember correctly, his name is Dorian and he lives at her house. Apparently, his language is a bit too colourful for the office."

Louise was grateful that Alex and his co-workers had decided to trust her, so the least she could do was drop some of the resentment she'd been harbouring for the past couple of days.

Her mood swings of late had to be confusing to Alex, because if she was being honest with herself, they were confusing to her too. Between the recent traumatic events and Alex's mystery surprise, which Daphne had mentioned earlier in the week, Louise was on an emotional roller coaster.

He was staring at her, obviously confused as to why she was discussing a bird when he'd been filling her in on information she'd been longing to know.

"Sorry about being snotty when you asked what type of bird that was. I honestly didn't know, but Sandra told me while we were waiting for you earlier."

Alex's confused look remained. Did he even remember asking? The man was dealing with multiple murders and carnage.

"Okay, good to know. Apology accepted." He smiled at her, then stood up and opened the door. He invited her to follow by stretching his arm toward the hall.

His forgiveness was good enough for Louise, even if he didn't remember why she needed it. Maybe his not remembering her bad behaviour was more important. Forget the small stuff and forgive everything, even the big stuff—that was Alex. He lived his faith every day.

"Any word on Bailey Nelson's whereabouts?" she asked.

"No. The team went through his property, and his computers. He appeared to be tracking ARSE, but they didn't find anything to explain why, or where he is now."

Louise gathered her things and followed Alex to the door. She left her backpack on the landing, then reached into the trailer to switch the lights off. The mobile building was now in darkness, except for a light in the window at the far end. It reminded her of something, but she couldn't quite place it.

Alex, who'd already descended the stairs and was walking across the parking lot, turned to look at her. "Everything okay?"

She glanced back at the window. "Yeah, that light didn't go out. No big deal. It's just that . . ."

"Just what?"

"I don't know. Lack of sleep is messing with my mind. Let's check on Major and get out of here. I think I hear my bed screaming my name."

As they made their way to Major, Louise turned to look at the trailer again. The light in the window seemed important, but why?

Chapter 28

THE PARKING LOT of the Black Creek Animal Hospital was overflowing by nine o'clock the next morning. Between the already scheduled appointments and surgeries were several other animals who needed to be seen before the weekend. After the airport bombing, their owners had cancelled their appointments out of fear, but the condition of a couple of these pets was now more concerning to the clients than the threat of further terrorist activity.

One such patient was Blue Brown, a young male Jack Russell terrier who'd been urinating with increasing frequency and had had a few accidents in the house. Mr. and Mrs. Brown were a sweet older couple who were long-term clients. When they called this morning, they reported that Blue was now going outside and squatting, but no urine was coming out. Louise, fearing that Blue might have a stone causing urethral obstruction, had directed Mary to have them bring the dog over right away.

Mary's voice came over the intercom in Louise and Daphne's office. "Blue's here. He's doing a lot of whining."

Louise looked at Daphne and grimaced, then pushed the talk button on the intercom. "Thanks, Mary. Can you ask one of the techs to take him right back for abdominal rads? He might be blocked, so we'll start with rads." After releasing the button, she said to Daphne, "He might need surgery. Will you be able to squeeze one more in?"

Daphne waved a hand in the air. "For the Browns? Of course."

Louise wanted to ask her how her night had been after being an arm's length away from a potential bomb, but they'd both had to start the day running. Upon arriving at the clinic that morning, they were each met at the back door by Mary, who had a stack of files and notes for each of them. Perhaps it was a blessing, Louise reflected, to have a distraction to take their minds off the close call they'd had last night at SWaRF.

When Louise arrived in the treatment area, Heidi and Jenny had already taken the X-rays of Blue's belly and displayed the images on the wall monitor. Louise smiled at the wonder of the technology. "A couple of decades ago, we'd have to wait for the film to be processed, then dried, before we could look at the X-rays."

Heidi placed Blue on the floor, then stood behind Louise. "Looks like there's a few stones in his bladder."

"And here's the culprit responsible for today's troubles."

Louise pointed to a tubular structure on the radiograph. "A stone in the urethra. His bladder is so full, poor guy." She turned to look at Heidi. "I'll go speak with the Browns and let them know what's troubling Blue. We'll sedate him and see if we can flush that stone back into his bladder. That'll give him some relief until Daphne can do the cystotomy. If it doesn't help, he'll have to be the first surgery of the day."

Louise made her way to the front office, where she explained to the elderly couple that Blue would need surgery to remove the stones from his bladder, but first they'd attempt to relieve the obstruction to make him more comfortable.

Mrs. Brown dabbed at her eyes with a tissue. "Whatever he needs, Dr. Miller. You and your team have always taken the best care of our pets, Blue included."

Mary took the Browns into an exam room to sign the paperwork allowing the recommended procedures, leaving Louise alone in the front office with Shirley.

"How are you feeling, Shirley? Do you have a date for your surgery yet?"

"I'm doing okay. Surgery is scheduled for a couple of weeks from now. I let Rita know last night."

"Perfect."

When Louise got back to the treatment area, Heidi and Jenny were already set up to sedate and catheterize the Jack Russell terrier. Jenny placed him on the treatment table and held his front leg out, allowing Heidi to place an intravenous catheter. Once the little dog was sedated, Louise placed a urinary catheter and flushed his urethra with saline. The obstruction cleared immediately.

"Well, that was easy. Thank God for small miracles!" Louise used the same catheter to empty Blue's bladder, allowing him increased comfort while awaiting surgery. "We'll have to watch him closely over the next couple of hours to make sure he doesn't re-obstruct. I think Daphne wants to get the dog spays done first, and then she'll do Blue's cystotomy." Louise removed her latex gloves and tossed them in the garbage. "Jenny, let's give Blue some pain meds and get him set up so he's comfy while he waits his turn." Louise wrote the instructions for Blue's medication on his chart.

"Will do, boss!" Jenny saluted.

Louise laughed and shook her head. Her staff were skilled at picking up when Louise was tired or stressed and needed a laugh, but before she could relax her tightened muscles, Mary came through the door.

"Your next appointment's here, and we have a dog on the way in. Hit by car. It happened last night, but they didn't want to go to the emergency clinic. They think he has a broken leg—he can't stand up. They're about twenty minutes out."

"Let's hope it's not a broken back." Louise took the file from Mary's hand and headed toward the exam room, where a litter of kittens was awaiting their first set of vaccines.

By mid-afternoon, the appointments and surgeries were completed, and Louise, Daphne, and crew were able to take a break. Miranda, who'd been called in to help them out, was at the front desk manning the phones while the rest of the staff sprawled their worn-out bodies over the staff room chairs.

Heidi shifted in her chair as she popped open a can of cola. "I think we should buy a couch for the staff room. Let me clarify that—I think *Louise and Daphne* should buy a couch for the staff room."

Louise rubbed her back. "I'm not arguing with that." She looked over at Daphne. "What do you say? Maybe a couple of couches."

Daphne, who was chewing on leftover butterscotch pie she'd found in the fridge, covered her mouth with her hand. "Sure, but where would we put them? There's not enough room in here."

"What about the AI room?" Heidi was referring to the room that had been set up several months earlier when a previous associate wanted to start an artificial insemination service at the clinic. Both the associate's employment and the service had ended in a surprising fashion. "There's lots of room in there now that we've sold all the equipment."

Daphne swallowed her last bite and washed it down with a sip of tea. "That's something to think about. If we're going to do that, we might as well include a TV, and maybe a bookshelf."

Louise knew what Daphne was thinking. "And maybe a couple of desks? Maybe for doing homework? You know, once Joe finishes paternity leave and goes back to work, it might be nice to have a place the kids could hang out in if needed."

"That's not what I was thinking at all." Daphne grinned.

Louise returned the grin. "Of course not, but it's still a great idea. And hey, it wouldn't hurt to have a comfy spot to stretch out and relax after a morning like this."

Heidi raised her can. "A toast to comfy couches at work."

Rita raised her mug. "Sounds good. I'll get right on that before they change their minds. Two couches—comfy ones, of course—two bookshelves, and a couple of children's desks, though it may be a while before Ben is ready to use his."

Rita finished her tea. "By the way, I've responded to Mrs. Theobald's review. I've requested it be taken down, but that could take some time, so I thought a response was in order. I kept it to the point and professional. Of course, I had to rewrite it several times to keep the emotion out of it, but I think I accomplished that. I'd encourage you, Daphne, to have a look—not at my response, but at the tons of responses left by clients. People aren't happy with Mrs. Theobald's review and they've let her know what they think about it, and her."

"Just like I told you, Louise, we have a lot of great clients," Shirley said.

"I never doubted you Shirley, but I'm grateful for the reminder you gave me. Sometimes it's hard to remember the good people when the bad people are so loud."

Louise went to the counter and grabbed a chocolate doughnut. "The hit-by-car dog is doing okay. He has some serious bruising, but nothing's broken. And to update every-one on Major, he was up and walking around when I checked on him last night. Sandra offered him a bit of gruel this morn-ing and he lapped it right up. We'll continue to monitor him over the next few days, but I think he's going to recover com-pletely, now that we've gotten that fish hook out of his belly."

The group was repeating their disgust at lazy humans who toss dangerous items onto the ground with no regard for others when Miranda appeared in the doorway. "Sorry to break up the party, ladies . . . Oh, and Eric." Was Miranda swooning? "But the mid-afternoon rush has started. Daphne, your next appointment is here. Louise, the Browns are on the phone asking about Blue. Heidi, your first heartworm test is here. And Jenny, there's a suture check for you in room one."

Eric tilted his head. "Hey, did you forget about me?"

"I could never do that!" Miranda blushed when she noticed everyone grinning at her. "Um, I think you're on lab duty this afternoon, so . . . you know . . . Do whatever it is you do in the lab."

Eric headed for the door. As he passed Miranda, he said, "I may need some help. Wanna learn how to run a CBC?"

Miranda smiled. "Sure. I'll meet you down there."

After Eric left, Mary stood up and stretched. "Is that all?"

Smiling, Miranda shook her head and rolled her eyes. "Um . . . no. Mrs. Victoria called to order dog food. When she realized it was me, she asked that I have Shirley call her back."

Shirley sighed. "Oh, lucky me."

Mary patted Miranda on the shoulder. "Good job, my young Jedi."

The staff went down to the main floor, except for Rita, who returned to her office down the hall. Louise and Daphne headed to their office, where Daphne retrieved her stethoscope and Louise made another cup of coffee.

"Did anything else happen at SWaRF after I left last night?" Daphne threw the stethoscope over her shoulder, then stood in the doorway staring at Louise.

Louise felt uneasy about the question, and Daphne's stance.

Daphne picked up on her confusion. "You haven't mentioned what happened last night at all today."

"We've been busy, that's all. Thankfully, they didn't find any more suspicious crates or anything else of concern. The bomb squad and forensics teams were there most of the night according to Alex. If there was so much as a misplaced leaf, they would have found it. And when I spoke to Sandra about Major this morning, I could hear the relief in her voice."

"Did anything else happen?"

Louise wasn't sure what Daphne was getting at because, other than her chat with Alex, nothing did happen. She'd given him her word that she wouldn't discuss the information with anyone. Louise gave Daphne a sidelong look. It wasn't like her friend to fish for information about a police investigation, so what was going on?

"Did anything happen between you and Alex?"

Louise frowned. "Why would anything happen between us?"

Daphne rolled her eyes and turned up her palms. "I don't know. Because he was almost blown up a few days ago, and you were almost blown up last night. For some people that might be a sign to stop wasting time and get on with things."

Louise feigned ignorance. "What things?"

"Admitting your feelings for each other. Not that Alex is the issue. We all know his feelings—he doesn't hide them like someone else does."

Louise wasn't ready to discuss her internal conflict about Alex, even with her best friend. And besides, too many other things were going on that were keeping her head spinning. No! This wasn't the time to talk about turning friendship into dating, and all that involved.

"You know, something *did* happen before we left SWaRF."

Daphne crossed her arms. "Oh yeah? What?"

"One of the lights in the trailer didn't go off when I flicked the switch. It struck me as familiar, but I couldn't come up with what—"

"Didn't you say there was a light on in the kennel across the street from Bailey Nelson's home when you and Sandra were there?" Daphne put her hand over her mouth. "Nuts! Why did I remind you of that?"

"Because you're a genius. And a good friend. And apparently tired, because I, too, am surprised you reminded me of that and didn't keep it to yourself."

Daphne said, "Hmph," then headed downstairs to start her hectic afternoon.

Louise sent Alex a text message. *I have an idea about the kennel near Bailey's house. Can you meet me there later?*

Alex responded unusually fast. *Yes, but can't say when. Waiting on a search warrant for Joan Williams's home, then going there. Do not go to the kennel without me. When I can, will let you know.*

She texted him again. *No worries. I have a busy day here. Won't be free for several hours.*

Alex's response was short. *Good!*

Chapter 29

A S LOUISE FINISHED up the last of her records, she thought back to her text exchange with Alex. The meaning of his single-word response—"Good!"—wasn't lost on her. He was hoping her schedule would keep her too busy to get herself into trouble doing her own investigating. She'd promised him she wouldn't and had to think that perhaps he didn't trust her. Sure, he had good reason, but the distrust still stung.

Louise glanced at the clock on the wall. Daphne, having finished her phone calls and records, had left an hour earlier, not long after the clinic was closed for the day. Patients who were able to go home were discharged, and those who needed overnight attention had been referred to B-REC. Once the patients were sent on their way, the staff went home or out to meet friends. She was only in her mid-thirties, but Louise wondered how the staff had the energy to go out and socialize after a day like today.

"Of course," she said to the empty room, "they weren't up all night playing cop like I was—getting involved in a dangerous investigation when I should have been home cuddling with Oscar." She paused. "*Oscar!*"

Louise shut down her computer, grabbed her backpack, and ran for the car. Oscar had been left alone most of yesterday and again today. If he was bored, and worse, if he was hungry and there was a mouse in the house, her living room didn't stand a chance of surviving the chase.

She hopped into her car and hit the ignition button. Before putting the transmission into drive, she glanced once more at her phone. Still no message from Alex. She wondered where Joan Williams lived and whether or not she was present while they searched her home. What Louise wouldn't do to be a fly on that wall. Was it possible Madame Grumpy Face's face could get even grumpier?

"Not nice, Louise. God, please grant me patience. Patience to wait for Alex to get in touch before heading to the kennel. Patience with the protestors. Patience with cranky clients." She put the car into drive. "Oh, and patience while driving home in evening traffic."

Thankful that the traffic was unusually light—a blessing from above, she was sure—she pulled into her driveway and parked close to her front door.

Leaving her bags in the car, she approached the house, then opened the door gradually. She switched on the entry light, then peeked around the corner into the living room. The TV was undisturbed on its stand. "So far, so good."

As Louise advanced into the foyer, there was no sign of Oscar. Where was he? Her heart skipped a beat as a torrent of horrible scenarios flew through her mind. Had he been grabbed by the protestors? They knew where she lived. Was he lying sick somewhere in the house—or worse? It wasn't unheard of for a cat to die without warning of a blood clot or from heart failure. Louise had seen this play out too many times.

She closed the front door behind her and crept slowly into the living room. The furniture was undisturbed, the papers she'd left on her desk by the window weren't on the floor, and her potted plants hadn't been upended. There was no sign that Oscar had been chasing a mouse, so where was he? Why hadn't he met her by the door, screaming for food?

Louise wandered through the kitchen, and despite knowing he had no access to the garage, she peeked in there anyway, calling his name. He wasn't there, or in the main-floor powder room. The door to the basement was closed and she hadn't been down there in days, so there was no possibility he'd gotten trapped there after she left this morning.

She headed upstairs, calling his name and shaking the bag of cat treats she'd grabbed while searching the kitchen. The door to the guest room stood open so she peeked in— he wasn't there. She glanced into the main bathroom as she passed it on her way to her bedroom. No Oscar.

The door to the primary bedroom was partly open. When Louise pushed on it, her neck muscles tightened, her heart racing. If Oscar was in the house, why hadn't he come running at the sound of the treats? The sun had set on her way home, darkening her bedroom. She reached for the light switch and flicked it on. In the same instance, something on the corner of her bed leapt into the air. Louise gasped, then placed one hand over her chest to steady her racing heart while holding the door frame to steady her startled body.

Oscar landed on his feet in the centre of the bed, then jumped down and marched over to his shaky human. He rubbed his face on her legs and yowled the sort of yowl only a poor cat who thinks he's starving can make.

Louise stared at him. "I think I need to take you to the clinic to check for wax in your ears, young fellow." Oscar followed her as she headed for the kitchen and continued to talk to him. "Come to think of it, I don't know how old you are. Maybe you're losing your hearing due to age?"

Oscar had arrived at the Black Creek Animal Hospital in the arms of a client who'd been feeding the little stray. One day he didn't show up, and when he returned to the client's home a week later, his leg was broken beyond repair. After amputating the non-functional limb, Louise took him home to recover, and they'd been housemates ever since.

"I'll have to do some research on hearing loss in older cats." She filled his bowl with a measured helping of canned cat food. "Or maybe you're just ignoring me." She rubbed the brown tabby's head, put the partly empty can in the fridge, then grabbed a frozen dinner from the freezer.

She popped the ready-made pasta meal in the microwave attached to the wall, then checked her phone. Alex still hadn't messaged her. She looked at the time. "It's getting late. How long does it take to search one person's house?" Louise shrugged, then carefully took the hot meal out of the tiny oven. "Maybe it's a big house."

As she wolfed down her pasta, smothered with what

the manufacturer claimed was cheese and bacon, she found herself thinking about how the ARSE members supported themselves. They'd been at SWaRF every day this week and were known to visit other animal care sites frequently. When she'd mentioned working for a living in front of them, Erica Cotton was proud to announce that Joan Williams worked, but what about Erica? Or Beth? Beth was old enough to be retired—perhaps she had a good pension.

The group was an odd assortment of people. A leader named Keith who appeared to be in his fifties. How did he support himself? Perhaps he had a job at night, or maybe he worked shift work and that's why he wasn't always with the women. Louise thought about these women. Every one of them looked over sixty, so perhaps most of them were retired. Her fork froze midway to her mouth. Were they supporting Keith? Was ARSE a true cult?

She shook off the thought. Most cults try to keep a low profile, and these people were doing anything but. On the other hand, they were protesting a facility that had little visibility. The main road was mainly travelled by farm vehicles during harvest and planting season, and by cottagers in the summer.

Louise emptied the contents of the fork into her mouth, then tapped the end of the utensil on the table. She looked at Oscar, who was cleaning his paws in the corner. "We know there's a connection between the airport bombing and Tina Purcell's murder. Tina was a member of ARSE. Joan worked at the airport, and so did Tina. Did they set off the bomb? If so, why?"

Louise checked her phone for messages again. If Tina and Joan had set off the bomb, they might have also been trying to do it at SWaRF, but for some reason it didn't work. Bailey had been researching ARSE—he had to be the key to all of this.

Alex remained silent. Louise had promised she'd wait for him before going to the dog kennel, but urgency was overwhelming her sense of caution.

"I'll just head that way, and hopefully you'll meet me there, Alex." She grabbed the car key fob and her jacket. Before heading out, she peeked out the window. "No sign I've been followed tonight—so far, so good."

She locked the door to her home and hurried to the car. Once safely inside, she locked it, then sent another text to Alex. *I'm heading over to the dog kennel. I'll park out of sight behind the property's main house and wait for you.*

She threw the car in gear and headed into the dark streets.

Chapter 30

LOUISE DROVE UP the deserted driveway, and as she made her way behind the little brick bungalow, she could see that the light she'd noticed two nights ago was still on.

"I thought it was a realtor who left it on, but I wonder . . ." She glanced around for any signs that she had company. The neighbouring house was dark except for a single light over the garage, and the street was quiet.

Louise turned her lights off, then without using the gas, crept closer to the kennel over the flattened gravel yard. The previous owner of this property had been a client of the Black Creek Animal Hospital—she and her dogs had moved away several months ago, and the place was put up for sale not long after they left. Louise wondered how much interest there would be in a tiny two-bedroom house with an oversized garage that had been converted to a dog kennel.

"You're distracting yourself, Louise." She again checked to see if Alex had responded. Nothing. Louise turned the ignition off and tapped her foot on the floorboard. It was getting late, and she didn't want to go home without checking the building for clues. She'd promised Alex she wouldn't do so without him, but Bailey could be in there. It could be his hideout from the police, or perhaps he was injured.

As she stared at the large wooden shed, complete with windows and a garage-style door at one end, she noticed that the gate at the end of one of the outdoor dog runs wasn't closed. Two standard-sized entry doors had been installed on the building's side, each leading to a fenced-in exercise area—a dog run. The doors appeared closed, but she couldn't tell from the car if they were locked.

Louise grasped her door handle as she debated her next step. Wait for Alex, not knowing if he'd even received her text, or do a little investigating before he arrived. In the time she'd been sitting there, no other vehicles had passed her. The area was quiet, but not eerily quiet, giving Louise a sense that she was alone and safe.

Within seconds, she was standing on her tippy-toes, peering into the converted garage through a window. Besides a multitude of spiderwebs containing dead bugs hanging from the ceiling and walls, Louise could see several rusted filing cabinets and dilapidated shelving in the near right corner. In the near left corner sat a sink decorated with rust stains. Towels, still folded, lined a shelving unit to one side of the sink, and a grooming table occupied the space on the other side.

Her attention drifted from the table to the far left corner, where there were closed cabinets and a couple of kennels. One kennel had a groomer's dryer hung on its bars. "Why didn't Nancy take that with her? It would be expensive to replace." Louise shrugged.

She was about to step down and return to her car when she noticed the corner of a towel poking around a box in the far right corner. It was draped over something long and tubular with a beige tip showing. Louise squinted, but no matter how much she tried to squeeze her cheekbones and her eyebrows together, she couldn't make out what the object was. She dropped to her heels—her toes were aching from bearing her weight.

Her phone sat quietly in her pocket. It hadn't vibrated to inform her of an incoming text. "Now what?"

Louise headed for the dog run with the open gate. She'd see if the door to the garage was unlocked, and if so, she'd have a quick look around while waiting for Alex. What could it hurt? She hadn't discovered anything to indicate a crime had been committed, or that someone was using it as a headquarters for criminal activity. There was no fear of disrupting evidence, and if that grooming table was in good shape, she'd mention it to Daphne—maybe they'd offer to buy it for the clinic.

As she crossed the length of the run, Louise used her phone's flashlight to help avoid stepping in any evidence that this place had once housed dogs. The doorknob turned easily, and with a slight push, the door opened with a creak. The smell of mould and mildew immediately assaulted Louise's nose, but this was soon overpowered by the odour of metal and decay. It wasn't unlike the smell of parvo that had invaded the clinic when Jack Morrison was admitted.

Jack's recovery reminded Louise that despite all the bad

things that had happened in the past few days, good things had been happening at the same time. Both Jack the parvo puppy and Flip the Great Dane with GDV were recovering quickly from their health scares.

She left the door open, allowing the room to air out, and covered her mouth with the sleeve of her jacket. Her first mission was to check out the grooming table. As she walked to the end of the building, she was stopped by an unexpected sound. *Was that a groan?*

She spun around and stared at the towel near the pile of boxes. She froze when the sound came again. Then the towel moved. Louise leapt backwards, hitting her back squarely on the edge of the towel rack. She started to scream in pain, then stopped. She wasn't alone.

"Who's there?"

Another groan. The towel moved a few inches away, as though it was being pulled or dragged.

"Are you injured?"

"Help. Me." The voice was weak but obviously male.

"Bailey? Is that you?" Louise moved closer to the source of the pleas for help, and the smell of infection grew stronger. "You must be injured. Can you get up?" Stupid question—if he could get up, he would have by now.

She peeked around the boxes. A man was curled up in the corner, one leg stretched out and covered by the towel. The beige tip she'd noticed earlier was his bare toe. She thought back to the photos she'd seen of Bailey. Could this be him? This man's face was swollen and bruised, the colour of his hair and beard masked by dried blood.

Louise suspected that he couldn't see, as his eyes were

hidden by severe swelling of his cheeks and forehead. "Can you hear me?"

"Help. Me."

"Help is on the way." Louise called 911 and informed the operator that she'd just found an injured man, then gave the address.

The operator wanted her to stay on the line, but the man needed help right away, so Louise placed her phone on the grooming table, allowing her to speak with the operator while she retrieved a clean towel.

Standing by the sink, she said, "Please work." She crossed her fingers on one hand while turning on the tap with the other. Clear water came flowing out. "Thank you, God."

She used the wet towels to clean the blood from the man's face. Several of the wounds were infected, and Louise gagged as she picked a maggot from one area of necrotic skin. She contorted her face while holding the wiggling creature between her fingers. "Thankfully, you don't have any friends—I hope." She squished the dead-flesh-eating intruder into the cement floor.

Louise examined the man for other injuries. His shirt and shorts were stained with blood, but worse than that, his right arm was lying in a direction nobody's arm should be lying in. "Your arm isn't meant to bend between the elbow and shoulder." Not seeing anything that could be used as a splint, she elected to leave the arm lying as it was. "I just hope there isn't any permanent damage to the nerves and other tissues."

She returned to the sink to grab another towel but froze in place when, through the open door, she detected movement in the yard. She hadn't heard any sirens; it couldn't be the ambulance already. When she called 911, she knew that help would be at least twenty minutes away, if they weren't already overwhelmed with other emergencies. And the operator would have told her if they were here.

She backed up so she couldn't be seen through the doorway, then crept over to the grooming table, and her phone.

Louise whispered, "I think we have visitors. Can you send the police?"

"They're on their way. What do you mean by visitors?"

"This man has obviously been beaten. I think he might be the missing employee from the rehab centre." Louise crouched down behind the table. It wouldn't hide her if someone came in, but she hoped that if they were looking in from a distance, she'd be hidden by the table's wide pedestal. "What if those people out there are the ones who attacked him?"

"How many of them are there?"

"I don't know."

"Stay out of sight. The police and ambulance are on their way."

"Good plan." Louise looked over at the injured man. She didn't want to leave him alone in the corner. How long had he already been alone, suffering, and scared? Bailey Nelson had last been heard from five days ago. If this was him, had he been in here all that time?

Louise crawled, starting her journey back to her human patient, but as she approached the door and looked up, a familiar face stared down at her.

Beth Gilley was pointing her scrawny finger at Louise. "That's the vet. The one who's been interfering with our work."

Standing beside her was one of the protestors from the news articles, Patrick Howard. The middle-aged balding beast with a cube-shaped head stood quietly, staring at Louise as he slapped a metal bar into the palm of his hand.

Chapter 31

LOUISE RESISTED THE urge to glance back at the grooming table that held her phone.

"So, if it isn't Beth Gilley." The phone was still connected; Louise could only hope that the 911 operator could hear everything that was being said.

"What are you doing here?" Louise glanced at the man, then back at Beth. "What's your friend's name?" Louise knew his name—she just hoped Beth would say it loud enough that it would be recorded.

Beth crossed her arms and jutted her chin into the air. "This is Patrick How . . ." She stopped short of saying the rest of his last name when the imposing man glared at her, his eyes telling her to stop talking.

"Names are not important." He slapped the metal bar harder into his palm and frowned at Louise.

She rolled her eyes. What was it with these people and their desire for anonymity? "Sure, Patrick, whatever you say. Um, listen." Louise started to stand.

"Not so fast." Patrick moved closer to her and held the bar over his head.

The bleeding man's injuries assured Louise that the beastly man wouldn't hesitate to do the same to her. She shielded her head with her arm. "Okay, okay." She rolled into a sitting position. "That's better. My knees can't take kneeling for long." She faked a smile, hoping it might calm him. It didn't work.

"No sudden movements."

Was that fear in his eyes? For a bully, his confidence seemed lacking, but they do say that bullies are often cowards in disguise.

"There's an injured man over there—in the corner, behind the boxes. He needs medical attention fast." Louise glanced at the corner. From this angle, she could only see the leg she'd uncovered earlier. "Maybe one of you could call 911?"

"No need." Patrick's lips formed a grin, and he resumed slapping the metal bar into his palm.

Why don't you slap that bar into your head? Maybe knock some sense of decency into it.

With a nod, Patrick indicated he wanted Beth to check the man in the corner. She limped over to the victim, then bent her already bent back down until she was face to face with him. "That's him, all right." She shook her bony finger at him. "There's no mistaking it. That's the same shirt he had on when we—"

"Beth!" Patrick's angry voice echoed through the garage.

His sudden outburst stirred the bleeding man, who pulled his leg closer to his body.

"Sorry." Beth turned her attention to Louise and glared at her through narrowed eyes, her nostrils flaring. "You shouldn't be here, but I guess it's a good thing you are. When I saw you pull into the driveway, I knew something was up, so I called Patrick. We've been looking for Bailey."

Louise now had confirmation it was him. "Why? Are you responsible for his injuries?" But if they were, why would they be looking for him? This was getting more and more confusing. She massaged her temples.

"Of course not. We just wanted to talk to him." Patrick closed the door to the garage, then pointed the metal bar at Louise. "Don't move." He strolled over to Bailey and grinned at him. "Looks like we left you with just enough oomph to crawl across the street and into here."

"What did you do to him?"

"We didn't do anything. He fell. Right, Patrick?"

Patrick straightened his shoulders and smiled. "That's right." He side-eyed Beth, then winked at Louise. "He fell."

Louise was certain that Patrick had beaten Bailey, then later convinced the gullible older woman that Bailey had fallen. Beth viewed Keith as the saviour of the animal kingdom, so in her mind it might also be reasonable that a man of Bailey's age and size could sustain such serious injuries from a fall. Unless . . .

"Did he fall from the roof? His arm is seriously broken."

"Nope." Beth scrunched her face and shook her head. "He's just clumsy. Foolish man tripped over his own feet when Patrick was chasing him to the back of his house."

"Beth! Stop talking!"

"Can I at least check on his wounds? He needs help now."

"No need." Patrick, who'd been staring at the front corner of the garage where the grooming table was located, retrieved his phone from his pocket, then tapped the screen. "I need to make a call. Beth, keep an eye on her." Patrick nodded at Louise, then exited the garage.

Louise's heart sank when she heard the click of a lock. She prayed a silent prayer that the ambulance, and the police, would arrive soon.

The temperature was dropping, and the unheated garage had cooled significantly since Louise entered it. "Hey, Beth, how about we cover Bailey with some of those clean towels over there? He's lost a lot of blood, and he's probably really dehydrated. The cold isn't good for him."

Beth shrugged. "Go ahead." She pointed her wrinkled finger at Louise. "But no funny business."

"You have my word." Was this woman for real? They were locked in a garage with a dying man inside and a crazy man outside. Until help arrived, there was little Louise could do other than decrease Bailey's risk of death from hypothermia, and pray for him.

"Why was Patrick chasing Bailey?" Now that she was alone with this genius, Louise hoped she'd talk freely.

"He tried to join ARSE to shut us down. He'd been taking photos of us from a hiding spot, and when he asked to join the group, he was told no. Our leader found out who he was and sent Patrick and me to tell him to stay away."

"Your leader? You mean Keith something?"

Beth's brow furrowed. "Yes. Of course." She crossed her arms and attempted to straighten her shoulders. "Who else but Keith Roberts would be worthy to lead this important operation?" She shook her head, her opinion that Louise was an uninformed idiot obvious in the woman's facial expression.

Louise smiled at their leader's last name being revealed and hoped it had been recorded on the 911 call. "So you found Bailey and told him to stop. Then what?"

"We followed him home one night. When he parked his truck, Patrick went to the driver's door and told him to stop bothering us. Bailey wouldn't listen. He held a wrench up and threatened Patrick. I got into the passenger seat and pulled on Bailey's arm so he couldn't hurt Patrick. Then that horrible man, he pushed me and . . . Look at this."

Beth twisted her shoulder toward Louise, then pulled down her collar to expose a healing gash on her shoulder blade. "I was injured. It bled, even."

Louise thought back to Bailey's clean truck. It seemed odd that anyone committing a crime would take the time to clean a vehicle, but if they were trying to remove trace evidence, like blood and DNA, it made perfect sense.

"I think you'll live. Bailey on the other hand, might not. We need to get out of here and get him help."

"I'm sure Patrick's calling for help now. He's not going to let anyone die."

"Um . . ." Louise rubbed her chin. It was official—this woman was beyond gullible. "He's not coming back, you know. Just before he left, he looked over at my phone and probably saw the light on indicating I was on a call. And, there's no way someone could sustain those types of injuries from tripping and falling. I take it when Patrick chased Bailey, you didn't follow?"

"I did, but they were way ahead. I don't move as quick as I used to, you know."

No kidding.

"By time I got around the back, Bailey was lying there, not moving. Patrick said we needed to leave."

"Why didn't you call 911? And why have you been looking for him?"

"Patrick thought the fall had killed him. We went back to Keith to get his advice on what to do. When we didn't hear the next day that a body had been found, we were all relieved he wasn't dead. They had me watch for him so we could make sure he was okay."

Louise's eyes widened more than was normal. "Seriously? You believe that?" She got closer to the older woman, and this time, it was Louise's turn to stick her finger in Beth's face. "You are insane if you believe any of that. Patrick tried to kill Bailey to shut him up. When there was no report of a body, your leaders were looking for him to finish the job." Louise shook her head and moved to the front of the garage to grab some towels.

As she passed the grooming table, she spoke into the phone. "I really hope you're still there and heard everything."

Louise looked at Beth, whose jaw dropped when she heard the operator's voice.

"I did. It's all recorded. The ambulance and police are only a minute or two away. They ran into a road blockage. Someone stole a dump truck, then left it blocking the roadway. How's your patient?"

Louise glared at Beth. "Not good."

After covering Bailey with a couple of plush oversized bath towels, Louise tucked them tightly around his body to offer further warmth and a sense of comfort. "I assume that was you the other night—the person in Bailey's yard. The person who took the bloody wrench. Why worry about the wrench if this was all an accident?"

"Patrick thought we should check out the yard to see if maybe Bailey was there and just hadn't been found yet. If I found him, I would have called 911. I'm not a monster, you know. We don't go around killing people. I didn't see Bailey, but I saw the wrench, so I took it. Just in case . . ."

Just in case what? This cemented for Louise that even though Beth was gullible and probably believed in the innocence of her comrades, a small part of her knew the truth about them.

"I'm not so sure about the 'We don't go around killing people' bit. Tina Purcell is dead, you almost killed Bailey, and he may still die. Oh, and then there's the five dead from the airport explosion." Louise covered her mouth. She hadn't intended to let Beth know that she knew of a connection between the SWaRF murder and the airport bombing.

"Tina tripped and fell, just like Bailey did. It's sad, but it happens." Beth rubbed her nose, then squinted. "And what *about* the airport? We had nothing to do with that."

"Brainwashing at its finest!"

Sirens were getting closer. Louise rubbed Bailey's forehead with her thumb. "Help is here, Bailey. You'll be okay."

She stood and approached Beth. "I've said this before and I'll say it again—your ride is here. Hopefully this time they'll give you a nice warm place to sleep where you can think about the foolishness that just escaped your mouth. You've been used to do others' bad deeds, and now you're going to jail and the folks who brainwashed you are still free."

The door burst open and Alex rushed in. When he saw the blood on Louise's jacket and hands, he yelled behind him, "In here—we have one injured." He rushed over and hugged her. "Are you okay?"

She hugged him back, happy to feel the warmth of his body and the safety of his embrace. "I'm fine." She pulled back and knelt by Bailey. "He's not. This is Bailey Nelson. He's badly injured." She nodded at Beth. "That woman and her buddy, who took off, did this to him."

Alex nodded at an officer, who placed Beth in handcuffs, then spoke into his radio. "It's clear in here. Send the EMTs in."

Chapter 32

THREE DAYS HAD passed since Louise had last been to the hospital—three days since the explosion had threatened to take Alex away from her forever. The corridors were no longer filled with the smell of burnt flesh and patients wrapped in bandages to protect their skin, and frantic paramedics trying to keep their patients alive while waiting for a nurse to triage them. The hours after the airport bombing had been filled with things that could cause nightmares in the most seasoned medical staff.

The death toll remained at five. A small blessing, Louise thought, knowing that with some of the catastrophic injuries victims were still battling, the number could go higher.

One death was too many. One person suffering a lost limb, burns, or other life-altering injuries was too many. As Louise sat outside the emergency room waiting for word of Bailey Nelson's progress, she bowed her head and prayed once again for the victims and their families. Now she'd add Bailey and his family to her prayers.

"Is he okay? Where is he?" She lifted her head to see a frantic Sandra Kelly rushing down the hallway, two nurses attempting to stop her. Sandra flung her arms behind her, thwarting their attempts to grab her. "Get away from me. I have to see Bailey."

Louise leapt to her feet and waved to the nurses. "It's okay. She's a friend."

In surrender, the nurses threw their hands in the air; Louise had come in with the patient, and the police detective had said she could wait near Bailey's room.

Louise was certain that the worn-out nursing staff had more important issues to deal with than a couple of crazy women hanging out in the hallway. While the corridors were no longer crowded with injured people, the rooms were filled to capacity. The hospital was still cancelling previously scheduled procedures as surgeries on the bombing victims continued.

Louise reached out to hug Sandra, to offer her comfort, but her friend pushed by her and attempted to enter Bailey's room. Louise placed her hand on Sandra's shoulder and guided her to the chairs pushed up against the wall. "Come sit, Sandra. You can't go in just yet."

Sandra sat and put her head in her hands.

"He's in really bad shape, but he's alive. They started him on fluids as soon as they got him into the ambulance, and it's helping. He was severely dehydrated and probably anemic from blood loss. They gave him a blood transfusion shortly after we got here, and now they're cleaning up his wounds. X-rays and possibly a CT scan will follow. They've been unable to reach his family. Do you know how to reach them?"

Sandra shook her head. "Not offhand. I'd have to check his personnel file. Why a CT scan?"

Louise debated how much to tell Sandra. Soften the blow and claim that the scan was merely a precaution? Or tell her the truth, that someone had beaten him viciously and repeatedly over the head. Bile hit the back of Louise's throat when the poor man's appearance as he lay dying in the kennel flashed in her memory. It truly was a miracle he was alive. She couldn't fathom how he'd gotten himself across the street and into the converted garage. Or why. Why hadn't he gone to a neighbour's house? Perhaps his brain injury had kept him from thinking clearly. His phone was found in his pocket, but the battery was dead, making it impossible to determine if he'd tried to call for help.

"It's a precaution, Sandra. He received trauma to his head, so they want to ensure he doesn't have a brain bleed or some other serious head injury."

Sandra jumped to her feet, then glared at Louise. "Who did this?"

"One of the people responsible is in custody, and the other fled. I'm not sure if they've found him yet."

The door to Bailey's room opened, and Alex entered the hallway. Sandra grasped his shoulders to push him aside, and he clutched her arms.

"He's in and out of consciousness, Sandra. You can go in and see him briefly, but I'll ask you not to ask him any questions about what's happened. He was able to talk to me a bit, and we'll fill you in on specifics as soon as we can. Deal?"

Sandra squinted with distrust at Alex. "What are you hiding? Is he a criminal like Louise thought he was?"

"Hey, I never said that."

Sandra shot a look of anger at Louise, then Alex. "You implied it a few times, and so did the police."

Alex released his grip on Sandra. "He may not be a criminal, but he's a very injured man who needs rest. Just sit with him, hold his hand, let him know he isn't alone."

"I can do that." Sandra removed her hands from his shoulders, then wiped her eyes before heading into Bailey's room.

Louise dropped into one of the chairs, but Alex pulled her back up by the arm. "Come on, let's find some coffee."

"That sounds great, but I'd rather go home to bed. My car's still out at Nancy Wells's place. I rode here in the ambulance."

"I know—I was there. I'll give you a ride in a bit to your car, but first I thought you'd want an update on a few things. Of course, if you'd rather not hear what we found at Joan Williams's house, I could take you home now."

"Cafeteria's this way." Louise quickened her pace to catch the elevator before the door closed. She threw her hand on the edge of the door to stop it, much to the displeasure of the people inside, then looked over her shoulder at Alex. "Are you coming?"

Louise held the warm cup tightly between her palms; the hospital was warm, but the events of the past few hours continued to cause her chills. She eyed the neglected cream puffs on Alex's tray and wondered when she'd last eaten anything healthy. When he asked her if she'd like a snack with her coffee, she'd declined the offer. Now her stomach was grumbling and she regretted the decision.

He's very fixated on his phone. Would he even notice if I helped myself to a cream puff? She reached across the table, and the back of her hand was met with a playful slap. After she withdrew her hand, Alex held the plate up, offering her a sugar-filled snack. She gobbled it down.

Nerves and anxiety overwhelmed her as she tried to be patient. Alex's phone had buzzed the second they sat down, and he'd been transfixed by a text exchange ever since. Still hungry after only the cream puff, Louise left her distracted companion alone at the table and headed over to the sandwich section of the café.

The ham and cheese sandwich hit the spot, and she followed it with the rest of her coffee. Alex hadn't touched his drink, but the tiny cream puffs were gone from his plate. Louise stared at his cup. He took his coffee black, but at this point, she'd be okay with the bitter brew.

Alex clicked on his phone and eyed Louise. "Don't even think about it." He picked up the cup of tepid coffee and finished it. "Ahh . . . nothing like cold, bitter coffee to wake you right up. I'm getting another. You?"

"Yes."

Alex fetched a refill for each of them, then sat back at the table. "You're probably wondering what that was about."

Louise shrugged. "No, not at all. I'm sure you were just putting in a grocery order after rescuing me and Bailey from a couple of maniacs."

Alex stroked his chin. "Hmm, come to think of it, I do

need a few things. There's a twenty-four-hour place in town. Putting in an order's not a bad idea—I can pick it up on the way home."

"Alex!"

He grinned. "You'll be happy to hear that Patrick Howard has been arrested. Turns out he has a record of white-collar crimes, but this is his first arrest for a violent one. Lucky for us, while he's an experienced criminal, he's not a smart one. When he left the kennel, he went straight home. Beth Gilley spilled her guts as soon as they got her to the station, giving the officers Mr. Howard's home and business addresses."

"He has a job? Who does he work for? Kneebusters Are Us?"

"He works for himself. Apparently, he owns a successful small parts supply store in Coverdale. They import auto parts or something."

"Wonders never cease."

"It gets better." Alex placed his elbows on the table and leaned toward Louise. "The missing wrench was found in the trunk of his car. We'll have to do DNA testing to confirm that the blood belongs to Bailey Nelson, but there's little doubt that it's the wrench from Bailey's car."

"Why so confident?"

"Besides Beth Gilley's statement to you that she retrieved a wrench from the backyard, there's a label on it that says SWaRF."

Louise grinned from ear to ear. "That's it! I hope they fry the little weasel."

"I know you're talking from frustration and lack of sleep, but remember . . . forgiveness."

"Sure. I'll keep that in mind. Do you think Patrick killed Tina Purcell?"

Alex shrugged. "That we don't know yet. We'll search his house and office over the next day or so—we'll turn every inch of every corner inside out."

"Speaking of searching homes, you said you'd update me on what you found at Joan Williams's place. I trust it's a lot, because you took a long time to respond to my texts about going to the kennel."

"Yeah, sorry about that. But no matter how long I took to reply, you shouldn't have gone there yourself."

"No. I see that now. It was dangerous and could have ended badly, but if I hadn't gone, Bailey might not have been found until the next house showing, and who knows how long that would have been. I can't imagine there's a big market for a rundown two-bedroom house with a dog kennel in the back."

"You never know. For the right price—"

"So what did you find at Madame Grumpy Face's?"

"We're back to the nicknames?"

"I'm tired, remember?"

Alex smiled. Louise stared back at him and wondered how he'd really been handling the past few days. He'd been jumpy at her house the other night, but she hadn't had much personal time with him since. Was he coping adequately with the emotional and psychological fallout of being in the midst of the explosion? Or was he holding on the best he could but ready to crack at any moment?

"Are you doing okay? Do you need to talk to anyone about how you're doing?"

"I thought we were discussing the search of a witness's home?" He frowned. "What are you talking about?"

Good timing, Louise. "Nothing. I was just thinking, but it can wait." Of course he didn't want to talk about his feelings in the hospital cafeteria in the middle of the night. "Tell me what you found."

Alex leaned back and intertwined his fingers. "Okay, then. We confiscated her laptop. It'll be analyzed by the crime lab to see if there is any incriminating evidence on it."

"I have to know, Alex, was she there when you did the search?"

"Ms. Williams? Yes. I caught her by surprise, because as I told you earlier, she'd been doing a good job of avoiding us since the explosion. If I'd known she was one of the protestors that would have sped things up."

"And this is why we should work together on these things. If you'd told me you were looking for a Joan Williams, I could have told you where to find her." Louise grinned a grin to beat all grins.

Alex smirked. "Right. I'll remember that next time."

He finished his coffee. "Anyway, where was I?" He pulled his notebook from his pocket. "We seized the laptop. Most of the house was clear of anything interesting—not so much as a family photo. The basement search, however, was rewarding." He paused.

"And?" Louise's eyes opened wide. That couldn't be the end of it. "What did you find?"

"Remember, this goes no further than this table."

Louise crossed her heart. "I promise."

Alex frowned but continued. "Wires, wire cutters, and a couple of metal canisters."

She shrugged a shoulder. "That's it? I have wire and wire cutters in my basement." She combed her fingers through her hair. "I think. No, no, I'm pretty sure. When was the last time I was down there? Maybe in the garage?"

"Louise!"

"Sorry. I just don't see the significance. Most people have tools and scraps of wire around the house."

"Wow. You must be tired. What happened to your suspicious mind and crazy theories?" Alex leaned forward and stared into her eyes, then said, "Wires and metal canisters?"

Louise thought about it for a few seconds, then said, "Oh . . . like what you need to make a . . ." She stopped talking when Alex brought his index finger to his mouth and glanced at the cashier.

He nodded. "You might be right that it's a coincidence, but finding those items gave us cause to seize the computer. Now we'll wait for the lab techs to decipher the contents."

She sighed. "There's a lot of waiting in police work. I'm not sure I'd be cut out for something that requires that amount of patience."

He tapped her hand. "That, my dear, is clear to all who know you."

Louise wanted to slug him—gently and playfully, of course—but she was too tired to lift her arm high enough. He'd lucked out this time.

Chapter 33

LOUISE SUCCEEDED AT dragging her tired and painful body into the clinic on time for morning rounds. Sandra, who'd spent the night at the hospital with Bailey, had called to give Louise an update on his condition. He'd wavered all night between the unconscious and conscious worlds, but testing for serious head injuries came up clear, and the doctor was positive he'd make a full recovery.

Louise didn't remember much of the meeting she'd just attended in the treatment room. She set up the Keurig behind her desk with a pod of dark brew, flopped into her chair, and leaned forward on the desk, her head in her folded arms. Her surroundings darkened as the air grew bitterly cold. In the distance she heard moaning, crying, and someone calling for help. She started to run toward the cries, but with every step the voice grew fainter.

"Hold on, I'm coming. Where are you?" In the darkness ahead, a voice echoed her words, but it wasn't her voice—it was a deep, sinister voice.

She turned and screamed. A man was standing in the distance, his form made visible by dancing flames that surrounded him. He held his twisted arm against his chest, blood seeping from his eyes and nose. Part of his skull was missing. He called out, "Help me!"

Louise wanted to go to him, to help him, but his sinister voice gave her pause. *Why does he sound so evil? Why did someone hurt him?*

She called out to him, "Are you a good guy or a bad guy?"

A hand grasped her shoulder. Louise screamed again and leapt into the air, ready to fight off the danger.

"Wow! Back down, Louise, it's just me!"

She shook her head and opened one eye. She wasn't in a dark, creepy forest but in her office. She rubbed her face with her hands. "I must have nodded off."

Rita appeared to be suppressing a laugh. "Must have been some nightmare. When I heard you scream, I ran in here thinking you were injured, only to find you sound asleep." Rita pointed at the coffee maker. "I think it's done, and not a moment too soon."

After watching Rita leave her office, Louise added extra milk to the hot drink, then consumed it in one long gulp. As she was setting another dark brew pod in the machine, a loud thump sounded behind her. Louise jumped and slammed her back against the wall. Her muscles relaxed when she saw

Daphne standing by her own desk, a new pile of files on the corner.

Daphne tilted her head. "Sorry, I didn't mean to scare you. Guess you didn't hear me come in. What's got you so jumpy?"

Louise sank into her chair. "Everything that went on last night. I have to admit, it's really shaken me up. Bailey looked awful. It's hard to believe that one person would do that to another. And we still don't know what Bailey was up to."

Louise stopped herself from revealing that Bailey might have been operating under a secret identity. Neither she nor the police knew his motive for being at SWaRF, or at the ARSE meetings. Sandra was confident he was a good person, but the ARSE members saw him as an intruder who needed to be eliminated. That scenario worked in his favour. A friend of Sandra's, but not a friend of ARSE.

"I think I'll need another cup or two before I'm ready to do surgery this morning." Louise held her mug in the air.

"Not to worry, my friend. You don't have any surgeries today."

"How did that happen?"

"It's Friday. We don't book surgeries on Fridays, remember?"

"Right."

"And we've been alternating Fridays off, remember?"

"Right. Whose turn is it this week?"

Daphne smiled broadly. "Well, I'm not usually here when it's my day off, so . . ."

Louise stared at her for a few seconds. What was her friend trying to say? Why were they both here if it was Friday? "Oh! What? Wait!" She glanced at the clock on the wall—9:00 a.m. "So, I'm not expected today?"

"No. I was surprised to see you when you walked into rounds, especially after last night. Did you get any sleep?"

Louise filled her lungs with air, then released it slowly. "A few minutes. Just now. On my desk."

"What happened last night? You sent that text saying Bailey Nelson had been found, but it was light on details."

"All I'm allowed to say is that two of the ARSE protestors, Beth Gilley and Patrick Howard, have been arrested on suspicion of assaulting Bailey." Louise yawned. It was a struggle to keep her eyes open. "I need to go home."

"Your options are to call a taxi or wait until one of us can drive you. I'm not sure how you made it here safely, but you shouldn't be driving."

"If only we had those couches across the hall already." Louise emptied her second cup. "I'll wait for a ride. In the meantime, I have some research to do."

An hour and four coffees later, Louise was struggling with both exhaustion and caffeine-induced hyperactivity of her senses. Her internet search yielded only a small amount of useful information. Her first stop on the World Wide Web was the CITES website. It was the one government vehicle she hadn't been familiar with when she and Daphne visited the airport. A quick search told her it was the agency responsible for overseeing international trade of endangered plants and animals. That tied in to the airport workers' talk of importing exotic animals, but Louise didn't know which animal they'd been referring too.

CITES had hundreds, if not thousands, of protected animals listed on its website. It would be impossible to review all of them, and even if she could, it wouldn't tell her which animal was the victim of this group of criminals.

Louise sighed and looked over her shoulder at the Keurig machine, then down at her trembling hand. "You've had enough coffee, Dr. Miller. Time for food."

"I couldn't agree more." Alex was standing in the doorway.

"Oh, hi. How long have you been there?"

He walked over to the window and perched on the windowsill. "Not long. Daphne called. Seems someone needs a ride home. She said she'd take you, but it's a bit of a zoo downstairs right now. With everything that's been going on over the past few days, she didn't want to send you in a cab, so she called to see if I could send an officer to take you home."

"Really? I'll have to chat with her about using the police department as her personal taxi service."

Alex shrugged. "She's worried about you." He grabbed Louise's jacket from the hook on the door. "Come on. I was heading for lunch anyway. We'll stop and eat, and then I'll drop you off at home."

"Sounds good." Louise yawned, then grasped the side of her desk to pull herself to her feet.

"Not enough sleep?"

"Too much caffeine." She followed Alex out the door but stopped at the landing to the staircase. "So, what species did you say was being illegally imported? You know, the one that got away?"

Without looking back at her, he shook his head. "I don't believe I said anything about any such thing."

Chapter 34

THE SIGHT BEFORE her startled Louise's senses. She combed her hand through her hair, then rubbed her eyes. Beyond the windshield of Alex's SUV lay a pile of twisted metal from cars and box trucks. Lying beside one truck was a mound of scorched plastic resembling the top of a giant ice cream cone, but the type of truck was no longer discernable. It, along with the other vehicles, were mere skeletons of their former selves. Metal skeletons with melted tires surrounded by a sea of shattered glass.

Is this another nightmare? Louise pinched herself. It hurt. She removed her seat belt and grasped the door handle, then saw a note attached to the dash. A note from Alex. *Got a call on the way to your place. Had to respond ASAP. You were sleeping. Stay in car. Won't be long.*

Louise glanced at the time on her phone. "You didn't write the time down, Alex. How long have I been sitting here, and how long have you been gone?" She pushed her head back into the headrest. Her frustration soon subsided when she realized she was being afforded an opportunity to view ground zero of the explosion.

The one and only time Louise had been to Tobin Memorial Airport prior to her foray here with Daphne was last summer, when they'd toyed with the idea of taking skydiving lessons. Joe quickly put an end to that notion when a colleague of his spotted Daphne and Louise in line to register. Daphne's phone rang, and Joe let her know his feelings about the mother of his two small children jumping out of an airplane. After ending the call, Daphne twisted her lips and toed the ground. "Um, Louise . . . I think I'll have to pass on skydiving lessons for now. At least until Ella and Ben are older. Joe suggested I wait until they're fully functioning professionals in their chosen fields."

While Louise didn't share her relief with her best friend at the time, she later admitted to Daphne that if Joe hadn't called when he did, she would have feigned vertigo or some other ailment so she could back out. Jumping out of planes wasn't on Louise's bucket list, and how they'd ended up in that lineup, she still wasn't sure.

Back then, the building that housed the airport offices, staff rooms, and public areas was a two-storey concrete structure no larger in square footage than the average fast-food restaurant. It was a small airport that didn't require a lot of public or office space. Attached to that building was a hangar large enough to house two small four-seater airplanes. Larger planes, like the one that would have been used for skydiving, were parked several hundred feet away at the base of one of the unused runways.

It was the office building that suffered the worst of the impact from the explosion. From what Alex had been allowed to tell Louise so far, and from what had been leaked to the press, she knew that the bomb had been placed in the staff room. Two planes were in the hangar at the time, and a good deal of the fire damage was from jet fuel igniting in the plane closest to the bomb. The second plane was protected from the blast by the first, and by some miracle its gas tank didn't explode in the fire.

The two-storey building had been reduced to a quarter of its original size, with only the corner farthest from the bomb still standing. Louise's heart froze momentarily as the image of Alex lying below that rubble flashed into her mind. "Thank you, God, for keeping Alex safe." She knew how fortunate she was that her loved one had survived when five others hadn't.

What was once a hub of short-flight commuter traffic now looked like ancient ruins, wires twisting through the wreckage like deranged snakes. The metal rebar sticking through the crumbled walls and floors reminded her that this was a modern-day structure destroyed by modern-day hate, not a building that was a casualty of a long-ago battle.

Louise's eyes were drawn back to the vehicles and the cone-like structure. Her bag was sitting by her feet, and she was relieved to find her binoculars still in it. As she looked through the lenses, the unusual object came into focus. It was a facsimile of a giant ice cream cone—the type found on top of ice cream trucks. The happy symbol of so many people's childhoods had been reduced to rubble, a victim of evil.

Two police officers had been killed in the explosion, as well as one airport employee and two volunteers. Was the driver of this truck, a person who brought so much joy to local children over the summer months, a victim of this atrocity?

She felt pressure in her chest and heat rising to her face as she looked at the chaos before her, and she remembered the chaos at the hospital when she was desperately searching to determine whether or not Alex was alive. She'd felt as though her world was spinning out of control when she saw the empty hospital bed and thought the worst.

She was fortunate that her grief had lasted only seconds, as others were now experiencing life-long grief. Why? What could have brought someone to the point of placing a bomb in a small airport? And at a time when it could have been filled with families. Was it meant to go off the day it did? Or the next day when the charity event was to start?

A purple-clad figure whipped past a parked pickup truck on the far side of the off-limits parking lot. Louise guided her binoculars there and waited. When the person stepped out from behind the truck, Louise had to convince herself she wasn't seeing things. "What are you doing over there?"

She stepped out of Alex's vehicle to look for a police officer. Two were stationed out of earshot by the entry to the parking lot—and they wouldn't have seen the figure in purple. Louise waved her arms, hoping to get their attention, but they were engrossed in paperwork. She'd have to approach them. Surely Alex would be okay with her leaving the car if it was to alert the officers to an intruder.

Her plans were foiled when the intruder slipped under

the police tape and disappeared behind a utility building. Louise couldn't lose sight of her. "I don't know what you're doing here, Erica Cotton, but it can't be for a good reason." She threw the binoculars into her backpack, slung it over her shoulder, and started her hunt for the woman also known as Plump-in-Plum.

Chapter 35

NOT WANTING TO be seen by the various agents from the various agencies still on site, Louise used the trees north of the bombed-out building as cover. The bushes closer to the building had been reduced to singed remnants of their former selves by the fire, but by the grace of God, the wind had been blowing south that morning, saving rows of beautiful thick coniferous trees from the same fate. If the fire had reached that line of trees, the entire forested region north of the airport might have been lost, including a small number of homes.

Several officers from the department's Forensics Investigative Services (FIS) Unit were sifting through rubble and placing anything that might be evidence into plastic bags, while others were taking fingerprints from materials that hadn't melted. All of the officers and agents were wearing blue jackets, their various agencies identified by black lettering on the back. Two RCMP officers were speaking with a CITES agent, while two officers from the Bathurst Region Police Department were pacing along the periphery of the debris pile that marked where the building's outer walls had stood.

One of those officers was Louise's friend Wayne Carter. She was tempted to call out to him and wave but reminded herself that she was hiding. She was facing west with north to her right. When she and Daphne were here the other night, they'd left before venturing to this point, after hearing airport employees talk about an animal that had possibly escaped. This was the closest she'd been to the blast site.

Where did you go, Erica? You must have gone this way, because unless you want to get lost in the woods, there's nothing east or north. Louise wandered several yards deeper into the woods, then headed west toward the hangar that had housed the planes. If Erica was heading to the hangar, perhaps she was looking for evidence the leaders of ARSE were concerned about. And with Beth Gilley in jail, Erica must be their new pawn.

The ground was dry but littered with twigs and stumps. Louise forged ahead cautiously, careful not to stumble and fall. While the fire hadn't reached this area, there was no way to know how much debris, including glass shards and scraps of metal, might have been blown this way. The heavy rain a few days ago would have driven the dangerous material closer to the ground, under the leaves and out of view. Louise shuddered at the thought of falling into that mess, and what a mess it would make of her.

The airport buildings weren't visible from behind the thick vegetation, but she did see a piece of purple cloth caught in a low branch a few feet away. As she grew closer, it was obvious it was a mitten. A purple mitten. "I must be on the right trail. I can't think of anyone else who'd leave a purple mitten hanging in a tree. Did you leave it as a way to find your way back?" Louise was tempted to retrieve it and shove it into her pocket, but she resisted the urge. If Erica did need it to find her way out of the woods, Louise didn't want to be responsible for stranding the woman.

More importantly, it was evidence that Erica Cotton had been in the secure area; Louise would tell Officer Wayne about it when she saw him later. "With all the law officials wandering around here, I'm pretty sure someone will catch me eventually. I wonder if they'd believe I was simply looking for the washroom?"

A clearing was visible ahead. Louise stopped short of it and peeked around a large tree. She froze at the scene in front of her. Two planes sat in the hangar, visible because the wall had melted in the fire. The one on the left, closer to the office building, was reminiscent of planes that had crashed and burned, as documented on the TV show *Mayday*. The metal frame of the plane was there, but little else of it remained.

The second plane was truly an oddity. One wing was severely damaged, causing the body of the aircraft to tilt down, lifting its other wing up. That wing, and the body of the plane, were undamaged. Forgetting she might be seen, Louise made her way in zombie-like fashion to the hangar to get a closer look.

There was a series of letters and numbers on the tail of the plane. Louise suspected it was a licence number, similar to one she'd seen on a yacht not long ago.

The smell of burnt materials and fuel burned her eyes and throat. She pulled her shirt up over her mouth, then stepped closer to the intact plane. The passenger-side door hung open, the tilted angle of the plane making the interior easily accessible. Certain that the forensics teams would have already removed anything important, Louise grasped the frame of the doorway, stuck her head in, and had a look around. Without entering the cockpit, she scanned every inch she could, including under the seats, and under and on top of the console.

"Ah . . . look at that." She was about to reach in.

"Find anything interesting?"

Louise froze, then slowly turned to find Alex standing behind her, his arms crossed.

"In fact, I did. There's a cigarette butt in there. It could be the same brand as the one found at SWaRF. Another connection."

"I asked you to stay in the car, but when I got there and you were gone, I, well . . . I guess I wasn't surprised."

She shrugged. "I was accused not long ago of lacking patience. What can I say? I guess it's true."

Louise stepped aside to allow Alex access to the cockpit. He reached in with a gloved hand to retrieve the cigarette butt, then stopped himself. "Hmm. I hate to say this, but you may be on to something. I'll call Julie Corridor. Her team will have to photograph and bag the butt. They'll check it for DNA, and if they find any, they'll compare it to the other one you found."

Louise slapped him on the shoulder. "Splendid. Good thing you brought me here with you. By the way, what was the ASAP all about?"

"The missing animal was found earlier today."

"So there *was* a missing creature."

"Yes, but sadly it was dead when they found it. Do I want to know how you knew there was a missing animal? We've discussed the crates, but not the contents."

"The trip Daphne and I took here the other night. We overheard a couple of airport workers talking about it."

Alex slapped his forehead. "Right! Anyway, the CITES agents identified it. Have you heard of a pangolin?"

Louise massaged her neck muscles to remove the kink caused by her nap in the car. "No. Pan-go-lin? I've no idea what that is. Where did it come from?"

"Wendel Mitchell—he's the agent from CITES—says it could be from either Africa or Asia. He needs to do a little research before he can identify which type of pangolin it is."

"Hey, speaking of CITES agents, do you know if they're missing any?"

"Why would you ask that?"

"Because Bailey Nelson was working at SWaRF, which was accused of importing exotics, and he was spying on ARSE, a group that might have links to the airport explosion. And then there are the crates found at both sites that can be used to transport animals."

Alex stared into her eyes and held her gaze for more than a few uncomfortable seconds. Every nerve in her body was on edge. Was this it? Was he about to have a complete breakdown from the trauma he's suffered? He wasn't moving or talking. His face was without expression. She readied her phone to call 911 in case he was having a stroke.

Louise studied his eyes for any signs of nystagmus. As she raised her arm to check his eyelid response, he suddenly turned and headed for what remained of the office building.

"You might be on to something there too. Let's go have a chat with Wendel."

They found Wendel Mitchell, a tall man with Harry Potter glasses and long grey hair pulled into a ponytail, hovering over a laptop computer in the CITES van. Laid out on a table beside him was a small animal with scales covering most of its body. It had a long tail, a blunted nose, and a head that reminded Louise of a pyramid. She estimated it to be about two to three feet long, but its weight was hard to judge because of the scales.

"The poor little thing. I've never seen anything like this little guy, but . . ." Louise sniffled. "People can be so cruel." She wanted to run out of the truck and scream into the air at a week so full of death and trauma and cruelty. How many lives were lost because of the greed of a few people? She couldn't bear the thought of the bigger picture—of how many people, and animals, were suffering every day around the world because of the greed of many. Instead of running and screaming, she lowered her head and whispered a prayer to God: "Please help me to trust that you're in control. That good really does outweigh evil in this world."

Alex put his arm around her shoulder and pulled her close. The warmth of his embrace was calming—Louise was assured that Alex knew her well enough to realize that the terror this creature had gone through was tearing her up inside.

"Hey, Wendel, we have a question for you," Alex said.

Wendel looked up from the computer. "Shoot."

"Do you have any missing colleagues?"

Wendel frowned at Alex as though the detective had had

one too many martinis for lunch. "Why would you ask that? We didn't have any agents here when the explosion happened." He rubbed his chin. "Not that I know of, anyway." He swivelled around in his chair and punched a few computer keys. "Nope, no one was here that day. We do have an agent in the area." Wendel punched a few more keys, then swivelled back around to look at Alex, concern on his face.

"Bailey Newman. He hasn't checked in all week. He was assigned to—"

Newman? Bailey Newman? Similar to Bailey Nelson! Louise interrupted the CITES agent. "To Sydney's Wildlife Rehabilitation Facility?"

"Yeah. How'd you know?"

Alex took his notepad from his pocket. "I'll need the name and contact information of Mr. Newman's supervisor."

A few parking spots from the CITES van, the FIS van was parked beside a transport tent that housed a mobile laboratory. As Louise followed Alex closer to the white canvas structure, she watched three forensics technicians running samples through various machines and another person looking into a microscope.

The set-up reminded her of her veterinary technicians at the clinic—they were probably running labs right now. She hadn't seen much of them this week, and a flood of guilt swept over her when she realized she still hadn't had a heart-to-heart with Daphne. Daphne seemed back to her usual self this morning, but Louise might have imagined that in her severely sleepy state. She'd make it up to Daphne and the staff once this case was over.

Alex placed his hand on Louise's shoulder and guided her into the tent. "Julie, this is my associate, Dr. Louise Miller."

Alex wore a huge grin as he said "associate." Was she the butt of some joke? Julie didn't return the smile, setting Louise's mind at ease that Alex's joke was his alone.

"Nice to meet you, Louise." Julie offered her hand, which Louise accepted. The forensics officer nodded over her shoulder at a young man behind her. "This is my assistant, Larry."

Larry nodded a greeting, then returned his attention to the microscope.

"I hear you found a few bits of evidence for us," Julie said.

"I got lucky when I literally stumbled at the rehab centre earlier this week, and there in front of me was a piece of fabric. Alex says it won't be of use, though, unless there's something to match it to. Makes sense," Louise said.

"True, we need a shirt that matches the material you found, or DNA from a suspect, as well as the victim, to identify the source of the blood. Rest assured though, we keep evidence like that as long as needed to identify and convict the culprits."

Alex hadn't confirmed to Louise that there was blood on the piece of plaid fabric she'd found. She glanced back at him; his expression was neutral, suggesting that Julie sharing this information wasn't a concern.

Julie continued. "The cigarette butt could be useful. We recovered a male DNA profile from it. It doesn't match Bailey Nelson, the man you found last night, so we entered it into the national database to see if we can get a hit. We haven't gotten word yet about whether or not he's a match to the fabric."

Louise's adrenalin was skyrocketing. Listening to an actual forensic investigator talking about real evidence was far more exciting than watching it on TV. She fought to control the giddy feeling overwhelming her. *Keep it professional, Louise. Don't make a fool of yourself. You're not at a celebrity meet-and-greet.*

Alex cocked his thumb toward the hangar. "We have another cigarette butt for your team. It's in the cockpit of the second Cessna."

Julie raised her eyebrows. "Impossible. My guys swept that cockpit clean of anything that wasn't attached. They've been done with the plane since yesterday."

"There's definitely a cigarette butt on the floor. I can't imagine they would have missed it . . . unless?" Alex ran his fingers through his hair, then rested his hand on his head as he gazed at something in the distance.

"Unless, what? I didn't put it there. Is that what you think?" Louise crossed her arms.

"Humph. No. Why would I think that? I have no doubt you didn't do it, but someone did."

"Maybe that's why Plump-in-Plum—I mean Erica Cotton—was sneaking around earlier. That's why I left the car, by the way. I spotted her crawl under the police tape and I couldn't get the attention of the officers guarding the parking lot. I didn't want to lose her, so I followed her. But I lost her. Then I found the hangar. Well, I did find a mitten first. A purple one, so it's probably hers. I left it hanging in the tree."

"Erica Cotton? From ARSE? Why didn't you mention this earlier?"

"Slipped my mind after I found the cigarette butt. Now that Beth Gilley's in jail, I bet Erica is the new pawn—sent to do the others' bidding so that they can keep their hands clean."

Alex radioed the on-site team with instructions to keep an eye out for an intruder. "What did you say she was wearing?"

"A brimmed hat with a purple band around it, and a

purple coat. Not the best outfit when you're trying to sneak into a secure area undetected, but the only bright thing about that woman is her coat."

Alex relayed Louise's description of the suspect, minus the unkind remark, to the officers on duty at the airport.

While he was doing that, Julie dispatched Larry to photograph and retrieve the cigarette butt. Then she turned to Louise. "If she lost a mitten, she might have left a fingerprint on the cigarette butt with her bare hand. And if we're really lucky, she's also left us some DNA."

"Wouldn't that ruin the DNA sample of the person who'd been smoking the cigarette? You said the DNA from the other butt was from a male, so if this is the same smoker . . ."

"We might get a mixed sample, but if the sample's good enough, we can separate it and come up with two profiles."

Louise couldn't hold back her excitement anymore. "Cool!" *Acting mature is so overrated.*

Julie addressed Alex. "The Electronic Crimes Unit gained access to Ms. Williams's laptop and told me they found some interesting files. The computer was delivered to your office earlier."

"Thanks. I'm heading to the department now, after I drop my associate here at home."

Louise frowned. "Come on, you can't cut me out now. We're too close."

Alex shook his head and headed for his car.

Chapter 36

"THERE'S NO NEED to take me home right away. I've been helpful so far, so why not just let me tag along? I'm sure the CITES agents are busy. I can do some research on the pangolin for them. You know, free up their time. What do you say, Alex? Alex?"

Louise, who'd been walking a couple of feet ahead of him, stopped and glanced over her shoulder. Alex was several yards behind her, standing still, staring at one of the burnt vehicles. Why hadn't she noticed it earlier? The car she and Alex rode here in was his personal vehicle, one he rarely used in favour of his Bathurst Region Police Department car. Using his BRPD vehicle, he could respond quicker to crimes scenes when he was on call.

Now the latter vehicle, no more than a burnt frame with shattered glass and melted seats, sat sadly alongside two Bathurst Region squad cars, also destroyed.

Louise moved to Alex's side and held on to his arm.

He remained frozen in place. "You know how lucky I was that I wasn't in there when the bomb went off? Much of the blast came this way and sent flaming shards of"—he shivered—"I don't know, but whatever it was, it went into these cars. I was one of the lucky ones."

"I've been thanking God every day for sparing you." Louise tightened her hold on him. "What about"—she pointed at the other squad cars—"those officers. Are they okay?"

"Norman will be, because he was in the building with me when the bomb went off. I spoke to Jean this morning, and he's doing well."

"That's good news. His wife is the woman who thanked you at the hospital?"

"Right." Alex pulled away from her and walked toward his car. "Officer Truman wasn't so lucky." He picked up a rock and flung it toward the shell of the airport office building. "He was trapped in the vehicle and, well . . ." Alex's head drooped.

They walked silently back to Alex's SUV, through the graveyard of a place meant to be the site of a happy occasion this past week. Families gathering for a fun-filled week of festivities to raise money for the children's hospital. Hopes of ice cream, rides, and an air show had been replaced by the burnt and crumbling evidence of death and destruction.

Alex unlocked the doors with the fob, then climbed into

the driver's seat. Once Louise was seated on the passenger side and buckled in, he threw the car into drive.

"You know, it would be faster to go to the station first. Then I'll drop you off later. Would that be okay? I know you're tired, but . . ."

Was he kidding? Not only did she want to keep abreast of what was going on with the investigation, but after what she'd just witnessed, she wasn't ready to let Alex out of her sight.

"Tina Purcell worked at the airport." Stress and fatigue emanated from his eyes.

"You mentioned that before. She and Joan Williams both worked there."

"Yup. The airport manager informed us that Joan had been hired on several months ago. She only recently recommended Tina Purcell for a receptionist position."

"Joan got Tina the job at the airport?" Louise mouthed *Wow*.

"That's what I said. Remember, you can't share any of this information with anyone outside of the investigation."

"I remember. So do you think Tina planted the bomb at the airport?"

"That was the initial theory, but Ms. Purcell didn't have access to the secure staff area. Her clearance hadn't been approved yet. Joan Williams, on the other hand, did have access."

"And she'd been avoiding the police all week. I can't wait to find out what they found on her computer. It sounds pretty juicy."

Alex pulled onto the shoulder of the road and slammed on the brakes. "Maybe I should take you home first."

"Why?"

"*Sounds juicy?* This is real life, not a crime drama on TV."

"I know that—I don't need to be reminded. I saw the victims at the hospital. I saw the damage today. I don't know what it's like for you and the others to have had a near-death experience, but I did find a dead body the other day."

Louise had found one body—how many had Alex had to deal with in his career? She could only imagine that as a homicide detective for Bathurst Region, Alex, who was on call 24/7, had witnessed more heartache and horror than one person ever should. How often had he had to give the news that someone's loved one wasn't returning home?

"I'm sorry. I didn't mean to sound flippant. I'm just functioning on way too much caffeine and not enough sleep. And add to that, stresses at the clinic."

Alex sighed. "Okay, let's start over." He manoeuvred the car back onto the road. "We've both had a very bad week."

They purchased a couple of decafs and sandwiches at a drive-thru. Dark clouds were slowly approaching from the west. Louise rolled up her window before unwrapping her Mediterranean sub. "Mmm . . . feta cheese and Greek dressing. What did we do before drive-thru service?"

"We made food at home and used lunch boxes. Hand me a napkin."

"Right." Louise passed him a napkin, then wasted no time consuming her lunch.

Alex parked near the private entrance at the back of the police station, then escorted Louise through the locked doors to his office.

Not wanting to reignite Alex's regret at bringing her to his office, she hid her excitement when she found a laptop marked Evidence sitting in a clear plastic bag on the desk.

Alex tapped the keyboard of Joan Williams's laptop while intermittently stopping to flip through his notebook. Louise yawned; the benefits of her short nap on their way to the airport were wearing off, and the cost of multiple nights of disrupted sleep once again threatened to overtake her. She stood up and paced Alex's small office.

"Wow, Julie's techy guys weren't kidding—this is definitely interesting!" Alex massaged his chin, then leaned back in his chair.

"What? What's interesting?" She positioned herself behind him so she could read over his shoulder, but he closed the laptop. "Hey, I thought we were sharing?"

"We're sharing what I can, but not everything."

"So you're proclaiming things to be interesting just to tease me?"

"No. I can't show you Joan Williams's bank account information, but I can tell you that she won't be going on any fancy vacations anytime soon."

"Why's that?"

"Her account balance is close to zero. Three dollars and twenty-two cents, to be exact."

"Really? But if she's involved in smuggling animals—"

"Exactly. We'd expect her to have funds available to cover the costs of the operation, and some evidence of profits."

"Unless . . ."

"Unless?"

"Unless she's a beginner. Maybe she blew out her savings

on one job, then couldn't complete the mission and so blew up the airport."

Alex frowned. "That's a pretty drastic measure to take because you drained your bank account. What would her purpose be? And with the airport closed down, she's out of a job, at least temporarily."

Louise shrugged. "I don't know. I'll have to think on it. Anything else interesting in there?" She pulled the chair she'd been sitting on to the desk, trapping Alex between herself and the far wall.

He scooted his chair over to give her more room, then lifted the laptop lid, bringing the screen to life. "There is. I'll go back into her emails."

Alex opened the email app and scrolled through the inbox. "Right here—an email thread between Joan Williams and Tina Purcell. Initially, they're discussing the job Joan recommended Tina for. Nothing too interesting there, other than the connection between ARSE and the airport. It gets more interesting later on."

He opened the thread and scrolled to the later messages, then held the cursor over a point of interest.

Louise read the text out loud. "'Tomorrow morning is a go. Meet us at the arranged time. Enter the way we showed you on the map. Beth will drop you off before joining the others at the front.'"

She slapped Alex on the shoulder. "Look at the date—the day of the bombing! I wonder what they were meeting about, and where."

"Was Beth Gilley with the group of protestors the first time you saw them at SWaRF?"

Louise inhaled deeply and held the breath while staring

at the ceiling. Then she exhaled and shook her head. "Sorry. I don't remember, but Sandra's crew was filming the protestors, so there's probably some video evidence. Why?"

"It sounds like they were meeting at SWaRF. Joan tells Tina that Beth will meet the others around the front after dropping her off. So, if Beth was with the protestors that morning—"

"Then Beth Gilley drove Tina Purcell to her death?"

Alex gave Louise a sidelong look. "Very dramatic way to put it, but yes, that's what I'm thinking."

"So that crinkled-up little old lady I didn't take seriously in the woods might be an accomplice to murder?"

"Yes. That's one of the many reasons you should leave police work up to the police. You can't rule out someone as dangerous based on physical appearance alone."

"But she's just so little, and . . ." Louise glanced out the window. In the parking lot sat a couple of squad cars, one of the RCMP Tactical Armoured Vehicles, and the CITES van.

"And?"

"What are the RCMP and CITES doing here?"

"They're here to interview Beth Gilley and Patrick Howard—the RCMP about the bombs, and CITES about the pangolin."

"I don't suppose . . ." Louise tilted her head and gave Alex the best puppy dog eyes she could muster.

He wasn't swayed. "No, you cannot watch the interviews."

Louise shrugged. "Doesn't hurt to ask. Anything else interesting on there?" She pointed at the laptop.

"Besides Joan Williams's search history on ways to construct a bomb?"

"Wow. That's surprising."

"Why surprising? We already suspected she was involved in the bombing."

"It's not that. I'm just surprised that people use their own computer to search for something like that, or if they do, that they don't wipe their search history after the fact. You know, in case they get caught."

"Most bad guys don't think they'll get caught, so they don't worry about covering their tracks."

"Or, as might be the case here, they're just not all that smart."

Brian Tomlin, one of the police officers who'd initially responded after Sandra and Louise discovered the body in the pond, entered Alex's office with a file in his hand. He handed it to Alex. "Julie and her team have completed their work on the crates. I was on my way up here anyway, so I offered to deliver the results to you."

Alex flipped it open. "Hmm." He looked at the uniformed officer. "Thanks, Brian."

Once they were alone again, Louise tapped the back of the file Alex was holding up in front of his face. "More interesting evidence you can't share?"

He slowly lowered the yellow folder, revealing a grin. "I can reveal this to you—I just wasn't sure if I should."

She nodded. "You should."

"Remember, it doesn't go past this office." He held her gaze.

"I haven't blabbed yet."

"Yet?"

She slapped his leg. "And I won't. Come on, what does it say?"

"Fingerprint analysis was done both on the crate you found at SWaRF and the salvageable crates at the airport. The

SWaRF crate had multiple prints. Some matched our victim, Tina Purcell. Some matched prints found at Joan Williams's home. They might be from her, but they could be from someone who visited her home. And some prints weren't matched."

"So Tina handled the bomb?"

"We only know that she handled the crate that was at SWaRF. We don't know if she had anything to do with its contents or purpose. They'll be checking the wires and other contents of the box for prints and DNA."

"What about the airport crates?"

Alex shook his head. "Lots of prints, but none belong to our victim. Some do, however, match prints found in Joan Williams's home." He gave Louise a knowing glance, then leapt to his feet.

She moved her chair, freeing him from the corner. He threw open the office door and called out to Brian and Wayne, who were chatting by the water cooler. "Hey, guys, I need you to pick up Joan Williams. Tell her she's being arrested on suspicion of terrorism and murder."

Chapter 37

LOUISE PACED THE hall outside Alex's office. Her pacing was becoming a bad habit. How long could it take to go through the formalities of booking Joan Williams before questioning her? She knew it was unlikely that she, a civilian, would be allowed in the interview room, but would Alex agree to let her observe from elsewhere? Perhaps watch a live video feed, or observe from an adjoining room with a two-way mirror. Did they have such rooms at the police station? Or was that just something they did on TV crime shows?

Needing to keep her mind occupied, she used the array of shadows, created by beams of light cast through the windows at the far end of the hallway, to perform her own psychology exam. She knew it as the inkblot test; Daphne had told her the proper term long ago, but "inkblot" was all Louise could remember.

The combination of the open door and the fire extinguisher created a large syringe with a short needle attached. With a great deal of imagination, the shadow from the fake fern in need of dusting mimicked a shaggy dog, and that the shadow from a chair looked like, well, a chair. She reached the chair, sat, and dropped her head into her hands. A short nap wouldn't hurt.

The nap that never happened was interrupted by an ear-piercing, screeching voice around the corner. Louise focused her attention in that direction as the alien-like screams grew louder, and soon the noises took on the form of distinguishable words.

"Let me go. You have no right to touch me. I'm going to sue every one of you. You'll all be charged. You just wait and see. He'll come and get me out of here."

The voice was familiar, but it wasn't Joan Williams, who'd already been brought into the station through a different entrance. While Louise was happy to hear the news that Madame Grumpy Face was in custody, she was saddened to have missed the opportunity to see the nasty woman in handcuffs. No, this wasn't her—Joan's voice was lower pitched and grumpier. This woman sounded upset but more delusional and frenzied than grumpy. When the police dragged a large figure into view, Louise recognized the hat and coat immediately. Plump-in-Plum, otherwise known as Erica Cotton.

Louise wanted to follow the tiny crowd of struggling officers dragging a very uncooperative giant plum, but she knew she'd be shooed away. She'd save her energy and use the time to make some calls.

She was about to hang up after several unanswered rings when she heard "Hello?"

"Hey, Sandra, it's Louise. I thought I'd call for an update on Bailey and Major."

"Where are you?" Sandra sounded more tired than Louise felt.

"At the police station. They've made a few more arrests. I'm waiting to hear for any updates before heading home. How are you doing?"

"Heading home soon myself. One of the staff from SWaRF called earlier to let me know that Major's doing really well. Eating, drinking, and he's had a bowel movement. All normal."

Louise's heart leapt at the good news about the coyote, but what about the man she'd found in the kennel? "How's Bailey?"

"He's fully conscious now. He'd been coming in and out when I first got here, but he's been awake for an hour or so. They offered him some soup, but his lips are so swollen he can't eat."

"Has he told you anything?"

"Not really. He can't talk very well, but even if he could, the officer guarding his door instructed him not to talk to anyone except law enforcement. Have you heard anything about what happened to him? Or why? Is it related to that Tina woman we found in the pond? He didn't do it, did he?"

Louise had promised Alex she wouldn't reveal any information about the case, but surely telling Sandra that her trust in Bailey wasn't completely misplaced wouldn't be so bad. "He didn't kill anyone, Sandra, or hurt anyone. That's all I can say at this point."

Sandra sighed in relief. "That's fine, Louise. It's heart-wrenching to think of him all alone in that kennel, cold and in pain and unable to call for help. Every time I think about it, I get this feeling of deep sadness." Her tone changed from a reflective one to one of conviction. "But you know, I knew he wasn't a bad person."

No, he wasn't, but he hadn't been completely honest with Sandra. He was working at SWaRF under a false name, and Louise still wasn't sure if he was investigating Sandra or helping her.

"Sandra, do you have video of the protestors from earlier in the week? The first day I was there to check on Major?"

"Sure. Why?"

It pained Louise to keep information from her friends, but she'd made a promise to Alex. "I can't say, but I think it might help the investigation. Can you send me what you have?"

"I'll do that as soon as we hang up so I don't forget. If any of those protestors were involved in this mess, anything I can do to help send them away for a long time would be my pleasure."

They said their goodbyes, then Louise hit End. Within seconds, a text message from Sandra arrived with three video clips attached. Louise was eager to view them, but first she wanted to check in with Daphne. They still hadn't had a heart-to-heart about what had been stressing Daphne all week—besides the nasty client with a nasty review, the airport bombing, and the events at SWaRF, that is.

Louise was about to tap on Daphne's number when Alex came around the same corner the Plump-in-Plum parade had emerged from earlier. She waved to him from the hall. Alex stopped at the entrance to his office and, with a wave of his hand, indicated she should join him inside.

Louise's head dropped back, the fatigue in her legs encouraging her to stay seated, but the desire to get an update on Joan Williams propelled her out of her chair and down the hall.

"I have three videos of the protestors at SWaRF from earlier this week." She opened the first video and viewed it. "Beth Gilley was definitely there." She handed the phone to Alex.

He watched the video, then scrolled to and watched the other two. "That's odd. I thought you said Joan Williams was with the group that day."

"She was." Louise pointed to the phone in Alex's hand. "She's in all three videos. The one with the grumpy face."

He scrolled through the videos again. He stopped on one and with two fingers enlarged the image. He then held the phone closer to his face, his brow wrinkling. "This is the grumpiest face of the group, but that's not Joan Williams." He turned the phone to show Louise.

She took the phone from him. "Yes, it is. That's her. The woman Erica Cotton referred to as Joan, the woman I identified via facial recognition as Joan Williams, and"—Louise paused to take a breath—"the woman named Joan Williams in the online articles I found about ARSE."

Alex squinted and rubbed his chin. "Well, that's not the woman who was just processed, and it's not the woman who was at Joan Williams's home when we executed the search warrant. And if that isn't Ms. Williams we have in custody, why didn't she speak up?" Alex took back the phone and stared at the screen for a few seconds. "If this is Joan Williams, who's the woman we have in the cells?"

He flew by Louise and headed back around the corner, still holding her phone.

Chapter 38

LOUISE WAVED GOODBYE to Alex before getting into her car. She'd finally had a good night's sleep, but when she woke up this morning, the first thought she had was *I don't have my car*. It was still at the veterinary clinic. By the time Alex had finished interviewing the mystery woman impersonating Joan Williams—and it didn't take long because she'd refused to talk—and sent out a warrant for the real Joan Williams's arrest, he was eager to drop Louise off at home so he could get home himself.

Oscar had been in the kitchen howling for breakfast when Louise made her way to the main floor. She fed her furry companion and grabbed a muffin and coffee before calling Alex to request a ride to the clinic. Within half an hour he arrived at her door, and after a quiet ride to the parking lot, which was empty other than her SUV, Louise again became independently mobile.

Sitting in her vehicle, she stared at the building that housed the Black Creek Animal Hospital. They were coming up to their nine-year anniversary, and while they were doing well, there had been bumps in the road. Some were tiny bumps, but others felt like a ride at a poorly maintained mobile amusement park. They'd grown busy enough to justify hiring a part-time associate, but when they did hire someone to cover Daphne's last maternity leave, it ended in an unexpected fashion.

Louise and Daphne hadn't voiced their hesitation at hiring again—they both knew they needed a third veterinarian—but they were reluctant to go that route so soon after the last debacle. This past week affirmed to Louise that they needed to let go of the past and find an associate.

Even with the cancellations they'd had earlier in the week, brought on by the explosion, they'd been busy. Daphne was feeling the stress, and Louise hadn't yet had a chance to talk to her about it. How did two best friends get to the point where they couldn't take a few minutes to chat about how they were doing mentally and physically?

The empty parking lot was evidence of their decision to close the clinic on the occasional Saturday. They'd closed it this Saturday, anticipating the festivities that were supposed to happen at the airport.

Louise checked the time—it was a few minutes past eight. She knew that Daphne and Joe didn't have any plans this weekend, so there was a good chance Daphne would be home.

At this hour, she'd probably be in the barn feeding her horse, Jo-el. As a doting godmother, Louise would grab some treats for Ella, then head to Daphne and Joe's country home.

The lane to Daphne's farm was a long S-shaped gravel road bordered by traditional wooden log fences. On a working farm, the fence would be meant to keep livestock in, but in this case, it was merely decorative. There was a paddock behind the barn for Jo-el to exercise in, and this was where Louise spotted Daphne as she drove up the lane.

At the sound of the car door closing, Daphne turned her head and waved, then disappeared into the paddock side of the barn. She reappeared through the door adjacent to Louise's SUV, holding a basketful of chicken eggs.

Louise smiled at the sight of her best friend in coveralls, a ball cap, and dirty boots.

"What are you doing here this early? I thought you'd be sleeping in today."

"Oscar had other ideas. There's no sleeping in when you have a cat who lives to eat."

"He *is* getting a bit on the pudgy side. Have you thought about putting him on the new weight loss diet? Rita said we've been getting some good results with it."

Louise frowned. She hadn't stopped by to discuss Oscar's dietary needs. "He's fine. You're starting to sound like Alex."

"Well, if he's saying Oscar needs to go on a diet, I'm happy to sound like him." Daphne waved for Louise to follow her. "Come into the barn. I want to show you my new chickens."

Louise followed her cheery friend to the stall at the far end and peeked in. She counted six chickens. "These are the new birds? What happened to the old ones? You didn't—" When was the last time she'd eaten at Daphne and Joe's? Did they have chicken? Louise wasn't such a city girl that she didn't know where her food came from—she just preferred not to have met it first.

Daphne laughed. "No! You know I couldn't do that. I'm as big a goof as you are in that department." Farmer Daphne placed the eggs onto the ground, then entered the stall and picked up a chicken. "This is Sheba." She pointed to a couple of birds in the corner. "Those two are Gunny and Sparky."

"Weren't there always six chickens? What happened to the three old ones?"

"Two died of old age. The third went missing. It's been eating away at me all week."

"Poor choice of words when there's a missing chicken."

Daphne rolled her eyes at Louise's sad attempt at humour. "I think the dog might have gotten her. Not our dog, Max, but a neighbour's. It's been getting into the barn at night. I've had to leave Jo-el in the paddock because it was upsetting him, but I can't leave the chickens outside. Joe and the new man who moved in down the road have had a few words."

Louise opened her mouth to offer a platitude about loving one's neighbours, then resealed her lips. Joe was a mild-mannered man, so hearing that he'd had words with a neighbour made her wonder how bad the newcomer was. Even in the country, where the nearest house could be over two hundred yards away, no one was completely safe from acquiring an unfriendly neighbour. "Is that why you've been so stressed this week? I mean, I know we've all been stressed by the explosion and the murder, not to mention good ol' Mrs. Theobald, but . . ." Louise leaned against the stall wall.

"No, you're right. It's been hard to sleep when I'm worrying about that dog getting in here. When I'd finally fall asleep,

Ella would wake up crying over the lost chicken, or excited about her school play. We secured the loose boards Thursday. I'm hoping that'll take care of the problem."

Spiderwebs decorated the corners of the barn, one of them home to what looked like a larger-than-normal spider for this area of Ontario. "What is that?" Louise pointed at it.

Daphne returned Sheba to the ground, then gently touched the spider. It ran from the intruding finger. "Her name is Charlotte."

"You name your spiders? I guess I shouldn't be surprised." When they'd first met, Daphne had a name for her pen. Louise had forgotten the name long ago, but she knew that naming inanimate objects was one of the character quirks that would make Daphne a friend worth having. Who named their pens if they weren't full of fun and imagination?

"Not me—Ella. She not only named this spider, but all the others as well."

Louise scanned the barn. "How can she keep track of them all?"

"Easy." Daphne grinned. "They're all named Charlotte."

They enjoyed a giggle session, then headed into the house to have tea and biscuits with Joe and Ella, and to afford Louise some cuddle time with the baby, Ben.

Now that one mystery had been solved—hopefully permanently with the newly secured barn keeping Jo-el and the chickens safe—Louise's mind drifted back to the criminal mysteries that had occupied so much of her time over the past week.

Beth Gilley, Patrick Howard, Erica Cotton, and one

unnamed woman were in custody—Beth and Patrick for the assault on Bailey, and Erica for sneaking into the airport and tampering with evidence. Louise guided her SUV from Daphne's gravel driveway to the main road. She had suspected early on that Beth and Erica were under the control of Joan Williams and Keith Roberts, the man in the hoodie. It stood to reason that the woman posing as Joan Williams was also under their control. Louise shook her head as she dug into her bag for a snack bar. What could lead a group of seemingly normal older women to blindly follow another person to the point of being arrested?

Louise had been full of questions when Alex picked her up to fetch her car earlier that day, but he was unable to answer any of them. The police were as baffled as Louise was at having arrested someone who'd willingly posed as a murder suspect. She slowed when she noticed a squirrel darting across the road, unaware of the danger of its actions. Perhaps the imposter was unaware of the dangerous actions she was taking—had she succeeded in convincing the authorities that she was the real Joan Williams, an unlikely scenario, she could have faced a lifetime in prison for crimes she didn't commit.

The fuel gauge was approaching the red zone, so Louise pulled into the gas station on the right side of the road. She filled the tank with regular unleaded, then replaced the cap. As she was getting back into the car, two men near the entrance to the gas station's store drew her attention when the smaller man shoved the larger one.

Louise mouthed *"no way"* and sank down in her seat, hoping they hadn't seen her. She used the camera app on her phone to spy on the men by raising the lens above the dash. There was no mistaking who they were—the tightly curled hair on the bearded man in a hoodie identified him, and Louise would never forget the face of the man who'd beaten up Bailey Nelson.

Keith Roberts and Patrick Howard were having a heated argument, but about what? And more importantly, what was Patrick doing out of jail?

She called Alex, then plied him with questions before he could say hello. "What's Patrick Howard doing out? Why isn't he in jail? Is someone following him to see if he leads them to more clues? What's going on?"

Alex jumped into the conversation when she paused to take a breath. "Calm down. Where are you?"

"At the gas station not far from Daphne's. I needed gas. Howard and Roberts are here arguing."

"Roberts?"

"Keith Roberts. The cult leader I told you about. Well, he seems like a cult leader. They're shoving each other around. What's that Howard guy doing out of jail?" Louise heard the fear in her own voice. That man knew who she was—a witness to his crimes and someone whose testimony could send him to prison for a very long time.

"We couldn't hold him—not enough evidence. His fingerprints weren't on the wrench, and Beth Gilley insists she was the one who hit Mr. Nelson with it. Her fingerprints were all over the weapon, so we couldn't immediately dismiss her confession." Alex paused. "Listen, drive away and act as though you don't recognize them. I'll send a squad car. Maybe we can pick both of them up for public disturbance."

"Howard was at the kennel when I found Bailey. His voice will be on the 911 recording."

"Beth Gilley is claiming he wasn't there, and Howard's lawyer made a motion to suppress the 911 recording."

"How'd they do that so fast?"

"Money talks. We already knew he's a successful business owner. I suspect he's got some connections in political circles—it's not unheard of. Give a large donation to the right campaign and well . . . you get it. Fortunately, though, even millionaires have limits to the amount of influence they can acquire through donating, and Howard's far from being a millionaire. We just have to be patient while we gather all the evidence."

Louise lost sight of the arguing men, then found them again when they moved out from behind a parked van. They walked farther away from her car, then disappeared around the far end of the gas bar. She sighed with relief that they hadn't seen her. *Let's hope you're heading to your car and leaving.*

"Have you left yet? I don't hear your engine," Alex said.

"No. They've gone around the back of the store. It's a strange alliance, Patrick and Keith. Why is a businessman hanging out with a cult leader?"

"We'll figure that out later. For now, just get moving before they return and spot you."

"Got it." Louise hit the engine button.

Alex continued to talk as she shifted into drive. "The good news is, Erica Cotton has been very talkative. She's confirmed that Ms. Williams ordered her to plant the cigarette butt, but she claims she doesn't know why."

Louise returned the transmission to park. The two men hadn't returned, and her curiosity overwhelmed her caution. "Do you think Williams is trying to set someone else up? Maybe the woman who was at her house. Is Mystery Lady a smoker? Does the DNA on the butt found at the airport match hers?"

"It was male DNA on the SWaRF butt and the results on the plane butt aren't in yet. Ms. Cotton also confirmed that Mystery Lady, as you call her, isn't Joan Williams. But listen, don't worry about any of that right now. Just drive to the nearest populated place, and call me when you get there."

"Will do. I'll head for the grocery store near my house." Louise ended the call, slipped the phone into her pocket, and started the engine. She was ready to shift the car into drive when she heard rapping in her left ear. She turned toward the driver's window and froze, unable to see anything beyond the barrel of a handgun.

Chapter 39

LOUISE INSTINCTIVELY LOCKED the car doors, knowing deep within her that this wouldn't stop a bullet from shattering the glass before it shattered her skull.

"Open the door." Keith Roberts banged on the window with one fist while his gun-wielding hand remained steady.

"Not a chance." It was unlikely the bearded man could hear her response—Louise herself could hardly hear the timid whisper that escaped her lips. If only she was still on the call with Alex. Then he'd know she was being threatened and would come to rescue her.

If she left the car and allowed this man to take her, she'd disappear, never to be seen again. When her abandoned car was found, Alex would deduce she'd been taken but wouldn't know how to find her. As far as she knew, the police knew nothing about this man in the hoodie—his true identity, where he lived, or what he was doing in Bathurst Region.

His dirty hand with yellow-stained fingertips continued to batter the window. *Think Louise, think. How are you going to get out of this one?*

"Open the door and get out. Now!" His upper lip lifted, exposing his damaged teeth, the result of poor dental hygiene, and making him appear like a vicious dog ready to attack.

Patrick Howard, who must have gone into the store, appeared at its door and turned in their direction when Keith Roberts resumed banging. Behind Patrick, a man and woman exited with three small children. A family on a day out. Louise glanced at Keith, then back at the family. She wasn't alone. Would the presence of others be her saving grace, or was she putting them in danger too?

Shaking his head and raising his palms, Patrick stomped toward Louise's car. He appeared to be questioning Keith's banging, suggesting that he hadn't yet recognized that Louise was the woman at the dog kennel.

"What are you doing, man?" Patrick nodded over his shoulder at the family. He faked a laugh. "Woman issues, bud? Let it *go*." He sang the last word as though attempting to soften the situation.

Patrick's actions bought Louise time to think and scan the immediate area. Two men were pumping gas. Could she get their attention without putting anyone in danger?

Keith banged on the window again. "Get. Out. Of. The. Car!" Spit flew onto the window. Louise gagged at the sight of the mucousy yellow slime slowly running down the glass.

She swallowed hard, sat up straight, and spoke loudly enough to be heard. "I'm not going anywhere with you."

"Get out or I shoot you now."

"Or you'll shoot me later. We both know you won't shoot me now." She nodded toward the men at the pumps. "Too many witnesses. Besides, we know you don't like to do your own dirty work."

Patrick stared at Louise, recognition dawning on his face. "Come on, Keith. Let's go. Let's get out of here."

Patrick's tone of voice told Louise that he wasn't telling Keith to stand down but *pleading* with him to do so. Keith was obviously the dominant personality. It was as she'd suspected: Keith was manipulating the strings and the others were his puppets.

"You've been following us. Get out of the car now, or we'll drag you out." More yellow spit landed on her window.

"I haven't been following you. I stopped for gas, and to call a friend." Uncertain it would work in her favour, she was hesitant to reveal that her friend was a homicide detective, as some criminals might believe that taking a police officer's friend hostage could get them what they wanted in a bargaining situation. No, she'd keep Alex's profession to herself for now.

Keith moved the handgun from the window and positioned it under his opposite arm. Louise took a deep breath. The madman was seeing the futility of trying to get her to exit her car. He'd given up and would be on his way. But why wasn't he moving away from the car?

She froze when she realized he was now pointing the gun at the unsuspecting family.

Keith grimaced. "How about I don't shoot *you* here? How about I shoot someone else?"

Would he really do it? Take an innocent life because she wasn't willing to play his games? She watched as Patrick moved around to the passenger side of her car, his scowl forcing the memory of Bailey's beaten body into her mind. These men were ruthless. Were they responsible for the bombing and Tina's murder?

The children were laughing, and the smallest one, a boy of maybe three, hugged his mother's leg. The ice cream cone he was holding tilted, dropping the best part of the sweet treat onto his mother's pants before hitting the ground. When he started to cry, his mother picked him up and returned inside—probably to get him a new ice cream cone. Louise's heart melted at the sweet moment, then raced at the thought that this family might be injured or killed if she didn't cooperate with Keith and Patrick. She unlocked the door and cracked it open.

Keith, who was again aiming the gun at Louise's head, stepped back. She watched Patrick as he made his way to Keith's side.

The other drivers were still pumping gas. The family man was loading the older children into the van that had hidden the two crazed men from view earlier. Louise prayed that one of the customers would notice what was going on and call the police, and that they'd be able to give a good description of Keith and Patrick.

Patrick threw the door open and grabbed Louise's left arm, then dragged her out of the car. "Keep quiet, or daddy over there gets a back full of bullets."

Without a struggle, Louise allowed Patrick to escort her to a silver BMW sedan. It was a bad idea allowing these thugs to take her to a second location—she knew that—but she had no doubt they'd follow through on their threats to kill the children's father.

As she sat in the rear seat with her hands bound behind her back while Patrick drove past country fields, her fears were confirmed: they had no intention of her surviving the trip. They'd made no attempt to prevent her from knowing their destination. No cloth around her eyes or bag over her head. She was sitting up, able to see everything around her. If they released her, she could easily give a description of their hideout to the police.

Louise estimated it was about twenty minutes before Patrick turned into a short driveway that ended at a small weather-beaten cottage. A dilapidated picnic table on the front porch was leaning on its side, reminding her of the airplane where she'd found the planted cigarette butt. Hints of green paint, washed away long ago by rain and faded by the sun, created a blotchy pattern on the wood siding. Most of the windows were cracked, except for one that had what Louise thought might be multiple bullet holes. Had they been shooting into the cottage, or out? The land around the cottage had been taken over by weeds long ago, and the once paved driveway was returning to a natural gravel roadway.

Patrick parked the car beside the cottage, then dragged Louise out and forced her toward the building. As soon as he opened the door, she gagged at the smell of sweat, cigarette smoke, and what could only be rotting tissue. She pulled back, not wanting to enter what could be her final resting place. The police hadn't located Joan Williams. Did these men kill her and leave her body here to rot? Were they about to do the same to Louise?

Patrick pulled her farther into a shabby living room decorated with worn, dirty furniture and spiderwebs. When the door behind them slammed, Louise screamed at the burst of noise, then spun around. Keith was standing there grinning, his yellow-stained teeth more nauseating than the smell that surrounded them.

"You've been seen hanging out at the airport and at the police station. My gals tell me you're friends with that Sandra Kelly woman at the wildlife place, and"—he grimaced and tilted his head—"you're friendly with the cops." One side of Keith's upper lip raised—he really had the vicious dog thing down pat.

Louise shrugged. "Yeah. So?" So much for hiding her relationship with the police department.

Keith stepped closer to her. The foul body odour emanating from him, mixed with the other stomach-churning smells, became too much for her to handle. The contents of Louise's stomach landed on Keith's shoes. Patrick snickered, then quickly stopped. Louise glanced back at him and was surprised to see fear in his eyes. If she had to bet on a fight between the two, she'd have picked Patrick—the younger, taller, more muscular of the men.

Keith shook his foot, flinging bits of partially digested scones and cheese onto the dirty, worn carpet and baseboard. Louise gagged but managed to hold on to whatever remained of her snack with Daphne.

"I need to know what you know. More importantly, I need to know what the police know about our little operation here." Keith turned away from her and removed his hoodie. Under it, he was wearing a red-and-green plaid shirt.

Louise already knew he wore plaid from her first encounter with him at SWaRF. Wearing plaid didn't make him a murderer, but when he turned around, she held her breath to prevent a poorly timed "Aha!" from escaping her lips.

A pocket was missing from the front of the shirt as if it been torn off, and along with the pocket, a large piece of missing fabric left a hole in the shirt the same size and shape as the fragment she'd found at SWaRF.

Louise lifted her chin, indicating the hole. "Did Tina do that when you were strangling her?"

That was the wrong thing to say. Keith lunged at her, ready to wrap his hands around her throat. She instinctively tried to raise her hands to shield her neck, but they were still tied behind her back. She lowered her head to block access to her windpipe, but in an instant, her feet left the ground as she was flung backwards. She landed on a couch, her tailbone hitting the exposed metal frame.

"What did you do that for?" Keith screamed at Patrick, then pushed him out of the way, and lunged again at Louise, fire in his eyes.

Patrick grabbed the back of Keith's shirt and pulled him away. "If you kill her now, we'll never get the information we want. Calm down."

Keith redirected his anger to Patrick. The crazed man whirled around, his hand in a fist and ready to make contact with Patrick's face. Patrick ducked, then plowed his fist into Keith's midsection.

Keith bent over, then collapsed to the floor. He remained on his hands and knees for a few seconds to recover the breath that had been knocked out of him, then rolled over and leaned on his elbow. "You'll regret that, Patty boy!" He returned to his knees, then, clinging to a side table, raised himself to his feet. "I'm going out for a smoke."

In addition to the pain in her hands and back, Louise had a mix of emotions: relief that she was still breathing, anger at being kidnapped, fear that it wasn't all over yet, and a smattering of joy at seeing Keith Roberts brought to his knees. *There's always a silver lining, Louise.*

Patrick demonstrated that he could indeed beat Keith in a fight, but would he be willing to do it again? If she could convince Patrick to let her go, would he keep Keith at bay while she fled?

Patrick grabbed her by the arm and pulled her from then couch, then pushed her onto a chair. He released the bindings that held her hands behind her, then tied her right wrist to a table leg. "Don't get any ideas. I'm not going to help you. I only saved you from getting strangled so we could get the info we need from you. Then . . ." He made a slitting motion across his throat.

Louise's heart sank. This man wasn't going to be swayed easily, if at all. Her phone vibrated in her pocket. She'd forgotten she slipped it in after talking to Alex and was relieved it was on vibrate mode only, but what good was it if she couldn't use it? "Can I have a glass of water?" She'd wait until Patrick left the room, then try to loosen the twine that held her because she couldn't reach the phone with her free hand.

"Sure, and would you like to see the menu?" Patrick shook his head. "This isn't a café. No water, no food. Just answer our questions. Then you're out of here."

"And by 'out of here' you mean you're going to take me back to my car?"

Patrick smirked and whacked her on the back of the head. "Yeah, sure."

"The other guy killed Tina Purcell, didn't he? He smokes,

and a cigarette butt was found at the crime scene. And then there's his torn shirt. It all fits." Louise was giving away information about the crime scene to a suspect. Not something Alex would approve of, but if she could gain Patrick's trust, maybe he'd help her. "Do you really want to stand by someone with so much evidence stacked against him? The DNA on the cigarette butt will match his, and then its game over. He goes to jail and takes all his friends with him."

"You don't know what you're talking about."

"Maybe I don't, but tell me, what size shoes does your boss wear? Eleven? Eleven and a half?"

He squinted at her.

"Ten and a half?" She held his gaze for a moment, then glanced at his feet. "What size do you take?" His feet were obviously too small to have made the footprints she'd discovered in the woods at SWaRF. "There were footprints near the fabric torn from Keith's shirt. They made impressions of them. Once they examine his footwear, that'll just add to the evidence against him. He must have gotten his shirt caught on the tree after he, you know"—she paused for effect—"killed Tina. Was she a friend of yours?"

Patrick moved to what might have been a wingback chair years ago. He wiped the seat before plopping down. "Seems we were right about you. You have a lot of information that a member of the public would only know if they were chummy with the police."

"The important thing is that the police *do* know that information. Killing me will just add to the crimes you've already committed."

"I haven't done anything they can pin on me. Beth's already taken the blame for what happened to that Nelson guy. Idiot shouldn't have been snooping around—he could have ruined everything."

"Ruined what? Your animal cruelty operation?" Louise had no concrete proof that Patrick or Keith were involved in smuggling the pangolin, but it made sense that they were, and also involved in the bombing and the murder. It all had to be connected, but how? And why? Why would someone bomb the airport if they were using it for illegal activities? "There's a big difference in prison time for smuggling exotic animals and murdering someone."

"I didn't murder anyone. I had nothing to do with Tina—never even met the woman. And I had nothing to do with the airport bombing. Stupid idiots screwed up there. Keith was fuming."

"Fuming about what?"

"The size of the explosion. That damn bomb wrecked our plane and cost us thousands."

"*Your* plane?" The grumpy voice drew Louise's attention to the back of the room. Standing in the doorway, her arms crossed, was a grumpier-than-usual-looking Joan Williams. "What do you mean, your plane?"

Chapter 40

LOUISE LOOKED ON with a glimmer of fascination as Patrick attempted to backtrack. "What plane?" He desperately needed an acting coach. He rolled his eyes and crossed his arms as he proclaimed his ignorance.

"What plane? You just told this interfering moron"—Joan Williams nodded at Louise, who shrugged, too amused by the fight between the two cult members to be offended—"that the explosion wrecked your plane and cost you thousands of dollars." The woman with the permanently grumpy face pushed the outdated television set over. It crashed to the ground, shattering the screen and cracking the case. Years of dust and dust mites were flung into the atmosphere. "Don't try to tell me it was the TV I heard. That thing hasn't worked in years. So again. *What plane?*"

Before Patrick could continue to claim ignorance, Keith stormed through the front door. "What's going on in here?" He glared at the smashed TV, then shook his head and went to the adjoining room.

Louise held Joan's gaze and nodded at Patrick. "He definitely said that *his* plane was damaged. Yup, seems Patrick here is keeping secrets."

If you can't beat your enemies head-on, pit them against each other.

Joan's nostrils flared. "That plane was being used to smuggle animals into the country. It was owned by SWaRF. You work for SWaRF?" Her face took on a deep crimson colour as the blood vessels in her neck bulged.

"Work for those rehab nuts? You've got to be kidding." Patrick adjusted his collar and said, "Humph."

"I let Keith run the SWaRF protests his way because he said he had evidence that the Sandra woman and her crew were importing exotic animals to sell. He even showed me a report that said Tobin Memorial Airport was a probable entry point," Joan said.

"Hmm." Louise massaged her chin for effect. "Did the article specifically say that Sydney's Wildlife Rehabilitation Facility was involved?"

Joan pointed her index finger at Louise as she closed the gap between them. "What do you know?"

"I know that you've been misled. Well, I suspect you have been."

Keith returned with a bottle of beer, cracked it open, then flung the cap into the corner.

Joan thrust her finger at him. "That was your plane? Show me that article. The one about the imports."

Keith waved her off. "Calm down. I don't need to show you anything. I told you the rehab centre's importing animals, and that's all you need to know. I have it all under control."

Louise scanned the disintegrating room in the disintegrating cottage that apparently served as their base of operations. They blew up an airport, killing five people at last count, and were now obviously nervous that the police were on to them. Keith Roberts had a strange idea of being in control of a situation.

"You're the one that got that stupid Tina woman involved." Keith finished his beer, then flung the empty bottle. As it whizzed by, it just missed Joan's head and landed on the couch. He laughed. "You said you knew what you were doing, but I guess not. A small explosion to scare people is all you were supposed to do. Minimal damage."

"Yeah, well, it was more powerful than expected." Joan shrugged. "So what?"

Louise tried to jump to her feet, but she was pulled back down by the tie binding her arm to the table leg. "So what? So what? You killed five people at the airport, including two police officers."

Keith was mere inches in front of Joan now and bowed his head until they were face to face. "Your buddy Tina made the bomb too big and it damaged my plane. That's 'so what'!"

Louise thought back to a conversation with Alex. What had he said about Tina's security access to various areas of the airport? "Um . . . not that I'm looking to help you, Keith . . . Can I call you Keith? Tina Purcell didn't have security clearance for the area where the bomb detonated. A higher-level badge was needed, and she didn't have one. Nope, Tina didn't have access, but Joan did."

Keith moved closer to Joan, forcing her to step back. "Who made the bomb? Who planted it?"

Pinned against the wall, Joan swallowed hard. "Okay, I planted it, but Tina made it. She told me she knew how, so I trusted her."

Louise said, "Um, no. Tina's fingerprints weren't on the bomb remnants recovered at the airport, but—"

Joan edged along the wall to escape Keith, then rushed over to Louise. "Would you just shut up!"

"You got your friend a job, then you got her killed." Louise held Joan's gaze—she wasn't going to back down from Madame Grumpy Face. Besides being a terrorist and a murderer, this woman tried to ruin Sandra and her rehab centre.

"Tina wasn't my friend. She was just a stupid cling-on. Another retired empty nester looking for a good cause. I found her on Facebook cheering on an animal rights group she obviously knew nothing about. That bunch doesn't care about animals—they just protest wherever they can get lots of media coverage to bring in donor money. It didn't take much to get her to help me out with ARSE, and it didn't cost her anything."

"Except her life." Louise tugged at the string that bound her arm. It was tied tightly to her wrist, but not to the table leg. If she could get the three maniacs to leave the room, she could lift the table and free herself easily.

"Who decided to plant the cigarette butt in the plane? We know it wasn't Plump-in-Plum's idea."

The others glared at Louise, obviously confused.

"Sorry, you know her as Erica Cotton. I know her as

someone unlikely to come up with that idea on her own." If Louise could escalate the argument between her captors, perhaps they'd take it outside, giving her the chance to escape. She didn't want to cause any of them to get killed, but if it was between them or her, she was willing to take that chance.

Joan threw her shoulders back. "That was Erica's idea."

Keith advanced toward Joan again. "And just why would she put a cigarette butt into a plane? What's this about?"

Louise smiled at the creepy man, happy to reveal the truth. "To frame you for the explosion, of course. When the DNA on the cigarette is matched to you, Keith, you'll be suspect number one. That'll take the heat off Joan. She's not afraid of having others take the fall for her. One of her patsies is in jail right now after pretending to be her." Louise paused for dramatic effect. "That's my theory, anyway. The false evidence was planted after the police raided Joan's home, so I suspect she grew nervous and wanted to shift the focus of the investigation away from herself. No doubt the DNA will also match the cigarette found at SWaRF."

Keith's eyes widened as he rapidly and repeatedly shifted his gaze from Joan to Louise and back again. "DNA means nothing. It won't hold up in court. It's the mitochondria that's important, and that can only be found in someone who's a mother."

The man spewed his ramblings with so much confidence that Louise had to remind herself that while he was using real words, nothing about that statement was accurate. Was this how he drew Patrick, Joan, and the others in? Speaking nonsense with so much confidence that those listening didn't suspect he had no idea what he was talking about?

"The police can't touch me. I've been studying the law for years and they won't find anything to charge me with."

"Was that at the university of Google? Google research—a narcissist's best friend!"

Keith grabbed Louise's collar and pulled her up from the chair, the corner of the table following. His eyes were black and soulless, matching the description given by so many victims when they talked about their assailants on the true crime shows Louise was addicted to. The man wasn't just a narcissist, but also a psychopath. A dangerous one.

God help me. Where's Alex? How did I get into a mess like this again?

"Sorry, I got carried away." Pitting her captors against each other was Louise's plan—she had to remind herself of that. First, trust God. Second, keep them arguing until either there's a chance to escape or help arrives.

Keith loosened his grip, dropping Louise back down into the hard seat. She wanted to sarcastically say "Ouch," but this was no time for lame jokes.

Keith stormed out of the building, followed by Patrick.

Joan dropped onto the couch, fuming.

"They're playing you, you know. They're using ARSE to smuggle exotic animals into the country for sale to the highest bidder," Louise had been unsuccessful in gaining Patrick's help. Could she win Joan over?

Joan shook her head in disbelief.

"Why do you think they're so upset about the damage to the plane? They don't care about anything other than the plane."

Joan didn't appear to care about much either, not the death of strangers or even someone she knew.

Louise continued. "Did you know it was an animal called pangolin they were bringing in?"

Joan crossed her arms and started tapping her foot.

"Did you know that two of those poor innocent creatures died in the explosion? The explosion *you* caused?"

Joan's eyelids flew wide open and she jumped to her feet. "I didn't kill any animals!"

Louise softened her approach—she'd play the sympathetic friend. "I'm afraid you did. I know you didn't mean to, but we both know that you set that bomb using a timer and blew up the airport. The plane with the pangolins had just arrived from Halifax. The pilot parked it in the hangar, then went into the office to call . . . I don't know if it was Keith or Patrick . . . to let them know the delivery had been made. He barely made it out of the building before the bomb went off. There was no time to retrieve the living cargo." Louise lowered, then slowly shook her head. "It's not living anymore, that cargo. No, I'm afraid the animals are all dead."

Louise didn't know if more than one pangolin had died, and she had fabricated most of the other details of the story and added the dramatic ending to stir the woman's rage. She needed Joan to leave her alone so she could free herself.

It worked, and when Joan stormed out the front door, Louise had to act quickly. She could hear Joan shouting at the men. Glancing at the window riddled with holes, Louise wondered if Keith had his gun on him or if he'd left it in the car. If he had it on him, she couldn't just run out into the open; she'd have to free herself, then find somewhere to hide.

The table was easy to lift. She slipped the twine along the leg to the floor, then pulled it off the greasy piece of furniture. She grabbed her phone and checked for a signal. "Nuts! No bars."

The voices outside softened. Louise snuck over to the window and looked out. They were coming back. She quickly returned the twine to the table leg, then clicked Record on her phone. If she couldn't call for help, she could at the least get some evidence. Before returning the phone to her pocket, Louise noticed a flashing green light in the upper corner of the screen.

"What's that?"

The door opened. She replaced the phone to her jacket, leaned back in the chair, and crossed her legs. *Play it cool, Louise.*

Joan blew through the door first. "I knew I shouldn't have let you run things, Keith. You brainwashed my whole crew."

Louise eyed Joan and whispered, "never feed the ego of a narcissist." She didn't know why she bothered giving the advice and was surprised at the response.

With a sarcastic look, Joan whispered back, "no kidding!" She turned to address Keith and Patrick as they entered. "I'm not taking the rap for murder. This was all your doing. You killed Tina, not me."

Keith glowered at her. "Only because you told me she set the bomb. The bomb was meant only to scare SWaRF away from importing animals. You messed up!" He raised his hands, ready to engulf her neck. "You're the one I should have snuffed out. Your usefulness to me is over."

Patrick pulled him away. Keith spun around to punch the larger man, than stopped himself. He rubbed his stomach, then retreated to the kitchen.

Louise stared at Joan. "So Keith's the smuggler but convinced you Sandra Kelly was, then convinced you to bomb an airport to scare the smugglers? Why?"

"The bomb was Joan's idea." Patrick pointed at the woman. "Keith just went along with it as long as it was small. He even gave her the plans. One small bomb for the airport, and one small bomb for the rehab place. No casualties, little damage.

A little news coverage, and Keith's way to keep Joan and her ARSE crew convinced that SWaRF were the smugglers. That's it—keep the suspicion off us and on them."

Joan glared at him. "The plans he gave me were useless. I found a better design on the internet."

"Bigger isn't always better, woman. You wrecked our plane!"

Wanting to record as much evidence as possible, Louise continued to ask questions. If they killed her and found her phone, the information would never make it to the police, but she had to try. "So the morning of the airport bombing, you were all at SWaRF? Is that when you left the wired crate there? Another attempt to blow people up?"

Patrick waved his arm in the air. "Humph. I was nowhere near that place. I have a business to run. That's where I was, and I have plenty of witnesses who can attest to that fact."

Alex had told Louise that Patrick owned a business that supplied parts for the auto industry. While many industries used ships to import products, others had inventory brought in by international airlines. Smuggling animals into a large airport, then using a smaller plane to get them to Tobin Memorial Airport would fit the evidence. It would explain Patrick's role in the scheme.

Joan stood tall, but her eyes showed regret at her part in the death of what she thought were several pangolins. "I made sure Tina held the crate at the wildlife place in case there were fingerprints found. We were setting it up when Keith got a call. When he hung up, he came at me. He said I'd messed up and ruined everything. That the airport explosion was too big. He was crazy mad. Scary. What was I supposed to do? I told him Tina had set the bomb, and . . ." She shrugged. "He grabbed her by the throat. When she went limp, he pushed her into the pond. We took off when I heard that crazy Sandra woman in her golf cart. Guess I dropped the crate on the way over the fence."

"What are you doing?" Keith had returned with another beer in hand.

Joan shrugged again. "No biggie. She's not going to tell anyone."

The way Keith was looking at Joan, Louise wondered if Joan would be able to tell anyone anything ever again. Louise's mind returned to her phone. She hadn't seen that flashing light before. Alex had her phone for a while at the police station. Could he have . . . ?

"You know, I think the police might be on their way here. You were correct earlier—I do have a somewhat close bond with some of them. One in particular."

Louise thought over the events of the past week. She'd thought she lost Alex. She'd been reluctant to get romantically involved with a police officer for fear of losing him, but the pain she felt when she saw that empty hospital bed told her it was too late to avoid emotional involvement. Alex was a part of her, and she needed him in her life. Why hadn't she realized it earlier? Why did it have to come to her now, when she might never get a chance to tell him how she felt?

"You're bluffing. We aren't that far away. If they knew where we were, they'd be here already." Keith picked at his yellow teeth with his dirty fingernails, then rubbed the same hand through his tight curls.

Louise wanted to retch but held back the urge. "They won't be looking for *you*—they'll be looking for me. It would have taken time for them to realize my car was abandoned at the gas station, and then they would have had to set up a tracker to find me."

Keith leaned in until he was mere inches from Louise's face. "Then all we've got to do is get rid of you!"

The smell and sight of the diseased mouth was too much for Louise. She vomited on his shoes again. "You really need to consider some dental hygiene. Or at least stop standing so close to other people. It's not good for your shoes."

Keith grabbed her and pulled her up again. This time he dragged her, flimsy table included, to a window. "Do you see anyone out there?"

"No, but I can hear someone." Louise grinned as sirens grew louder.

Patrick escaped to the kitchen, then reappeared with a pair of scissors.

Louise gulped. "No need to be hasty. Really, I'm sure it's just an ambulance. Probably responding to a heart attack somewhere." Her own heart was beating erratically as she imagined the scissors being thrust into her jugular vein.

Patrick swung the scissors under the table and cut the twine that held Louise captive.

Keith lifted an old dining chair and swung it at Patrick. It missed the younger man, then broke into pieces when it hit the far wall. Keith stood fuming, threatening Patrick with the chair leg that remained in his hand. "What are you doing?"

"I'm letting her go. I'm not going up for murder. So far all they might have on me is smuggling some weird animal most people have never heard of. It's not even drug smuggling. A good lawyer will get me off with probation." Patrick grabbed Louise's arm. "Come on. I'll deliver you to your cop buddies. That'll work in my favour."

She pulled away from him and ran for the door.

Joan moved to block the way. "You're not going any-where."

Patrick shoved Joan aside. "Let her go." He opened the door and pushed Louise out.

Was this a trap? If she started to run toward the road, would Keith shoot her? How good a shot was he? Patrick might try to stop him, but he could shoot Patrick. Was Patrick really helping her, or was this a set-up?

She pressed her back against the outer wall of the cottage, then crouched down. The car the men had used to kidnap her was about twenty yards away; she'd stay low, then run and hide on the other side of it.

Louise started to get up, ready to run for the vehicle, when a patrol car turned into the driveway, sirens blaring and lights flashing. Behind it was a second squad car, a black SUV, and the CITES van. She inhaled deeply and leaned her head back. The cavalry had arrived.

Chapter 41

LOUISE WATCHED WITH trepidation as two soon-to-be convicts fled across the back field. She could only assume that Keith Roberts and Joan Williams had heard the sirens and thought they could get away on foot. The kidnappers were soon spotted by Brian and Wayne, who gave chase.

Relieved she'd gone unnoticed by the pair of criminals, Louise was fascinated by the almost humorous scene unfolding in the field. Keith, who'd been several feet ahead of Joan and only a few yards from disappearing into a wooded area, let out a high-pitched scream as his body was propelled forward. With the grace of an egg crashing to a tile floor, he landed face down onto the swampy field. He rolled over onto his back and lifted his head, revealing a wig of mud, reeds, and what might have been a frog.

When heavy-set Joan turned right, Louise could only assume she wanted to avoid Keith's fate of tripping in the wet field. The change in direction was pointless—her speed hadn't been impressive at the beginning of her attempt to flee, and now she was moving at more of a crawl than a dash. Having exerted every ounce of her energy in less a hundred yards, the woman with the eternally grumpy face bent at the waist and rested her hands on her knees.

Brian and Wayne, each carrying about twenty pounds of standard police gear, had no difficulty reaching Hoodie Man and Madame Grumpy Face. Brian pulled Keith to his feet, then placed the curly-haired narcissist in handcuffs. With Wayne only a few feet from her, Joan turned around and started waving her arms aggressively at him. When Wayne released the snap on his holster, Joan threw her hands behind her back, closed her mouth, turned around, and allowed him to adorn her wrists with handcuffs.

"Smartest thing you've done all week," Louise knew Joan couldn't hear her, but it gave her a sense of satisfaction to say it. She watched as the officers escorted the struggling criminals to the police cruisers, and shook her head at the foolishness of Keith and Joan's behaviour. Not only did the two very out-of-shape characters have no chance of escaping the fast and fit police officers, but they'd also added resisting arrest to their long list of charges.

But then, if you're already facing charges of kidnapping, murder, and possibly terrorism, perhaps you're not worried about adding on a misdemeanour.

Louise's attention had been so strictly focused on the capture and arrest of two of her kidnappers that she'd forgotten about the third. When the front door to the cottage squeaked open a second time, then slammed closed, Louise leapt to her feet and scrambled around the corner to the back of the building. How desperate would Patrick Howard be now to escape? Desperate people were as unpredictable as wild animals.

"Don't shoot. I'm unarmed." It was Patrick's voice.

"Turn around. Now back up toward the cruiser and keep your hands in the air."

Alex was here!

Louise's respiration became shallow and broken as the gravity of her situation sank in. She'd been kidnapped by cold-hearted murderers—psychopaths who had no qualms about killing people to accomplish their goals. If the authorities hadn't arrived when they did, she could have been their next murder victim.

Her life had been in danger, but as always, Alex was nearby. He had her back.

Not only Alex, but more importantly, God was always there for her. Watching over her. Louise was determined to work on her trust issues—to let God be in control. Did He want her to be with Alex? Had He allowed her to be in yet another life-threatening situation so she'd realize she was wasting time being overly cautious, and not trusting? Those were questions that would take some time to think, and pray, about.

Officer Wayne's voice, calling out from the distance, cut into Louise's musings. "Hey, Brian, throw me another set of handcuffs. We have another candidate for night court."

She peeked around the corner at the police vehicles. The three psychopaths had been apprehended by law enforcement, but they weren't all handcuffed yet. Patrick was still bare wristed, and none were yet locked away in the police cars. Anything could happen. Louise decided to stay put until all three of her captors were fitted with silver bracelets and securely belted into their ride to the jail.

A rusty patio set adorned the neglected, cracked patio. Louise lowered herself into one of the metal chairs, then lowered her head into her hands. It was time to have a serious talk with God.

"So, you've done it again!"

"God?"

"Nope. Just like at the hospital, only me. Alex."

Louise spread her fingers and looked up. "I know it's you. You're interrupting an important conversation."

If Alex had been trying to look annoyed at her—after all, this was the second time in two days she'd needed to be rescued—his face betrayed him. He looked as relieved as Louise felt that he'd found her.

Louise placed her hands on her lap. Her chat with God would have to take place later. She squinted against the setting sun as she stared up at Alex. "Tracker on my phone?"

"You know it."

"Hmm. I should be angry about that invasion of my privacy, but the truth is, I'm very grateful you were looking out for me."

"You're welcome." Alex flashed the grin that had first attracted Louise to him. He offered his hand.

"I didn't follow them, you know. And I didn't come here willingly. I was going to drive away, just as we'd discussed."

He helped her to her feet. "I know." He wrapped his arm around her shoulder and guided her to his SUV. "We have a lot to talk about."

"Yes, we do." Louise knew he was referring to the case. Not only the Bathurst Region Police Department, but also CITES and the RCMP would be very interested in the information she had for them. She had recorded much of the conversation in the cottage, and the rest she'd write down while it was still fresh in her mind.

However, there was more than the case to talk about. Earlier in the week, Alex had mentioned a surprise to Daphne but hadn't given her any details, and the chaos of the past few days prevented Louise from drilling Alex about it.

Was it a ring? That would be premature—they weren't even officially dating. Did Alex get a promotion at work? If so, he could be leaving Bathurst Region. Why would he think Louise would be excited about that?

Because you've been pushing him away, Louise. He probably thinks you'd be happy to see him go.

Louise's heart raced and her palms became sweaty. She had to speak up before it was too late. She had to tell him how she felt.

Alex opened the passenger-side door for Louise. She partially lowered her buttocks into the car, then stopped herself. She grabbed the door frame and pulled herself back out. If she didn't say something now, when she was feeling brave enough to be vulnerable, the opportunity would be lost.

As she stood in front of Alex, her olfactory senses were overwhelmed by vanilla with a hint of cinnamon—evidence of the handsome detective's bath soap. She'd noticed it before, but now the familiar scent brought a mix of comfort and fear. He was here to save her, but was he getting ready to leave? To leave town? To leave her?

She put her hand on Alex's shoulder. What she really

wanted to do was to kiss him, but he was on duty and his co-workers were all around them. Even if they weren't there, why bother kissing him if he was getting ready to move on with his life? Why complicate things?

"Look, Alex, I've been thinking a lot this week . . ."

Officer Wayne slapped Alex on his other shoulder. "Hey, boss, we got Williams and Roberts packed away in the squads. Can you take Howard in your vehicle?" Wayne smiled at Louise. "So relieved we found you in one piece, Louise. Everyone at the station was worried."

She smiled back, but what she really wanted to do was to shoo the officer away. "Thanks, Wayne. You have no idea how grateful I am that you all found me."

Alex addressed Wayne. "Of course, put him in the back of the Bronco."

After Wayne walked away, Alex gently massaged Louise's cheek with his thumb, then frowned. "Sorry. It looks like you'll have to get a ride back to town with Wendel in the CITES van."

He offered his hand for a second time and directed her away from the car, then shut the door. "What was that you were about to say?"

She shrugged. "It can wait." Louise let go of his hand and headed for the van. *I hope.*

Chapter 42

"HEY, STRANGER, WHAT are you doing here on a Saturday morning?" Daphne entered their office at the Black Creek Animal Hospital and tossed her jacket onto the windowsill.

"I had a few patient files to finish up before heading down to the marina." Louise downed the remainder of her herbal tea. She'd decided to take a break from caffeine for a while. She'd drunk so much coffee during the investigation around the airport and SWaRF incidents that even when things calmed down, she couldn't sleep properly for two nights. "What are you doing here?"

"I forgot a gift I have for Ella here when I rushed out

Wednesday evening." Daphne plopped into her desk chair and opened the drawer. "Here it is. We're having the grandparents over later to watch the video Joe took of the school concert. Ella's so excited, and she wanted to wear a special outfit. I found this when I was on lunch Wednesday." Daphne held up a pink-and-white dress, decorated with a large bow on the back.

"Very cute. Thanks for covering for me, by the way. I could hardly walk by Monday. My muscles were not my friends."

It had been a week since Joan Williams, Keith Roberts, and Patrick Howard had been arrested for kidnapping Louise, on top of charges related to the explosion at the airport, the resulting five deaths, the illegal import of exotic animals, the attack on Bailey Nelson, and the murder of Tina Purcell.

The day after her ordeal at the cottage, Louise was unable to ambulate normally due to the pain in her back and leg muscles. She had called her best friend and business partner early Monday morning, and Daphne agreed to work solo from Monday to Wednesday, then take Thursday and Friday off, leaving Louise to finish off the work week.

"I stopped by SWaRF last night. Major has made a full recovery, so they released him while I was there. It was pure joy watching him regain his freedom and bound off into the woods." Louise beamed at the memory of the happy coyote who'd she'd been able to help.

"That's amazing, and I want to hear more about it, but I'd better get going. Joe's waiting in the van with the kids." Daphne scooped up her jacket. "We're going to stop by the festivities at the marina for a couple of hours. I'm sure the organizers of the children's hospital fundraiser must be grateful that the marina offered a place for the event. They have rides for the little ones set up—Ella's very excited."

"Sounds like she's not the only one. I'll finish up here, then see you all there."

Daphne made her way to the door.

"Oh, Daphne, before you go, I should let you in on something. I haven't seen you all week so I haven't had a chance to tell you—"

Mary burst through the door and pointed at Louise, a huge grin on her face. "I knew I'd catch you here! My friend, Michael Ellis, called me earlier today. Seems he saw you and Alex in the park last night." As though in a dreamy state, Mary swayed and looked at the ceiling. "Holding hands . . . walking along."

Louise's gaze shot from Mary to Daphne. "Um, I was just about to tell you." She glared at Mary. "I haven't told Daphne yet."

Mary laughed. "Sorry. On the other hand, I'm sure she's not surprised. The only person who didn't know about your relationship, Louise, was you. Anyway, I'm off to the marina for a hot dog and funnel cake."

Mary turned and exited as fast as she had entered.

Daphne frowned at Louise, but soon her frown turned into a silly grin. "Mary's right. You were the only one who didn't know. Glad you've come around."

The Georgetown Marina was situated at the southwest corner of Georgetown, the town just west of Coverdale. It was home to a small number of houseboats and fishing tour boats, and it also played host every year to many privately owned yachts that docked in the slips for days or weeks at a time. Boats were guided into the marina by a narrow canal marked by a little lighthouse at the end of a pier.

As Louise drove down the curved road toward the tiny restaurant that serviced the boaters, she was reminded of her first misadventure. Alex and his co-workers had rescued her a week ago from her captors at the cottage, but several months ago, he and the coast guard had rescued her from a different band of bandits here at the marina. Louise slowed her car as she turned into a parking spot, then turned off the ignition. *How do you get yourself into these situations, Louise?*

She spotted Alex by one of the concession stands. The vendors were still setting up, as the event didn't start until 11:00 a.m. The Bathurst Region Police Department, as well as officers from CITES and the RCMP, were on hand to help out in any way they could, in remembrance of their fallen comrades. Beside Alex were Norman Talbot, the injured officer who'd shared a hospital room with Alex after the explosion, and his wife, Jean.

When Alex looked up and noticed Louise, he shook Norman's hand, then rushed over to her. "You made it. I have to admit that I was a little concerned when you said you were stopping at the clinic first. I thought I wouldn't see you for hours."

Louise slapped his shoulder. "Don't be foolish. When have you ever known a veterinarian to be delayed for a social function because she gets stuck at the clinic?"

Alex laughed and playfully palmed his forehead. "Right. Silly me." He entwined his fingers with Louise's and led her to the centre of the activity.

"How's Norman doing?"

"Really good. I was surprised to see him here today, but Jean says he insisted. The doctor okayed it as long as he stays in the wheelchair. They're confident he'll walk again, but they don't want him rushing it and doing more damage to his pelvis and back."

"Makes sense. Have you seen my crew? The clinic staff all volunteered to help set up."

"I've seen a few of them. Sandra Kelly is here too, somewhere." Alex balanced on the tips of his toes and scanned the array of vendors. "She has a tent for the rehab centre, but I think she's helping set up other booths."

"That woman is amazing. With all she's been through recently, she's still putting others first. No doubt she was up earlier than ever this morning to check on all of her patients before heading over here."

They walked past a food stand advertising popcorn, candy apples, and cotton candy. The buttery scent caused Louise's stomach to growl. Mary had mentioned funnel cakes, one of Louise's favourite carnival treats. She scanned the area to see if she could spot the vendor offering them.

A large bearded man wearing a black leather jacket and jeans ran toward her. She yelped, jumped behind Alex, and pressed her forehead into his back.

"Sorry, Louise, I didn't mean to scare you."

Louise peeked around Alex. A man she didn't recognize stood before her, compassion on his face. Did she know him?

Alex reached behind his back, and placed his arm around Louise's shoulder. "Louise, this is Bailey Newman, otherwise known as Bailey Nelson. This is what he looks like when his face isn't swollen and bleeding."

Louise let out her breath. In her flight behind Alex, she hadn't noticed the bruises on the man's face, or the cast on his arm. "Oh man, you scared me." She offered her hand. "It's good to meet you properly, Bailey. You know, without all the bad guys—and blood."

Bailey took her hand. "I couldn't agree more. I need to tell you how grateful I am. If you hadn't found me when you did, I probably wouldn't be standing here right now."

Louise blushed. "My pleasure. Can I ask you something?"

"Sure. Anything."

"Were you spying on Sandra the whole time? Why?"

Bailey grinned and rubbed his head. "Well, initially I was. We'd gotten a report that SWaRF was importing exotics. It soon became obvious that this wasn't happening, but while I was there, ARSE started harassing the centre. It got me thinking, if ARSE was trying to shut SWaRF down, maybe they'd made the false report, so I started investigating them. We did have some information that animals were being brought to this area via the Montreal airport, and it seemed too coincidental that ARSE would be making up a story that had some truth to it. I guess that Howard guy saw me at one of the rallies and recognized me as a CITES agent." He shrugged. "The rest, as they say, is history."

Bailey shook her hand again, then Alex's, before joining the lineup for cotton candy.

Louise picked up the faint sound of bagpipes. "Do you hear that?"

"I sure do. Let's head over and say hi to Sandra. But first, I have a surprise for you."

Louise's heart pounded. This was it. Was he going to propose? They'd only been dating officially for a week, and marriage had never been mentioned. No, it must be something else. Louise's mind raced with possibilities as she allowed Alex to guide her toward the slips. At this time of year, only a few yachts were in the water, as the summertime visitors hadn't arrived yet.

Alex pointed at the far end of the marina where a couple of yachts were docked. "That's it!"

She looked where he was pointing, then scratched her head and stared back at him. "That's what?"

"Don't you see it? I bought it for us so we can do some sailing this summer. Of course, I'll have to take lessons and learn how to pilot a yacht, but it can't be that difficult." He scrunched his face and ran his fingers through his hair. "Can it?"

"You bought a yacht? That's the surprise?" She glanced up at him, her brow furrowed and palms up.

"Yup." Alex's chest was puffed out and he had a huge grin.

Louise was torn. The last time she'd been on a yacht, it wasn't a positive experience. On the other hand, the surprise wasn't an engagement ring, so that was a plus.

"Do you recognize it? I'll get it painted—and change the name, of course."

Louise squinted to make out the words written on the side: Finding Freedom. "You bought the boat I was held captive on? Are you insane?"

She gave him the evil eye, slapped his shoulder, and walked away.

After a disappointed mumble, he said, "I thought you'd like it. A sign of your victory over the bad guys."

Alex had a point. Owning the prized possession of those who'd tried to harm her wasn't a bad idea. It might be a good reminder to trust God in times of peril. She smiled. "Well, you'd better go buy that cottage too, then."

He ran to catch up with her and held her hand. "Don't tempt me."

About the Author

Dr. Karen Cullen graduated from the Atlantic Veterinary College at the University of Prince Edward Island in 1992. Since then, she has been caring for companion animals in southern Ontario, including 23 years as a mobile sonographer. Along with caring for our furry friends, Karen has always had a passion for storytelling. This second installment of the Louise Miller Mysteries series is her third novel in the cozy mystery genre. When not driving between veterinary clinics east of Toronto, or working on her next mystery, she can be found playing with the world's cutest Shih Tzu.

If you enjoyed this novel, please consider a review on Amazon.

Thanks

A special shout out to my friends Mary Asaaf, Laurie Hancock, and Wendy Korver for being my beta-readers. Thank you to my editor, Caroline Kaiser, for cleaning up the manuscript, grammatically and structurally, and for all of your sound advice and recommendations. Thank you also to Chrissy Hobbs and Brittany Wilson of Indie Publishing Inc. for giving my novel its professional look.

www.ingramcontent.com/pod-product-compliance
Lightning Source LLC
Chambersburg PA
CBHW051323190726
48290CB00001B/284